If I am able to determine t
while at the same time I c
concentrate and he must di

—Sun Tzu, 400–320 B.C.
*The Art of War*

The enemy will never see me coming. By the time
I have executed my plan, they will have turned on
each other and divided their ranks, allowing me to
strike at their core.

—Mack Bolan

# THE
# MACK BOLAN
## LEGEND

Nothing less than a war could have fashioned the destiny of the man called Mack Bolan. Bolan earned the Executioner title in the jungle hell of Vietnam.

But this soldier also wore another name—Sergeant Mercy. He was so tagged because of the compassion he showed to wounded comrades-in-arms and Vietnamese civilians.

Mack Bolan's second tour of duty ended prematurely when he was given emergency leave to return home and bury his family, victims of the Mob. Then he declared a one-man war against the Mafia.

He confronted the Families head-on from coast to coast, and soon a hope of victory began to appear. But Bolan had broken society's every rule. That same society started gunning for this elusive warrior—to no avail.

So Bolan was offered amnesty to work within the system against terrorism. This time, as an employee of Uncle Sam, Bolan became Colonel John Phoenix. With a command center at Stony Man Farm in Virginia, he and his new allies—Able Team and Phoenix Force—waged relentless war on a new adversary: the KGB.

But when his one true love, April Rose, died at the hands of the Soviet terror machine, Bolan severed all ties with Establishment authority.

Now, after a lengthy lone-wolf struggle and much soul-searching, the Executioner has agreed to enter an "arm's-length" alliance with his government once more, reserving the right to pursue personal missions in his Everlasting War.

# The Executioner®
## Don Pendleton's®

### HELL NIGHT

A GOLD EAGLE BOOK FROM
# W♦RLDWIDE®

TORONTO • NEW YORK • LONDON
AMSTERDAM • PARIS • SYDNEY • HAMBURG
STOCKHOLM • ATHENS • TOKYO • MILAN
MADRID • WARSAW • BUDAPEST • AUCKLAND

First edition February 2008

ISBN-13: 978-0-373-64351-6
ISBN-10:    0-373-64351-9

Special thanks and acknowledgment to
Jerry VanCook for his contribution to this work.

HELL NIGHT

**Printed in U.S.A.**

# The Executioner felt blood dripping down his back

The cuts from the glass were deep—he could tell that from similar wounds he'd experienced in the past. But they didn't appear to have severed any arteries or major vessels. This was, however, no time to be thinking about superficial injuries. He still had work to do and he swung the AK-47 slightly to target a man in green-and-brown camouflage fatigues.

The Hamas terrorist had a puzzled look on his face, as if he still couldn't believe that a man had just come crashing through the basement window. But that bewilderment didn't make him any less dangerous as he attempted to raise a heavy Bren automatic rifle.

The weight of the weapon saved the Executioner's life.

# MACK BOLAN®
## The Executioner

# Prologue

The quiet ambience of the small Parisian café was in direct contrast to the proposed topics of discussion—mass murder and destruction.

Beneath the large shade umbrella on the patio, Benjamin Franklin Davis shifted his chair slightly to block out the setting sun. Behind him, a good-looking Frenchwoman sat on a tall stool, a guitar in her lap, singing a folk song. Although he couldn't understand the words, Davis listened to her voice. Not bad. Not bad at all.

Davis focused his attention on the café's door to the patio as his contact arrived. Davis nodded. He would have known the man even if Ibrahim Nasab hadn't told him he'd be wearing a brown sport coat and an open-collared white shirt. The look in Nasab's eyes gave him away as a man accustomed to violence.

It was the same look Davis saw in the mirror each morning when he shaved.

Nasab walked to the table and pulled out the chair next to Davis just as the sun sank below the horizon. The woman on the stool continued to strum her guitar, her voice low and husky.

"Do you speak French?" Ibrahim Nasab asked as he settled into his seat.

"I speak English," Davis almost spit. "The American version. Or I don't speak at all."

For a brief moment, Nasab's eyes filled with hatred, but

then the Arab forced a smile. "Then we will speak English," he said in a thick Middle Eastern accent. "For we have much to discuss."

Davis nodded. "Indeed we do," he said. He leaned forward, closer to Nasab so he could lower his voice when he spoke. The odor of some pungent spice filled his nostrils. He was telling himself to ignore it when another pretty Frenchwoman with long brown hair approached their table. She said something Davis couldn't understand, but Nasab answered for them.

"I have ordered you another cup of American coffee," the Arab said when she'd left again. "And one for myself."

Davis nodded, cleared his throat, then glanced around him to make sure no one was paying them any attention. An elderly couple three tables away were the only other patrons on the sidewalk patio, and they hardly looked like potential police or intelligence agents. Davis scanned the office building across the street. Surveillance equipment had become so sophisticated in the past few years that a hidden microphone might be trained on them from any of the windows.

But that wasn't the case, and he knew it. He had chosen this café at random less than ten minutes ago, and given Nasab the name and address by cell phone. Even if the French or the Americans or the Arabs were on to them, they wouldn't have had time to get their listening gear set up.

For a moment, the two men sat silently, sizing each other up. Then Nasab asked quietly, "Do you really think this can work?" He had leaned in slightly, too, and if the look on his face meant anything, the movement was as distasteful to him as it had been to Davis. "Our philosophies of life are so very different."

"Yes," Davis said. "They are different. But if North Korea can work with Iran and Syria for a common goal, I don't see why my American Rough Riders and Hamas can't do the same thing."

Nasab leaned back in his chair as a gentle breeze began to blow along the sidewalk. The woman on the stool behind Davis continued to sing.

"How do you propose that we join forces?" Nasab asked.

"I see things going down in two parts," Davis said. "The first part will consist of the same things we've been doing separately all along. Bank robberies, random machine-gunnings at shopping malls and other areas where there are lots of easy targets, small bombs and the like." He glanced at his watch and calculated the time difference between where he sat and Kansas City, Missouri. "Even now, some of my men are preparing to rob a bank later in the day." He rested his arm on the table. "We'll make sure everyone knows who it is behind the robbery, and we'll make sure there are plenty of bodies left at the scene."

Nasab nodded, then said out loud what all terrorists, the world over, knew in their hearts. "Each death sends horror through a thousand still-beating hearts."

"That's right," Davis confirmed. "And in addition to the strikes you've already set up here in Europe, I'd like you to send some of your men to the U.S." He glanced at the Hamas man's sport coat, slacks and the rest of his Western attire. "And I'd like them to wear more-traditional Islamic clothing than you have on, if you don't mind."

"We can disguise ourselves as Christians and Jews when necessary," Nasab said. "Won't robes and headdresses draw attention to us?"

Davis almost burst out laughing. "Of course it will," he said. "And that's exactly what we want. It'll scare the hell out of people, but they won't get in your way. You've heard of political correctness?"

Nasab nodded. "Of course."

"Well," Davis went on, "the average American doesn't know the difference between the Muslim sects, and they'll be so afraid of offending you that you could probably hide a howitzer under your robe and no one would say anything." He stopped talking long enough to pull a French cigarette from a crumpled package he'd purchased the day before at a tobacco shop. "They can call it political correctness if they want," he said as he lit the tip, then cleared his throat. "I call it stupidity. But it's a stupidity we can use to our own advantage."

Nasab smiled his understanding.

"We'll get the anthrax-mail thing going again," Davis said. "But on a larger scale than whoever did it before. I don't know who it was, but it was a damn good tactic. I want people afraid to even open their electric bill."

"That is easily accomplished as soon as my men and I arrive in the U.S.," Nasab said. "We already have a large supply of anthrax at our disposal. And much of it is already in the possession of our cells in America."

"Good," Davis said. "And I want to begin a food-poisoning campaign. It's easy enough for someone to walk through the fruit-and-vegetable section of any supermarket and inject fresh foods with the poison of their choice." He stopped talking as the waitress set their coffee on the round metal table. He didn't open his mouth again until she had turned to go back into the café and was well out of earshot. "Even one death like this'll make all of America afraid to eat anything that didn't come out of an airtight can."

Nasab smiled. "I like the plan so far," he said. "Then, perhaps once they have quit eating fresh fruits, vegetables, meat and other foods, we can plant men in the canneries. Your Americans will be less suspect than my darker-skinned brethren, and they can poison the canned food, making your countrymen afraid to eat anything." He paused, chuckled and took a sip of coffee. When he had replaced the coffee cup in its saucer, he said, "And what is the final part of your plan?"

Davis leaned even closer. "Part two?" He grinned. "We attack and destroy the very heart of the American government."

He went on to tell Nasab the exact site, and what he had planned as a joint strike by the Rough Riders and Hamas. "Not as many people will die as they will in the events leading up to it," he finished. "But just think about the symbolic shock to the United States. No one will ever feel safe again, even in their homes. They'll know that if we can get in there, we can get in anywhere."

The smile remained on Nasab's face. "It will be a true jihad," he said quietly.

"For you, yes," Davis said. "I've been calling it the Night of Hell. My men are already in America, so they'll be easy enough to move to the attack sites. You have men in cells all over the country, as well. But I'd like you to start bringing in even more. Through Mexico is always a good way—you've proved that. And the Canadian border is still unguarded for the most part. There are dozens of back roads you can take, and no one will even know your men are here. And don't forget the coasts—both Atlantic and Pacific. One ship pulling up to an isolated spot can off-load hundreds of Hamas operatives." He paused for a sip of coffee. "You'll need to bring your own small arms for the most part. If you run short, I can arm some of your men. But I don't have enough rifles or sidearms for all of Hamas. And we'll need as many of those suicide-bomb vests of yours as you can smuggle in."

Nasab frowned. "Your men are going to use them?"

Davis laughed out loud. "Of course not," he said. "Killing ourselves isn't quite our thing. But it's yours, isn't it?"

"Well," Ibrahim Nasab said slowly, "it is one of the tactics we employ when necessary, yes. And it is a path directly to Paradise."

"In any case, suicide bombings are what you're most famous for, aren't they?" Davis continued. "The World Trade Center and the Pentagon? All your buddy Bin Laden missed that day was the White House with that last flight. And you've blown up thousands of people—including the bombers themselves—in smaller ops against Israel and other spots around the world."

"You expect all of the suicides to come from *my* men?" Nasab asked.

"Like I said," Davis replied. "It's what you do, isn't it?"

The Arab forced a smile. "Yes," he said. "It is what we do. But why stop with the vests? We have small backpack nuclear bombs in our possession. One is all it would take."

Davis shook his head. "Uh-uh," he said. "I want this to be a surgical strike. Controllable. Besides destroying ninety percent of the United States infrastructure—which we'll need once we step in and take the reins—a nuke would indiscriminately kill my men, as well as yours."

An expression of loathing and disrespect curled Nasab's lips into a frown. "So you do not mind if my men die, only your own?"

"Exactly," Davis said. "But don't forget it was you guys wrote the rules on suicide bombings, not us. We don't do suicide. Or windows."

The puzzled look returned to Nasab, the joke obviously lost on him.

A long pause followed as the men finished their coffee. Finally, seeing only tiny black grounds in the bottom of his cup, Davis said, "Then it's decided, right? My American Rough Riders and Hamas will work together for our common goal—the attacks leading up to the big one, and then the one we're calling the Night of Hell. I'm not kidding myself—it won't bring the American government completely down. But it ought to drop it to its knees, and from there we may be able to pound it on into the ground." He started to stick out his hand to shake Nasab's, then drew it back, remembering whom he was dealing with.

Nasab had almost lifted his own hand. But now he dropped it again. "You have called it the Night of Hell. We have been referring to it simply the American jihad."

"American jihad," Davis said. "Night of Hell. Same thing."

Nasab nodded. "We have one major strike planned right here, tomorrow night in France. It will come the next day after your bank robbery in America, and can serve as one of the attacks leading up to the big night."

Davis nodded. "We've got a few things already planned in the U.S., too. In the meantime, start smuggling your operatives across the border."

"It is agreed," Nasab said. "But what are we to do once our joint mission is accomplished?"

Davis stood up, leaving several euros on the table next to his empty cup. Nasab followed him to his feet. "We'll have to work something out between us," he said. "But there's no sense worrying about that now."

Nasab nodded hesitantly.

Davis could see on the Arab's face that they were thinking the same thing.

Once the Night of Hell was over, the alliance between them would end. And it would become time for Hamas and the Rough Riders to start killing each other. But that didn't matter right now. And by the time it did, Benjamin Franklin Davis's other plan—the one about which Nasab was completely unaware—would have corrected the problem.

"We'll stay in touch by cell phone," Davis said as the two men left the sidewalk café and began walking down the street. "My electronics expert has worked on them, and they're all but untappable."

"When do we begin?" Nasab asked as they passed a florist's shop and the pleasant odor of freshly cut spring flowers filled their nostrils.

Davis glanced at his watch. The bank robbery should be well under way by now. "We already have, my friend," he said. "We already have."

# 1

The huge windowpane closest to the bank's front doors shattered, the tiny shards glistening like snowflakes as they fell through the bright sunlight. But before they had hit the ground, the bank robber in green coveralls and navy blue ski mask dropped the 9 mm Uzi and toppled to the pavement, dead.

Mack Bolan, aka the Executioner, crouched behind the Kia he was using as cover. Up and down the row of cars parked outside the bank in Kansas City, Missouri, SWAT operatives in dark blue BDU blouses and matching pants had their own rifles pointed toward the building.

Bolan had used up most of his 30-round magazine from the M-16 A-2 in taking out the window and the would-be bank robber, and now he shoved a fresh box mag into the rifle. The robbers still inside the bank and the cops behind the cars exchanged gunfire. If the gunfire continued long enough, Bolan knew it would accomplish nothing except getting the hostages inside the building killed.

Turning to the ruddy-complexioned SWAT captain next to him, the Executioner yelled, "Tell your men to cease-fire, Tom! If we don't establish some kind of dialogue fast, the good guys still inside are going to get killed."

"Cease-fire!" the captain screamed. Leaning his chin toward the microphone clipped to the epaulet on his left shoulder, he flipped a switch on his nylon utility belt and repeated the order. "Cease-fire!"

As the roar of the gunshots died down, Bolan thought about the strange situation in which he now found himself. He had been at Stony Man Farm, America's top-secret counterterrorist command post and training grounds. In addition to fielding top-notch assault teams like Able Team and Phoenix Force, Stony Man handpicked exceptional soldiers and police officers from the U.S. and friendly nations for advanced combat training. These men were flown to the Farm blindfolded, then left the same way—never knowing exactly where they'd been or who had trained them. What they did know was that they'd never received such pragmatic or intense instruction anywhere else in the world.

Tom Glasser, the sturdily built Kansas City captain next to the Executioner, had just completed a Stony Man session. When a local snitch informed the Kansas City PD of the upcoming bank robbery planned by the Rough Riders—a faction of the American Nazi Party—Glasser and Bolan had been flown straight from Stony Man Farm.

Bolan let the bolt on his M-16 slide home, chambering a round. The air seemed eerily quiet now. He watched quietly as a uniformed officer, hunkered low beneath the vehicles, approached Glasser's other side. When he was near enough, the uniform whisper-shouted a phone number.

Glasser wasted no time pulling a cell phone from a nylon carrier on his belt and tapping in the number. A second later, he had one of the bank robbers on the line.

"All right," he said into the instrument. "Let's cut the formalities. What do you want in exchange for the hostages?" He thumbed another button and activated the speakerphone so Bolan could hear the other end of the conversation, too.

The raspy cough of a heavy cigarette smoker sounded over the speakerphone. "Every damn penny we'll be hauling out of this bank," the bank robber declared. "And five million more for the inconvenience you've caused us." The voice paused and took in a hacking breath. "After that, the usual. A chopper big enough to take thirty people—that'll include some of the hostages—to the airport, a plane full of fuel ready to take off and a pilot who isn't a disguised cop." The man coughed again. "We find a weapon of any kind on him, or anything else that makes us think the flyboy's a pig, and we'll blow his head off."

Glasser looked toward Bolan. Even though he was technically in charge of this operation, the SWAT commander had just spent a month enduring the most rigorous cutting-edge training he'd had in his career, and Bolan had taught several of those classes. Hostage negotiation had been one of them.

Bolan answered the unasked question by silently mouthing the words, "You know what to do. *Stall.*"

"I don't have the authority to meet your demands," Glasser said into the cell phone. "It can be done. But it's going to take time."

"You've got time," the man across the street rasped. "Twenty minutes."

"I can't even get clearance for the chopper and plane in that length of time," Glasser said. "Let alone raise five million bucks for you."

"Well, you'd better try," the gravelly voice snapped. "Because each minute you're late means another dead hostage." There was a pause, then a low, phlegm-sounding chuckle. "I'll just shoot them, then toss them out the front window you guys blew out so you can see them." He finished with, "You've now got nineteen minutes." The line clicked dead.

Glasser cut the call at his end and turned once again toward the Executioner. He had known Bolan as Matt Cooper while training at the Farm, and still did. "Any suggestions, Cooper?" he said.

"Yeah," Bolan said. "Get on the phone and start trying to get clearance for the chopper and plane. And check with the local Secret Service field office. See how much counterfeit money they've got on hand." He looked the burly man in the eye. "These guys aren't going to have the time or the equipment to check out good fakes, and it'll be a lot easier than trying to talk any other bank or rich individual into gambling with five million real dollars."

Glasser nodded and began tapping numbers into his phone.

Rising to his feet, the Executioner stayed low, bending over to whisper into Glasser's ear. "You're never going to make the twenty-minute deadline," he said.

Glasser had just hung up the phone. "I know," he said.

"And if the guys inside are from the Rough Riders, they aren't bluffing," Bolan said just as quietly. He remembered a recent intelligence report that Aaron "The Bear" Kurtzman—Stony Man Farm's chief computer expert—had put together about this militant faction of the American Nazi Party. The Rough Riders were suspected in several murders and—like so many homegrown American terrorist groups—relied on bank robbery as their primary means of support.

"Do we know how many hostages are inside?" the Executioner asked.

Glasser shook his head as he touched the cell phone to his ear for the next call. "Not exactly," he said. "There'll be twenty to thirty employees, plus however many customers happened to be there at the wrong time."

Bolan nodded and started to move past the man.

Glasser reached out and grabbed Bolan's arm. "Where are you going?" he asked.

The Executioner squatted again. "I've got an idea," he said. "And if you don't know it, you can't accidentally give it away to the enemy." He paused for a deep breath, then went on. "Just conduct this operation as if I wasn't here. But when you hear shots fired inside the bank again, move your men in as fast as possible. Got it?"

"Got it."

"And give me one of those two-ways so I can keep track of you," the Executioner said.

Glasser waved at one of his SWAT men, a slender sergeant with dark brown hair. "Give Cooper here your radio and mike," he said. "Then go back to the van and get another one for yourself."

The sergeant didn't even bother to ask who Cooper was. Jerking the radio from his belt and the microphone from his shoulder, he handed them over.

The Executioner snapped the radio onto his belt, checked the earpiece connection, then shoved the tiny plastic receiver into one ear. He clipped the microphone to the shoulder of his blacksuit. He looked at his watch.

Not quite ninety seconds had passed since the raspy voice inside the bank had given them their twenty-minute deadline.

The innocents inside had roughly eighteen and a half minutes.

Police cars completely surrounded the bank. Three of the building's four sides faced streets, and here the vehicles were lined up practically bumper to bumper. To the rear of the bank—beyond the drive-through windows—was a housing complex. Here, the police cars had pulled directly onto the grounds beyond the windows, doing their best to provide a buffer zone between the innocent residents in their houses and the miscreants in the bank. Behind the circle of cars knelt uniformed officers, plainclothes detectives and the rest of Glasser's SWAT crew, each of the men training a weapon on the bank.

Moving to the rear of the bank, Bolan sprinted for one of the marked units separating the bank from the residential area. But no shots followed him.

Dropping down behind the black-and-white patrol car, Bolan found himself next to a portly patrolman resting his Glock 21 across the hood and aiming it toward the drive-through window into the bank. The man's uniform cap had been discarded and lay next to him on the ground. Coarse but sparse red-and-gray hair stuck up from his receding hairline and balding pate.

The patrolman glanced at Bolan, then back to the bank.

"You seen any activity through that teller's window since you've been here?" Bolan asked.

The patrolman nodded. "Some. There's a guy with a ski mask just out of sight below the glass. He pops his head up every few seconds and—" The blue head suddenly appeared as the officer spoke. "There! You see him?"

Bolan nodded. "You see anyone else?"

The balding man shook his head. "Just him."

The Executioner drew back slightly, taking in the rear of the bank as a whole. The First Fidelity Bank was a one-story building. Awnings covered the three drive-up windows with brick columns supporting what looked like shake-shingle roofs. He wondered whether they would support his two-hundred-plus pounds.

He suspected he was about to find out.

"What's your name?" Bolan asked the cop next to him.

"Coleman," said the man. "Call me Ron."

"You might want to hold back on that familiarity until you hear the rest of what I'm about to say," Bolan told him.

"Huh?"

"You wearing a vest, Coleman?" Bolan asked.

"You better believe it," said the man with the sparse red-and-gray hair. "I've got a wife and kids I like to go home and see every night."

"Shock plate inserted?" Bolan asked.

"Right over the old ticker. Thickest steel they make 'em in."

The KCPD officer's voice was starting to sound suspicious now. "Why?"

"Because I need to use you as a decoy," the Executioner said. "I'm going up on the roof. And if that blue ski mask happens to pop up at the wrong time and see me, it'll ruin what I have in mind."

Now the patrolman's voice took on a true tone of trepidation. "What is it you expect me to do?"

"Just get up and start walking toward the window. If Mr. Ski Mask shows his head or a weapon or both, take cover behind one of those brick columns. I just need his attention on you and not me."

"In other words, if someone has to get shot you'd rather it be me than you?"

"No," Bolan said. "It's just the way this thing has to go down, that's all. If you don't want to do it, say so now. I'll try to think of something else." He glanced at his watch. "But I've only got eleven minutes to come up with it and pull it off." He paused, then finished with, "So, Coleman. What'll it be?"

Bolan could see the concern on the man's face as he weighed his responsibilities to the job versus those to his family.

"All right," Coleman finally said. "Tell me exactly what you want me to do." He paused, then added, "And you can still call me Ron."

The Executioner smiled. It was a brave man he was working with.

"When I give you the word, just stand up and start walking directly toward the window. If you see the ski mask, make tracks for the brick column. After that, just stay where you are."

"What are you going to be doing?" Coleman asked.

"Scaling the wall. But don't look my way under any circumstances. I need that lookout's attention focused on you, or the inside of the bank's going to look like a Chicago slaughterhouse."

Coleman reached up and adjusted his vest, making sure the steel plate was in place. "Makes me wish I'd sprung for the steel-plated jockstrap you can get with these things," he said. "But what the hell. I've already got three kids and the wife and I were talking about a vasectomy anyway." He turned to face the Executioner. "Say when."

Bolan slung his M-16 A-2 over his shoulder and waited until the blue ski mask made another quick appearance, then disappeared. "Now!" he said under his breath and rose to his feet at the same time Coleman stood up. Coleman rounded the trunk, and the Executioner cut in front of the front bumper as both men made their way toward the building.

Bolan was running, Coleman walking—as he'd been instructed. So the Executioner reached the brick column supporting the carport several steps in front of the man. Sprinting at full speed, he lifted his right knee almost to his chin as his leather-and-nylon combat boot hit the bricks. His momentum carried him upward, and he got one more step with his left boot before he felt gravity beginning to overcome his own velocity.

Reaching skyward, the Executioner got his fingertips just over the edge of the shake-shingle roofing.

A second later, he had pulled himself up and out of sight on top of the carport.

No sooner had he risen to his knees than he heard several shots fired below him. Looking down, he saw Coleman driven back a step as the rounds clanged off the steel plate in his vest. But the balding cop he didn't let that stop him. Before the man inside the window could fire again, he dived behind the brick column.

Bolan leaned over the side and looked down. He could see Coleman sitting with his back against the bricks, the sparse and spiky reddish-gray hair pointing straight up at the top of the carport. The Executioner whispered downward, "Ron, you okay?"

The KCPD patrolman was savvy enough not to look upward when he answered. "If you call feeling like you just took three straight hooks to the chest from Buster Douglas okay, then yeah—I'm just peachy."

The Executioner chuckled. At least the man was out of danger now. He could sit out the rest of this encounter. "Okay," he said. "Stay where you are."

Bolan looked down at his wrist. He had a little under ten minutes before the hostages started dying. Switching on the microphone mounted to his shoulder, Bolan realized he had no call letters or numbers of his own, and he didn't know what Tom Glasser's were, either. So he said simply, "Cooper to Glasser. Cooper to Glasser. Come in, Glasser."

"SWAT 1," Glasser's voice came back. "This is Glasser, Cooper. You got a call name?"

The Executioner lowered his voice until he suspected it could barely be heard on the other end of the line. "I go by Striker, SWAT 1. And I'm on the roof," he whispered. "Have you had any more contact with the subjects inside?"

"Negative, Striker," Glasser came back. He was whispering, too. "But we've got the funny money on the way here, compliments of the Secret Service."

"How about the chopper?" Bolan asked.

"We're trying to find one big enough. And that's not easy if you don't go to the military."

Bolan immediately understood the reason behind the SWAT captain's words. The regular military was forbidden from taking action in police matters inside the U.S., and most of the time that was a good thing—it ensured that America would not become a military state ruled by its armed forces. But there were exceptions to that rule, when the use of the armed forces seemed like the only logical answer.

This was one of them.

"See if you can go through the state's National Guard," the Executioner said. "If they don't have a chopper big enough on hand, they ought to be able to get one from the regular army." He paused and felt his eyebrows furrow as he thought further. "And use this as an excuse to stall some more. Call into the bank on your cell phone and explain the problem with the chopper. See if you can buy some more time."

"Affirmative, Striker," Glasser said. "May I ask what you're doing?"

"Negative, SWAT 1," Bolan said as he made his way carefully across the shingled roof one shaky step at a time. "And the fact that I'm up top is for your ears only. We can't expect fifty men—no matter how good they are—to keep from glancing up and being seen by the bad guys."

"Roger, Striker," Glasser said. "That intel stays in-house."

Bolan finally made it off the carport roofs and onto the flat tar roof of the bank proper. His eyes skirted the building, seeing ventilation shafts, heat and air-conditioning equipment, and a variety of other pipes and housings sticking up out of the dirty black surface. He walked slowly around the perimeter of the building, staying just far enough from the edge that his head couldn't be seen by the police officers on the ground.

He had meant what he'd told Glasser. All it would take would be for one of the Rough Riders below him to see one cop straining his eyes toward the roof to know someone was above them. Then the element of surprise would be gone.

The Executioner had hoped to find a return air shaft or some similar means to enter the building below, but he had no such luck. Banks were built with the hope of keeping people *out* after business hours, and the rough roof of First Fidelity was no exception. There were holes leading down into the building, all right. But the Executioner would have had to have been the size of a house cat to get through them.

With one exception.

Near the street side of the building, above what Bolan assumed would be the bank's front lobby, was a large skylight.

Slowly, he crept toward it, formulating his plan of attack as
he went. If the skylight was plastic, he'd be out of luck here,
too. He'd have to shoot enough holes through the plastic with
the M-16 A-2 to create an opening large enough to drop
through. And by the time that had been accomplished, the
Rough Riders would have had time to kill the bank employees and other hostages several times over.

But if it was glass…

When he'd drawn near enough that he feared he might be
seen be someone looking upward, Bolan dropped to his belly
and used his elbows to pull himself the rest of the way to the
skylight. Then, slowly—almost ceremoniously—he reached
out with his left hand and tapped the clear surface in front of him.

Both the sound, and the feel, brought a smile to his face.

The skylight was made of glass. It would shatter just as
quickly, and as surely, as the picture window next to the front
door had.

Crawling back a few yards, the Executioner rose to his feet
again and activated the mike on his shoulder. "Striker to
SWAT 1," he said. "Come in, SWAT 1."

"I hear you Striker," came back into his ear.

Bolan looked at his watch. He had a little over a minute
before the twenty-minute deadline. "You buy us any extra
time with the National Guard story?" he asked Glasser.

"Negative," said the SWAT commander. "The guy just
laughed, told me he knew a stall job when he heard one, then
repeated his threat to start killing one hostage for each minute we were late."

"Okay," Bolan said. "Then it's Plan B time." He glanced
at his watch once more.

Forty-five seconds remained.

He was about to speak to Glasser again when he saw another man in green coveralls and a blue ski mask shove a
middle-aged woman directly under the skylight. The late-

afternoon sun was at an angle that gave him an almost perfect view through the glass and, he suspected, would block or at least distort what could be seen by anyone looking up through the skylight.

But at this stage of the game he was taking no chances. Bolan took another step back until only the tops of the man's and woman's heads were visible. He had already seen all he needed to see.

The man in the coveralls had wrapped his left forearm around the woman's throat. The short, stubby muzzle of an Ingram MAC-11 submachine gun was pressed against her nape. The watch on his wrist was clearly visible, and Bolan could see the Rough Rider staring at it, counting off the final seconds just as the Executioner was doing above, on the roof.

Bolan glanced at the MAC-11 again. Those submachine guns cycled at a phenomenally fast rate of fire. Unless the man firing the weapon was extremely experienced with it, he could empty the entire 30-round magazine before he let up on the trigger. All of which made the Ingrams less suitable for combat than for assassinations.

But an outright murder was exactly what was going to happen in less than thirty seconds unless the Executioner acted swiftly. The woman's head would be almost completely gone before the Rough Rider even had time to let up on the trigger.

Bolan looked at his wrist. Twenty-eight seconds.

"Listen and listen fast, SWAT 1," he whispered into the mike. "Fifteen seconds from the time I stop talking I'm coming down through the skylight. You should hear a few shots from me up top here, then glass breaking. Tell your men that's their cue—when they hear the gunfire and then the crash it's time to charge the building."

"You've got it," Glasser said. "Anything else?"

"Yeah," Bolan said. "Make sure that your men know that once they're inside the bank, they're to take orders from me."

"I'll make sure they understand it," Glasser said. "When do we begin the countdown?"

"Fifteen seconds from…*now*," Bolan said.

He took a deep breath and squinted through the glass. From where he stood, he had a good angle at the head of the man in the green coveralls. He switched the M-16 to 3-round burst mode, then lined up the sights on the back of the man's head. The holes he was about to drill through the glass would weaken it and make it shatter even easier.

The Executioner took a final glance at his watch, then returned his eyes to the sights. Slowly, he squeezed the trigger and watched the back of the Rough Rider's head blow off as three tiny holes appeared in the skylight.

A second after that, he leaped onto the glass in a sitting position and crashed through the skylight into the First Fidelity Bank.

THE EXECUTIONER STRAIGHTENED his legs as he fell through the glass, thankful that the blacksuit was made out of cut-resistant material. Still, he felt a few shreds of glass scrape his hands and face, and by the time his feet hit the floor of the bank's lobby he could feel tiny drops of blood running down his cheeks.

They mattered little in the grand scheme of things.

The Executioner landed on his feet, right behind the screaming woman and the dead Rough Rider who had fallen to her rear. To his right was a popcorn machine designed and built to look like the type found in old-fashioned movie theaters. Such fake antique popcorn machines seemed, for some reason, to be standard fare in modern banks. They were made out of thin metal and glass, and offered concealment but not cover.

Bolan pivoted on the balls of his feet, turning toward the cashiers' windows. The first thing he saw were the hostages. Roughly a dozen people who looked like customers lay on their faces on the floor, their hands clasped behind their heads. Next to them, at least twice as many bank employees—both males and females wearing tan slacks and maroon polo shirts sporting the bank's logo—lay in the same position.

The Executioner's sudden descent through the skylight had come as a complete surprise to the bank robbers. Like the pair he had already encountered, they also wore green coveralls and blue ski masks. But Bolan noted one major difference.

The masks of these men had been rolled up into simple blue stocking caps. This aided their vision, but it told the Executioner something else, as well.

These Rough Riders weren't worried about the customers or bank employees seeing their faces, which meant they intended to kill all the hostages.

A Rough Rider with a wide handlebar mustache was the first to recover from the shock of Bolan's aerial entry. He lifted the Uzi in his hands toward the Executioner.

But Bolan was a fraction of a second faster. The Executioner's first 3-round burst hit the mustachioed Rough Rider squarely in the chest. Above the explosions of the rounds Bolan heard a high-pitched ringing sound. He immediately realized that Coleman, the uniformed cop outside, wasn't the only one wearing a Kevlar vest with a steel insert. At least some of the Rough Riders had them, too.

While the trio of rounds from the Executioner's assault rifle had driven the man with the mustache several paces backward into a desk, they hadn't stopped him. The Rough Rider began to raise his Uzi again, and more rounds from another direction whizzed past the Executioner's ears, sounding like angry bees.

Bolan's next triburst was aimed at his target's head. The first slug took off the upper right half of his face and blew brains, blood and fragments of skull out the back of his head. The second and third rounds disappeared somewhere in the gore before the Rough Rider slumped to the tile floor in front of the desk.

The Executioner ducked behind the popcorn machine as more rounds from behind the tellers' windows zipped past him. As he hit the floor, a barrage of fire from a variety of weapons shattered the glass of the popcorn machine and tore through the thin red metal stand.

Suddenly, the First Fidelity Bank lobby appeared to be snowing popcorn and glass, both raining over Bolan where he lay on his side. The unusual combined odor of exploding gunpowder, popcorn and butter filled the Executioner's nostrils.

Several of the rounds that had ripped through the red metal stand had missed Bolan by millimeters. And the bank robbers knew that sooner or later, if they simply kept peppering the popcorn machine with fire, some of their rounds would find vital organs.

The Executioner knew that, too. Slinging the M-16 over his shoulder, he suddenly dived from behind the machine into the open. Hitting the floor on his right shoulder, he rolled under several bursts of fire just inches above him. The shoulder roll took him all the way to the desk where the man with the mustache lay in death, and the Executioner squeezed in between the dead man and the desk, using them both for cover now. He saw a flash of blue as one of the Rough Riders raised his head to fire through a teller's window.

Bolan triggered his M-16. The blue stocking cap blew off the top of the man's head. So did half of the head itself.

Two men in coveralls suddenly emerged through a formerly closed door next to the tellers' windows. Behind them, Bolan could see a private office. An employee wearing the same maroon polo shirt lay on the floor, bloody and battered but breathing.

Both of the men coming out the door carried Uzis, and both were well over six feet and broad shouldered. They made the mistake of trying to exit the office at the same time, and for a split second wedged themselves together in the doorway in a scene worthy of The Three Stooges. But the Uzis kept all humor out of the Executioner's brain as he flipped the M-16's selector switch to semiauto, then put one 5.56 mm bullet between each man's eyes.

They fell to the floor, dead.

For a moment, the gunfire died down and Bolan heard the sounds of running footsteps outside the building. He smiled grimly to himself. Glasser and his men were on the way. Their arrival was confirmed by the sounds of window glass breaking and side exit doors being rammed open.

Quickly, Bolan assessed the situation. The fact that the gunfire had died down meant there were a limited number of men who could see him. Which, in turn, meant the Rough Riders had to be scattered throughout the bank. The breaking glass and doors being rammed meant Glasser's SWAT teams were entering the bank at various positions. They would take care of the offices, vault area and other rooms behind the tellers' windows. But there was still one place just off the lobby that needed attention. The safe-deposit box room. And the Executioner was the most likely candidate to cover it.

Bolan could see the barred door was on the other side of the lobby, across from him.

And the barred door was *open*.

The Executioner squeezed out from between the desk and the dead man with the mustache, the M-16 aimed toward the tellers' windows. There was always a chance that he'd been wrong in his assessment as to the cease-fire, and one or more Rough Riders might be hidden back there, just waiting for an opportunity such as Bolan was now giving him.

But such was not the case. Making his way silently toward the safe-deposit box door, trying to avoid the broken glass, shreds of metal, popcorn and anything else that might make a sound and alert the men in the safe-deposit box room that he was coming.

When he reached the door, the Executioner dropped to one knee and peered inside. Row upon row of safe-deposit boxes were stacked to a height of seven feet or so, and they prevented him from seeing anyone in the room.

But they didn't prevent his hearing the conversation.

"I *can't* open them," a young female voice pleaded between sobs. "It takes both our key and the customers'."

"Then you'd better find some other way of getting into them," said the same cigarette-smoking voice Bolan had heard over Glasser's cell phone. "Because if I have to shoot the damn things open, and any jewelry or other valuables get damaged, my next shot is going right between those pretty little tits of yours."

The sobs increased in volume.

A moment later, a lone shot was fired, but Bolan continued to hear the young woman cry. So the round had gone into one of the boxes rather than her chest.

But it was only a matter of time before the raspy voice grew impatient, realized they were already under attack and killed her in order to concentrate his efforts on escape.

Because by now the Rough Riders could be pretty sure that neither a helicopter nor an airplane was in their immediate future.

"Find anything, Carl?" the raspy voice asked.

"Nah," said a new voice. "Nothing we can use anyway."

"Then shoot the next one."

Bolan squeezed through the small opening between the barred door and the wall, trying not to move the door in case its hinges needed oiling. When he'd accomplished that feat, he stayed low, duck-walking his way past the several rows of safe-deposit boxes until he came to a stack just beyond where the two men and the woman were standing. At least he *thought* there were only two men—because only two men had spoken. He reminded himself that there could be more Rough Riders there, assisting in the pilfering of the boxes, who had kept quiet.

Bolan flipped the selector switch to safety and set the M-16 on the floor. Slowly and silently he drew the sound-suppressed Beretta 93-R. If there were more than just the two men, he would take out as many as he could with the near silent Beretta. With any luck, he'd capture the man with the raspy voice alive. He hoped it went down that way at least. Dead men not only told no tales, but they also gave up no intelligence information.

But it was not to be.

Behind them, through the lobby and at the rear of the bank, came the roar of gunfire as Glasser's SWAT teams entered the building and engaged the Rough Riders spread throughout the bank. The raspy voice on the other side of the stack of steel boxes said, "Okay, that's it. We need to get out of here. Kill her, Carl, and let's get going."

Bolan could wait no longer.

Still squatting, the Executioner leaned around the corner and saw a short, stocky man with a three-day growth of beard lifting a Government Model 1911 .45 to the temple of the openly crying female bank employee. He had already made contact with the muzzle of the .45 by the time the Executioner lined up the Beretta's sights on him and flipped the selector to semiauto as he'd done with the M-16. But his other suspicions had been accurate. Besides the man with the unfiltered cigarette voice, three more armed men in coveralls stool in the aisle in front of the boxes.

One 9 mm round was all it would take to save the young woman, but it would have to be precisely placed, and he could control that placement better with the Beretta in semiauto mode. The shot would have to go directly into the Rough

Rider's brain stem and shut down all motor functions, lest the man called Carl pulled the trigger of the .45 in a convulsion of death.

Taking a deep breath, the Executioner let out half of it, stopped, then gently squeezed the Beretta's trigger. The sound suppressor coughed out the bullet. A subsonic, semijacketed hollowpoint entered the man's brain, and he dropped the .45 as he fell to the floor.

But the shot had drawn the attention of the other men down the aisle toward Bolan, and one of the coveralled men now raised a Heckler & Koch MP-5. With no time to switch to 3-round-burst mode, the Executioner aimed carefully again, hitting the main squarely in the nose. In his peripheral vision, he saw the raspy-voiced man he assumed was the leader take off down the aisle, away from him. But he had no chance to stop him because the second of the third men was now trying to fix the sights of a Glock on the Executioner.

Bolan remembered the vest on the man with the mustache and again aimed high. The shot took the Rough Rider in the scalp. But it was not a kill shot. The man got off one wild 10 mm round from his large-framed Glock. Miraculously it missed both Bolan and the female bank employee. The Executioner fired again.

And this time, his near silent 9 mm round caught the man in the right eye.

The only man left had taken off his ski mask completely, and Bolan could see it stuffed in a side pocket of the coveralls. He fired once more, and the 9 mm slug took out the last Rough Rider's left eye.

All of the men who had accompanied the raspy-voiced leader into the safe-deposit room were dead.

Bolan rushed up to the young woman, who was sniffling between sobs. "You all right?" he asked.

She nodded. "Thank you," she managed through the crying.

Bolan looked past her to the end of the aisle. The leader of the Rough Riders was nowhere to be seen. The Executioner carefully searched the rest of the room, but was not surprised when the cigarette smoker didn't turn up.

The man had used his own troops to give him time to escape.

Picking up his M-16 as he left the room, Bolan could still hear gunfire coming from the rear of the bank. One of the SWAT men was in the lobby, personally holding the front door open for the terrified hostages and telling each one to stay close—they'd need statements from them all.

"Anybody in the teller's area?" Bolan asked the man as he passed.

The SWAT trooper shook his head. "What's left of them is in the back. They've barricaded themselves in the vault."

Bolan stopped in his tracks. "You get a look at the vault?" he asked.

The SWAT man nodded.

"Can the door be opened from the inside once it's locked?"

The man holding the door for the hostages nodded. "I just caught a glance at it earlier when I ran by. And I'm no safe expert, but it looked like it to me."

Bolan hurried through the swinging door, stepping over several dead bodies in coveralls as he made his way to the back of the bank. He passed several private offices as he ran down an empty hallway. Turning a corner, he passed two more SWAT team members who lowered their AR-15s as soon as they recognized him.

The two men appeared to have gotten Glasser's orders that Bolan was in charge. They both saluted as he ran by.

At the end of the hallway, Bolan found both the closed and locked vault door, and SWAT Captain Tom Glasser along with more of his men. A half dozen more dead Rough Riders, all dressed in coveralls and blue stocking caps, had been piled unceremoniously against the wall, out of the way.

Which was fine with the Executioner. Terrorists deserved no ceremony when they were righteously killed.

"What's going down?" the Executioner asked the recent Stony Man Farm graduate.

Glasser's eyes reflected a deep confusion. "They've barricaded themselves in the vault, and they've got hostages," he said. "It's really no different than when they held the whole bank a few minutes ago. The playing field's just become smaller."

"How many of them left?" Bolan asked.

"The bad guys? Five, maybe six. And they've got three or four hostages. Can't be certain." He paused a second, then went on. "That raspy voice we heard on the phone?"

"Yeah?" the Executioner said.

"He's one of them."

Bolan nodded. "Same demands?" he asked.

Glasser nodded. "Yeah," he said, "but at least we can probably get them to settle for a smaller helicopter this time."

The Executioner nodded at the attempt at dark humor on Glasser's part. It was one of the ways cops and soldiers relieved tension.

Then he turned and looked at the vault door.

There would be no skylight to bust through here.

So he would have to come up with an alternate plan, and come up with it fast.

## 2

"You inside the vault!" the Executioner yelled at the top of his lungs. "Can you hear me?" He got no response. But a few seconds later, the walkie-talkie on Glasser's hip screeched. Then the voice of a female dispatcher said, "Base to SWAT 1. Come in, SWAT 1."

Glasser leaned toward the microphone on his shoulder and said, "SWAT 1, here."

"Ten-four, SWAT 1," the woman on the other end said. "Be advised we just received a cell phone call from a man claiming to be inside the vault at your location. He wants your cell phone number. Should I give it to him?"

Glasser's face turned into a mask of both outrage and astonishment. "*Of course* you should give it to him," he said, his voice dripping with sarcasm.

The woman on the other end either didn't catch the SWAT captain's tone or didn't care. Her voice remained colorless. "Ten-four, SWAT 1," she said, then ended the call.

Bolan and Glasser glanced at each other as they waited for the call they suspected would be coming from inside the vault. The Executioner had not been surprised that he'd gotten no response to his yelling—the vault door was thick steel and sealed tightly around the edges. What *did* surprise him was that the Rough Rider's cell phone had worked from within the vault. He'd have bet against it. But there was no rhyme or reason to cell phones, it seemed, and he was glad he'd been wrong.

Without some way to communicate with the Rough Riders still alive inside the vault they'd remain at this stalemate indefinitely.

Less than a minute after the radio transmission had taken place, Glasser's cell phone rang. Pulling it from his belt, he glanced to the Executioner.

Bolan reached out for it, and Glasser gave him the phone. Bolan thumbed the talk button, pressed the instrument to his ear and said, "Go ahead."

"We seem to be at a Mexican standoff," said the same raspy voice Bolan had heard over the cell phone's speakerphone earlier.

"I think we've got a slight advantage over you," the Executioner came back. "We've got access to all the food and water we need out here. We can just wait you out. Of course you could try eating the money all around you in there. Try the hundreds—I hear they're the best."

"Nice try," said the gravelly voice. "But you *don't* have the advantage. We do. You see, any time I decide to do it, my men and I can kill the bank people in here, drop our weapons, then open the door and come out with our hands up." He laughed in a low, guttural tone. "You're cops. We'll be unarmed and you'll have to take us into custody instead of killing us."

Bolan turned and walked away from the other men, going to the opposite end of the hallway, out of earshot. In a whisper, he said, "Everybody out here is a cop *except* me. And I promise you that if you kill those innocent people in there with you, I'll gut shoot every one of you and make sure you die slow."

"Bullshit," rasped the voice inside the vault. "If you weren't a cop, you wouldn't even be in the bank right now."

Bolan's jaw set firmly, his teeth grinding together slightly. It was the response he'd expected, so he wasn't surprised.

Ironically, it was the truth. He would execute the remaining men if they harmed their innocent hostages. But the man with the cigarette voice would never believe it.

"Okay," the Executioner said. "You have some plan on how we can all come out of this alive?"

"I've already given you the plan," the voice said. "Five million, and a chopper to take us to the airport." Then, ironically, he repeated what Glasser had said as a joke. "We can settle for a smaller helicopter now. But it'll need to carry nine people."

"How many hostages do you have?" Bolan asked.

"Four."

"I'll expect you to let one of them go when the helicopter arrives, you get the five million, and you're onboard."

"Fair enough," the Rough Rider said. "Got a pregnant woman in here I'll give you just to show good faith. Sort of 'two for the price of one' deal." He laughed over the phone, but the laughter brought on another coughing fit.

Bolan paused. Once the pregnant woman had been freed, there would be five of the terrorists, including the man on the phone, still alive to deal with. That could be crucial information down the road. "I'll expect you to give me the other three people at the airport," he said.

"I'll give you *two* of the three at the airport." the Rough Rider coughed.

"What do you plan to do with the last one?" the Executioner asked.

"I'll cut him loose him when we land." A chuckle brought on another cough. "You'll understand, I'm sure, if I don't tell you exactly where that's going to be."

The Executioner noted that the raspy voice rose a little with the man's final words. That was one of the indicators of a lie. Letting the final hostage go free when they landed would be too risky. What the cigarette-smoking Rough Rider really had planned was to kill the final hostage. They'd either throw him out of the plane once they were in the air or shoot him or cut his throat.

Which meant the Executioner couldn't afford to let them reach the airplane. He had to end this game either before they got into the chopper or somewhere between the helicopter and the airplane.

"All right," Bolan said into Glasser's cell phone. "When do you plan to come out?" He paused a second, then said, "I'd like to get all this done before you die of emphysema."

An eerie silence filled the wireless cell phone connection, and Bolan could tell he'd hit a sore sport with the man. The raspy-voiced Rough Rider either did have emphysema or lung cancer or some smoking-related disease that was slowly killing him.

Which, Bolan reminded himself, only made the man more dangerous and unpredictable. Men who knew they were dying anyway were often willing to take chances that other men weren't.

"We're coming out right now," the grating voice finally said into his cell phone. "So you boys move down to the end of the hall unless you want some dead bank employees on your hands."

The Executioner turned toward Glasser and the other SWAT men gathered around him. But he had no need to issue an order. All of them double-timed it down to the other end of the hall. Bolan followed them.

"Are you away from the door yet?" the gravelly voice asked.

"We are," the Executioner said.

The vault door began to swing slowly open. Then a blue-ski-masked face peered around the heavy steel at Bolan and the rest of the SWAT warriors. Seemingly satisfied, the man wearing the mask and coveralls pushed the vault door the rest of the way open to the wall, making sure no one was hiding behind it.

Stepping brazenly out of the vault, the man who had opened the door coughed as he waved for the men still inside to come out. One by one, they did.

But it wasn't *really* one by one. More like two by two. Because three of the men had duct-taped pistols to the backs of the hostages' heads. More duct tape secured the guns to the Rough Riders' hands, and a strip of the sticky gray tape was across the eyes of the young man and two women who were pushed out and down the hall. All of the terrorists had pulled their blue ski masks down over their faces again. Their right hands held the pistols. Two AK-47s and an M-16 similar to Bolan's were slung over their left shoulders, with their left hands grasping the rifles and their fingers inside the trigger guard.

Only the pregnant woman was free of the tape. She was ushered out last, a ski-masked Rough Rider jamming a revolver into her cheek as he guided her down the hall with his other hand.

The gravelly voiced man brought up the rear, cutting off his cell phone and dropping it into a pocket in his coveralls.

Bolan punched the Off button and returned Glasser's phone to the SWAT commander.

As the procession walked toward them, Bolan stepped slowly forward, reaching out for the pregnant woman.

"No!" the cigarette smoker shouted, bringing up his M-16 and aiming it at the Executioner. The rest of the Rough Riders ground to a halt.

"You get her *after* we get the five million, and *after* we're on the helicopter."

Bolan nodded and stepped back. At this point, there was nothing else he could do.

The Rough Riders and their prisoners turned the corner and walked down the hall that led to the cashiers' windows, then the lobby. Bolan, Glasser and the other SWAT men who had been inside the bank with them followed. When they reached the lobby, they saw more SWAT personnel, their AR-15s aimed at the Rough Riders.

Bolan held out a hand, palm down, then lowered it.

The SWAT men let their rifles fall to the end of their slings.

Outside, the Executioner could hear the whopping sound of helicopter blades. As he followed the Rough Riders and hostages through the front door of the bank he saw not one but two small choppers. The markings on their sides announced to the world that they were Kansas City Police aircraft.

The man with the hoarse voice turned in anger. "I said *one* helicopter," he practically spit. "And neither one of those is big enough for all of us."

A sandy-haired man in his late thirties, wearing a suit more expensive than any cop could afford, stepped forward out of the crowd of uniformed and plainclothes officers. "Sir, I'm Peter Johnson, Kansas City Police media officer. I'm sorry, but this was the best we could do at such short notice. After all, you only gave us twenty minutes." He paused, the smile on his face forced. Bolan also noticed his hands trembling slightly at his sides. "You're welcome to use both of the helicopters, of course."

Bolan continued to watch the media officer. Peter Johnson wasn't used to getting this close to the fire, and the man could feel his eyebrows getting singed. He probably wasn't even a commissioned police officer—more of a public-relations man. And he wanted his part in this little minidrama over quickly.

"You're more than welcome to both helicopters," Johnson said again, his voice shaking.

For a moment, the man with the raspy voice seemed frozen in place, not knowing what to do. Then he motioned for two of the men holding the pistols to the backs of the hostages' heads toward one chopper. The man guiding the pregnant woman went with them. The rest started toward the other helicopter.

Bolan frowned. This new kink in the situation both helped and hurt. It would be good to have the armed men separated so they had less collective firepower. But separating the hostages would make them more difficult to rescue. If the men in one helicopter heard gunfire from the other, they'd immediately pull the triggers on their duct-taped pistols.

The Executioner watched as the Rough Riders pushed their hostages into the choppers and took seats. The man with the rough voice took the arm of the pregnant woman and shoved her onboard with the others. "I've changed my mind," he shouted over his shoulder. "Since you welched on the single-helicopter agreement, I think we'll just keep this lady and the little bastard in her belly a while longer."

Bolan wasn't surprised. But the man's sudden refusal to keep his word settled a question that had been in the Executioner's mind ever since the hostages had been taken. If the man would lie about one thing, he'd lie about others. For all Bolan knew, he would keep all of the hostages when they got to the airplane, then kill every last one of them once they were in the air.

The bottom line was that the Executioner couldn't afford to even let these men get off the ground in the helicopters.

As soon as the Rough Riders and their hostages were seated, the man with the gravelly voice shouted out, "Where's the money?"

A uniformed officer holding a briefcase started past Bolan toward the choppers, but Bolan reached for the briefcase himself.

As he so often did, the Executioner came up with his plan of attack suddenly, ironing out the weak points in a few seconds. No, he could not allow the helicopters to take to the air—there was no third chopper handy. The KC police had wisely assumed that the Rough Riders would be on the lookout for an aerial tail. Which meant the terrorists and their hostages would reach the airport and be gone long before he got there via automobile.

It was time to act. The situation was much like he'd faced in the lobby only a few minutes earlier, when the man named Carl had held the .45 to the female bank employee's head. The difference was that instead of one life to save, this time he had four. And it would all have to be done before the men holding the pistols could react and pull the triggers of the guns taped to the hostages' heads.

Holding the briefcase in his left hand, the Executioner strode purposefully toward the chopper where the man with the raspy voice sat next to the pilot. With a quick glance to the other chopper, he made sure he was at an angle at which his actions could not be seen. Lifting the briefcase upward, he set it in the gravelly voiced man's lap. Then, in one smooth, lightning-fast motion, he drew the sound-suppressed Beretta from his shoulder holster.

It took a little less than a quarter of a second for Bolan to get the first shot off and into the brain stem of a Rough Rider holding a Walther PPK taped to the head of a pretty young blond-haired woman. Another quarter of a second, and the other terrorist holding a .357 Magnum pistol taped to the young male hostage's head went brain dead, as well.

The man with the raspy voice had just had time to look up from the opened briefcase in his lap when Bolan stuck the sound suppressed Beretta into the guy's mouth and pulled the trigger.

The Executioner had wanted this man alive so he could question him. But it hadn't worked out that way. So be it, Bolan thought. He'd just have to find another method of learning the ins and outs of the Rough Riders.

Less than one second had elapsed when the Executioner closed the briefcase, hid the Beretta behind it and started toward the other chopper. The angle of the sun made it difficult to see details inside the chopper. But at least he saw no flurries of movement that led him to believe the Rough Riders inside knew what had just happened in the other chopper.

He hoped.

"What are you doin' bringin' that thing here?" said a Rough Rider in a slow Southern accent. "It ain't me who needs to check the money." As Bolan walked confidently on, a cloud drifted over the sun behind him as if by an act of God, and suddenly he could see clearly into the helicopter. The man who had spoken had his hand taped to the gun which was, in turn, taped to the back of the head of a short, pretty brunette.

"Don't ask me," the Executioner said, simply to stall for time while he walked the last several steps. "Your boss told me to come show it to you, too."

It was enough to confuse the men in the second chopper while Bolan took the final steps to the open helicopter door. When his thighs were pressed against the deck, he dropped the briefcase and put another near silent 9 mm round into the brain stem of the man with the taped hand.

The final Rough Rider was the one who had guided the pregnant woman out of the vault. And though he had the muzzle of his .45 pressed against her head now, it wasn't taped. And he chose to swing his weapon toward the Executioner rather than kill the woman.

It was a mistake he would not live long enough to regret.

The man had the big automatic halfway to Bolan's chest when the Executioner fired his last round into the head. The .45 went off but blew past Bolan's side, harmlessly entering the bank through the broken window to lodge itself somewhere inside the lobby.

Suddenly, all of the Rough Riders were dead.

Bolan looked at the trembling little brunette and said softly, "Relax. It's all over." He reached up and flipped the safety on the gun still taped to the back of her head, then pulled a TOPS Special Assault Weapon knife—more usually referred to simply as a SAW—from the sheath on his belt. Carefully, he began cutting the tape away from the young woman's head.

Both she and the pregnant woman were crying, and Bolan had to stop the mother-to-be from hugging him. "Careful," he smiled as her arms reached out. "I wouldn't want to ruin your hairdo."

The woman giggled nervously. "My hair doesn't seem very important right now," she said, and circled her arms around the Executioner's chest, pressing her tear-stained cheek against his as well.

Bolan felt her extended abdomen against his belly. Inside was a totally innocent little boy or girl—a totally innocent baby who had come within a hair of dying by the hand of a group of whacked out, home-grown American terrorists. If not for him, both mother and child would more than likely be dead, and in a sudden epiphany the Executioner was reminded why he'd been put on this planet called Earth and given the special abilities that he had.

To save the weak and innocent from the strong and evil.

Bolan looked back toward the other chopper.

Glasser and one of his SWAT team men were cutting the pistols away from the hostages heads as Bolan had done. The rest of the men stood back, waiting.

As he started toward Tom Glasser, the cell phone in one of the pockets of his blacksuit suddenly rang.

The Executioner walked back into the bank lobby and thumbed the Talk button. "Striker," he said.

"Hello, big guy," came the voice of Hal Brognola from the other end of the line. "Anything happening on your end?"

Bolan suppressed a chuckle. "No, Hal," he said. "Things are actually pretty quiet where I am now."

"Yeah, now it is," Brognola said. "But ten minutes ago we were watching the whole bank thing go down on FOX news."

Bolan stiffened slightly. "Was I on it?" he asked. The last thing he needed was his face splattered all over the newspapers.

"I saw you," Brognola said. "But there was never a clear

shot of your face. The newshounds and ambulance chasers must have been using long-range equipment because the Kansas City PD wouldn't let them within a country mile of the action. I don't think you have anything to worry about in regard to being IDed." The high-ranking Justice official and director of Stony Man Farm's Sensitive Operations Group paused long enough to take a breath, and Bolan could almost see the unlit cigar sticking out between his teeth.

"Hold on," Brognola said. "Because we're about to get hooked into a three-way conference call to the White House."

Bolan frowned but didn't speak. While he often took advantage of the equipment, computers, communication networking and other benefits of Stony Man Farm, in truth he answered to no one, though he did operate with the sanction of the President of the United States. He rarely talked to the Man. The fact was, when he and the President actually did speak, it was always something big. Very big. Usually of global importance.

"Hang on a few seconds," Brognola said. "Aaron's connecting the three-way call right now." Aaron was Aaron Kurtzman, Stony Man Farm's computer wizard.

Outside, sirens sounded in the distance. Bolan waited silently as they grew louder, and then watched as ambulances and hearses arrived to cart off the bodies of the Rough Riders. He wondered exactly what was going on in Washington. The big story currently was that Israel and the Iran-backed terrorist group Hezbollah—based in Lebanon—was firing short-range missiles and rockets at each other with far more innocent civilians being killed than soldiers or militia. It had all started over the kidnapping of two Israeli soldiers by Hezbollah, and quickly escalated into a full-scale war.

Phoenix Force—one of the counterterrorist groups that worked out of Stony Man Farm—was in Beirut right now, trying to cull the terrorists from the innocent Lebanese among whom Hezbollah hid. So the Executioner suspected this call from the President meant he was about to join the other Stony Man Farm crew in the Middle East.

Bolan was rarely wrong. But this was one of those rare times.

"Hello, Hal?" the President's voice finally said over the line.

"Hello, Mr. President," Brognola replied. "I'm here. And Striker's tapped in with us, as well."

"Hello, Striker," the Man said.

"Mr. President," Bolan said. The noise level outside had risen again to the point where it was hard to hear the voices over the cell phone, so he moved into the private office just off the lobby and closed the door behind him. Through the glass wall he could see white-clad EMTs entering the bank to begin removing the dead men up and down the halls. And through the window to the street, he watched the Kansas City SWAT teams and other cops break into small groups to discuss what had just happened.

"We've got a problem," the President declared. "Actually, we've got a lot of them." He paused to draw in a breath. "But we've got one big problem, and you're the only man I trust to handle it. What's probably the worst, most organized threat to this country that's ever come across the board is sneaking in under the radar." He paused again. "If it's successful, it'll make 9/11 look like a Sunday School weenie roast."

Bolan waited silently. He knew the Man would go on as soon as he'd picked the right words.

"You'll probably find this as hard to believe as I did at first," the Man finally said, "but an alliance has been struck between the Rough Riders and Hamas."

Bolan thought about the two groups for a moment. The Rough Riders were fascists who believed in an America that was only for short-haired, white-skinned men and women—preferably of Aryan or Anglo-Saxon heritage.

Hamas, on the other hand, operated throughout the Middle East, with clandestine cells spread all over the world, just waiting to be called upon to create their own versions of September 11, 2001.

Two more disparate terrorist groups could not be found on the face of the Earth.

"You'll excuse me, sir," Bolan said, "if it takes me a few seconds to digest that thought."

"I thought you'd find it as hard to believe as I did," the President said. "But I'm afraid it's true."

"May I ask how you came upon this information?" the Executioner said.

The President sighed. "The CIA got it first. They've had a mole inside Hamas for some time now."

"Can this intel be confirmed?" Bolan asked.

"It's confirmed," the President said. "The FBI has a plant inside the Rough Riders. I just got off the phone with their director. The same story came from their informant."

Bolan felt his forehead furrowing. "These two groups have nothing in common upon which to base an alliance," he said. "Except the downfall of freedom, democracy and the United States. Their ideologies couldn't be more different."

"That seems to be enough for them," the Man said. "At least for now."

"Let me play devil's advocate for a moment if I might, sir," Bolan said, still frowning. "Assuming they were successful in overthrowing the U.S. government. What do they plan to do then?"

"I don't know," the President answered. "And according to the two snitches, neither do the Rough Riders or Hamas. But that doesn't seem to bother them at this juncture. It appears that they're willing to put their differences aside for the time being."

"They'd have to go to war with each other eventually," the Executioner said.

"Yes," the Man said. "But like I said, they appear to have agreed to put that on the back burner in order to achieve their initial, common goal."

"Destroying us," Bolan said.

"Exactly," the President affirmed.

"What else do we know?" Bolan asked.

"Not a lot," the President said. "But both sources report that there's a list of planned terrorist strikes."

Bolan stopped speaking as a white-clad man opened the door to the office and looked inside. Seeing no bodies on the floor, and the Executioner's head shake, he closed the door again and disappeared. "How do we get hold of this list?"

"That's one of the things I'm hoping you can find out," the Man said. "Neither the Hamas or Rough Rider informant is high enough up the food chain to have access to it, or know how to get to it. The Rough Rider infiltrator seems to know a little more. According to him, some of the strikes are to be carried out by Hamas, and others by the Rough Riders. But they also have some joint operations planned just to confuse police, militaries and governments around the world."

"Have you got a place for me to start?" Bolan asked the President.

"The CIA's informant heard that something's about to go down at the American Embassy in Paris," the President said. "But that's all he knows. He's got the where and who— Haas—but not the when or how."

"Tell me," the Executioner said. "Am I going to have access to either or both informants?"

"You'll have access to both," the Man said.

"And what kind of turf-jealousy problems am I going to have to deal with out of the CIA and FBI?"

"No more than the usual." The President laughed softly. "I've ordered both directors to inform their men that you've got free rein. I took the liberty of giving them your Matt Cooper name. I hope that's all right.'

"That's fine."

"Anyway," the Man said. "If you need any help from the FBI or CIA, they've been ordered to give it to you. On the other hand, if you want them out of your way, they're to make themselves scarce."

"With all due respect to both agencies," the Executioner said, "I'd prefer the latter. At least for now."

"Then I'll make two more phone calls as soon as we hang up," the Man said. "One man from each agency can hook you up with the informants. Then they'll disappear." The President paused for a moment, then added, "But are you sure you don't at least want one or two men to watch your back?"

The bodies had been cleared out of the building by now, and the Executioner walked back out of the office into the lobby again. With the phone still pressed to his ear, he looked through the broken window once more.

Tom Glasser was still in the parking lot, still glancing occasionally into the bank. The men around him appeared curious about his blacksuit. The stretchy, skintight material was nothing like the navy blue Battle Dress Uniforms they wore, and they were asking questions that Glasser looked like he was ignoring.

"I've already got my back covered, Mr. President," he said.

Brognola had remained silent during the conversation because he'd had nothing to add to it. Now, he did. "You're talking about the recent blacksuit graduate you're with at the moment, Striker?" he asked Bolan.

"I am," the Executioner said. "He's a good man, the training is still fresh in his mind and he's just proved to me that he can cross that bridge from classroom to practical application."

"He's covered, then, Mr. President," Brognola said. "The blacksuit he's talking about is with the Kansas City PD, and he graduated with honors at the top of his class. I can step back into my Justice Department role, make a call to Kansas City, get the man released for special assignment with us and then line him up with phony Department of Justice identification just in case it's helpful."

"You do that, Hal," the Man said. "And, Striker, you've got the direct number into the Oval Office, as well as the one in my living area. If you need anything else—day or night—give me a call."

"Will do, sir," Bolan replied.

"Then I guess that's it," the President said. "So if you'll excuse me, I've got a few other matters to attend to." Without another word, he hung up.

"You still there, Hal?" Bolan asked.

"Still here, big guy."

"This really is one of the oddest arrangements I've ever been around," the Executioner said. He felt himself shaking his head in awe. "Hamas and the Rough Riders. Who'd have figured on that one?"

"It is odd," Brognola said. "But it may turn out to be one of the deadliest combinations we've ever faced, too." The Stony Man director paused for a moment, then said, "You want to know what pisses me off almost as much as the terror these groups inflict, Striker?"

"Sure."

"The name these Nazi militants have taken," Brognola said. "The Rough Riders." He paused yet again to clear his throat. "Teddy Roosevelt was one of my favorite presidents."

"I suspect he's rolling over in his grave right now, Hal. He'd be the first to shoot every Nazi or Hamas terrorist he saw."

"Bully," Brognola said, using one of Roosevelt's favorite expressions. Then he went almost straight into another. "Want some advice from old Teddy on this mission, Striker?"

"Sure, Hal. Hit me with it."

"Walk softly," Brognola quoted, then slightly altered the rest of Roosevelt's other famous saying. "And carry your big gun."

The director of Stony Man Farm's Sensitive Operations Group clicked off as Bolan felt his hand slide down his ribs to the grips of the .44 Magnum Desert Eagle.

**3**

The Learjet had been gutted behind the cockpit. Four bolted-down beds—two on each side of the craft—took the place of the passenger seats. Between both pairs of bunks was a circular table with four chairs, all likewise fastened to the cargo area's deck. The walls of the aircraft were covered by lockers not unlike those you might find in a high-school football dressing room. But instead of holding helmets, shoulder pads and jerseys, these lockers were stacked with a variety of weapons, ammunition and other equipment.

Only two of the four beds were in use, however, as Jack Grimaldi, Stony Man Farm's ace pilot, guided the plane over the Atlantic.

Grimaldi turned and briefly glanced behind him. Bolan was asleep and breathing easily. On the bed next to him, the new blacksuit graduate, Tom Glasser, was doing the same.

They had changed out of their combat gear as soon as the Lear had leveled off, hanging their blacksuits, black nylon web belts and other equipment in the lockers, then changing into civvies. Now Bolan lay on his back, sleeping in a light-toned off-white shirt, and stone-colored slacks. The shoulder-holster system-containing the Beretta 93-R machine pistol and extra magazines had been slung over the shirt. He had transferred the mammoth .44 magnum Desert Eagle to a form-fitted, Concealex plastic belt holster on his right hip. Extra magazines for this gun, as well as his combat knife, rode on his left hip.

A light, camel-colored suede sport coat—which he would use to cover all of the weapons—had been hung over the back of one of the chairs at the table.

Stony Man Farm's top pilot checked his instrument panel and saw that the Lear was nearing the coast of France. He hated to do it but he had no choice but to awaken Bolan and this new blacksuit, Glasser. Turning yet again, he raised his voice slightly. "Okay, guys," he said. "Welcome to the land of wine, cheese, beautiful women and a nasty attitude toward us Americans."

The Executioner's eyes opened at once. Glasser had evidently been in a deeper stage of sleep. He didn't move until Bolan got up off the bed, maneuvered his way around the table and chairs and shook him by the shoulder. Finally, the Kansas City SWAT commander opened his eyes, sat up and turned to place his feet on the deck of the Learjet.

"Where are we?" he asked.

"France," Grimaldi said over his shoulder. "Where nine out of ten people wish they'd never given us the Statue of Liberty."

Bolan chuckled. "The French aren't all bad, Jack," he said.

"I know that," Grimaldi came back. "I only said ninety percent were."

Bolan chuckled again, letting Grimaldi know that the Executioner was aware that it was all just talk—the Stony Man Farm pilot was no more bigoted against the French people then he himself was. Grimaldi continued to watch as Bolan returned to his bunk, sat down and began lacing on a pair of low-cut hiking shoes.

In the rearview mirror, Grimaldi saw Glasser tie the laces of a similar pair of shoes. The SWAT man was wearing a double shoulder rig with a matching pair of Browning Hi-Power pistols. But they were not the time-honored and much copied

9 mm version that had been invented by Robert Browning in 1935. Glasser's sidearms were two .40-caliber S&W semiautomatic pistols. The beefed-up slides appeared to be coated with some kind of nonabrasive, rust-resistant finish, while the lower parts of both semiautos were made of brushed, nonreflective stainless steel.

The Executioner finished tying his shoes, stood up, walked to the seat next to Grimaldi, then sat down. "How far out are we?" he asked.

"Another twenty minutes or so to Paris," Grimaldi said. As Bolan fished for his seat belt, found it, then buckled himself in, Stony Man Farm's flying ace noted that the Executioner had put on the suede sport coat. His weapons were now completely hidden from view.

A second later, Glasser appeared between the seats, standing just behind them but being forced to bend low beneath the cabin roof. The Kansas City SWAT man was dressed in casual tourist garb, as well, wearing creased and pleated denim slacks and a light cotton OD green sport coat over a white sport shirt. With a hand braced on both seats, he looked at Bolan. "You've got the address where we're supposed to meet these guys?" he asked. "And their names?"

The Executioner nodded.

"Can I see them?"

Bolan shook his head, then turned to look at the SWAT man before tapping his temple with a trigger finger. "They're up here," he said.

And that, Jack Grimaldi thought, summed up the Executioner better than any other single gesture ever could. He had the fingers with which to pull the triggers. And the brains to organize and set up operations.

Not to mention memorizing addresses and names.

Grimaldi glanced at his controls again, then reached for the microphone clipped to the panel in front of him. A few moments later, he had clearance to land.

The President himself had cleared the way through French customs, and signing their names on a clipboard handed to them by a small, slender man with a curling mustache who looked very much like fictional detective Hercule Poirot was all it took to get their passports stamped.

"Well," Grimaldi said before Bolan and Glasser walked on through the turnstile into France, "good luck. Although I know you don't depend on luck."

"A lot of dead men did." The Executioner smiled as he shook Grimaldi's hand. "You'll be with the plane in case we need to go someplace in a hurry?"

"I will," Grimaldi confirmed. "Just give me about five minutes' lead time."

THE RENTED BROWN MERCEDES blended in perfectly with the rest of the Parisian traffic as Bolan guided it along the street that followed the Seine. Glasser—who had never been to Europe in his life—gawked like a schoolboy seeing his first female breast.

Bolan smiled inwardly. That was one of the things he liked about Glasser. The man didn't try to hide his thoughts or reactions to things. He was what he was, and didn't pretend to be anything else. So when Glasser's mouth fell open at the sight of the Eiffel Tower, the Executioner saw it as an honest emotion that came from viewing something he'd heard about but had never thought he'd actually see.

Amid honking horns, other cars cutting them off, and obscene gestures flung out of windows, Bolan guided the Mercedes over the bridge toward Notre Dame. Glasser seemed as impressed with the ancient cathedral as he had been the Eiffel Tower.

"What are those little monsters on top called again?" he asked the Executioner.

Again, Bolan kept his smile to himself. "Gargoyles," he said.

"Yeah, that's right," Glasser said. "Mary Ann used to have one in the flower bed in back of the house."

"Mary Ann?" Bolan asked. It was the first time he'd heard the name.

"Ex-wife," Glasser said. "She took the gargoyle when she left. Along with everything else, of course."

"Kids?" Bolan asked.

Glasser nodded, a sad expression taking over his face. "Two. Casey just started high school this year. Caitlyn's still in junior high. I don't see them much."

Bolan nodded and decided to change the subject.

They passed Notre Dame and Bolan began looking for a place to park. The streets were crowded with kiosks selling everything from old and rare books to T-shirts. Finally, he spotted a parking lot and pulled up to the gate. A wizened old man wearing a blue beret came painfully down the steps from a small building, took several euro notes from the Executioner and opened the gate.

After parking the Mercedes, Bolan used the remote control to lock the vehicle, then led the way along the sidewalk. "We're looking for a little bistro called Vincennes," he said. "It should be about a mile from here."

The two men kept up a brisk pace, dodging pedestrians coming from the opposite direction and passing people who were walking more slowly. They passed a park where old, and bent, men were playing bocce, making it look like each ball weighed twenty pounds. The Sorbonne appeared on their left, and they found Vincennes on the right a block later.

The bistro was tiny, dark and slightly humid as they entered through the glass door. A long mahogany bar ran the length of the downstairs room on their left, with several tables, covered in red-and-white-checked tablecloths, scattered directly in front of them.

A flight of stairs led up to a doorway over which a curtain had been pulled. But at the foot of the steps, a maroon felt rope, suspended between two movable posts, blocked entrance to the stairs.

A lone old man in a dirty brown canvas coat was the only customer downstairs. He stood at the bar, eating a plate of boiled potatoes and green beans, and drinking beer from a large schooner. He looked over his shoulder but gave Bolan and Glasser only a cursory glance before returning to his meal.

A waiter wearing a red vest and black bow tie approached, accidentally bumping into the old man as he passed him at the bar. The bump brought on a loud curse in French, which the waiter ignored. Stopping directly in front of Bolan and Glasser, the man in the bow tie said, "Party of two?"

"Yes," Bolan said. Then he added the passwords he'd been given during their flight over the Atlantic. "But only if you serve leg of lamb."

The look in the waiter's eyes intensified for a second, then returned to normal. Smiling, he said, "Only when it is in season."

"And it's out of season?" Bolan went on, using the rest of the code phrases.

"Only upstairs." The waiter completed the exchange, then walked to the staircase and unhooked the rope from one of the posts. Stepping to the side, he bowed slightly as the Executioner led the way up the steps and drew back the curtain.

Bolan stepped into a short hallway, still holding the curtain as Glasser ducked inside. The soft sound of voices could be heard at the end of the hall. Bolan led the way toward them.

The door to the room was open when Bolan stopped in front of it. Inside what appeared to be a small private dining room was a lone table with the same sort of tablecloth as those downstairs. Four chairs circled the table.

Two were already taken.

The two men who had been talking both looked up when they saw Bolan and Glasser in the doorway. The man on the right wore a dark gray suit with subtle pinstripes, black brogans, and had blondish-brown hair swept back over his head and carefully sprayed in place. He could have passed for an American businessman, a fraternity president about to start a meeting or a CIA agent.

Under these circumstances, however, he might as well have had CIA printed on his forehead.

The other man was small, dark and obviously of Arabic heritage. He was dressed less expensively in a white turtleneck sweater and the same blue beret that appeared more prevalent in Paris than cowboy hats at a Texas Ranger barbecue.

Both men stood up, and the man in the suit extended his hand. "Wilkens," he said simply, offering neither a first name or rank. His hand was clammy and the grip reminded the Executioner of holding a dead fish. "Matt Cooper," he told the man.

Wilkens turned to Glasser and shook hands with him, too. Since the SWAT captain was not widely known outside of the Missouri and Kansas regions, he had traveled under his own passport and name. "Glasser," he said. "Call me Tom."

Wilkens's smile was forced, and it was more than obvious that he didn't like turning over a good informant to someone outside the CIA. The fact that he didn't know this Cooper, or what government agency he worked for, made it even worse. But without even the merest crack in the smile, he said, "Gentlemen, meet Amad Nadir. He's our Hamas man in Paris, and knows what's going down most of the time in the rest of France, too." He paused, and for just a moment, the smile faded. "You can imagine I'm not all that crazy about giving him to you."

Bolan nodded. He didn't blame the CIA man. Good informants were hard to recruit, train and deal with. But Wilkens had his orders direct from the President, and he was being a good sport about it. The four men sat down at the table.

"I'm here to get you started," Wilkens said. "Then I'll fade away into the twilight zone." He reached into the breast pocket of his suit and pulled out a business card. Harold James Wilkens, it read. United States Embassy, Paris, France. "If you need me for anything, you can contact me at that number."

"One question before you leave," the Executioner said. "How long have you guys been meeting at this bistro?"

Wilkens frowned and looked at the ceiling. "Eight... maybe closer to ten months now," he finally said.

"You have some arrangement with the owner or manager?" Glasser asked, and Bolan could see that the SWAT captain shared his worries.

A lot could happen in eight to ten months. Bartenders, cooks and waitresses came and went. If Hamas or any other terror organization suspected Vincennes of being an American intelligence hot spot, it could have run any number of employees in and out during those months.

"We have a *great* arrangement with the management and owner." Wilkens smiled. "We're both. We own the joint."

"And the employees...?" Bolan asked, letting the statement trail off to form a question.

"They're all ours, too," Wilkens said. "In fact, it's become a sort of initiation rite. When an agent is first transferred here, they work Vincennes. None of them like it very much, but it does a good job of familiarizing the locals with their faces and establishing their false identities."

The Executioner nodded. "Makes sense," he said. Then, turning to Glasser, he said, "Tom, you have any questions for the man before we say goodbye to him?"

It was a polite way of telling Wilkens it was time for him to get the hell out of their way and let them go to work. And Glasser snapped to that fact immediately. Standing up, he extended his hand across the table. "No, I don't think I've got any more questions for Mr. Wilkens," he said. "It was nice meeting you, Harold. Maybe we'll hook up again sometime."

Wilkens smiled, and this time the expression seemed to convey genuine amusement at the way he was being gently ushered out of the meeting. Another round of handshakes took place, and then the CIA field operative disappeared behind the curtain. His footsteps grew progressively fainter as he descended the stairs.

Bolan turned to Amad Nadir, who sat quietly waiting for whatever was going to happen next. His carefully trimmed mustache, along with the beret and turtleneck, made him look as much French as Arabic.

"So," Bolan said to the man. "What can you tell us about whatever it is that's planned to go down at the U.S. Embassy?"

"Not a lot," Nadir said, shaking his head sadly. "I am not high enough in the chain of command to know the details."

"Then it shouldn't take you long to tell us what you *do know*," the Executioner said with only a trace of sarcasm in his voice. "So let's get that done."

"The planning has been going on for weeks," Nadir explained. "And it—whatever *it* is—is scheduled to go down tonight."

Glasser sat back in his chair and blew air out between his clenched teeth. "Nothing quite as comforting as getting plenty of notice to plan things," he said ironically.

The Executioner nodded in agreement. "We'd have plenty of time if we just knew how the attack was coming." He turned to Nadir once more. "Any particular reason Hamas picked tonight to carry out whatever it is they have planned?"

"I am sure that there is," Nadir said. "Every atrocity they commit is not only vicious but has some symbolic meaning attached to it." In an almost mirrorlike impression of what Glasser had just done, the Hamas informant clenched his teeth and sucked air into his lungs. "But I have no idea what it is."

"This isn't the anniversary of some great Muslim victory, or a holiday of some kind?"

"No," Nadir answered. "Nothing like that."

Bolan stood up and the other two men followed his lead. "Then the only thing I can think of to do at this point is to drive to the embassy and nose around a bit. Maybe we can come onto some leads there."

Glasser pushed his chair back beneath the table. "That's a pretty thin hope," he said.

"I know it is," the Executioner said. "But like I said, I don't have better ideas at this point. If you do, I'd be happy to listen to them." He walked to the curtain and held it open while Nadir ducked through.

As Glasser followed, he said, "Nope. Nothing better on my part. Guess we'll have to work with what we've got."

Bolan followed the other two men down the steps, out of the bistro and onto the sidewalk.

The Executioner flipped the keys through the air just before they reached the Mercedes, and Glasser caught them. "You drive," Bolan said.

He turned to Amad Nadir. "You're riding shotgun. I'll take the backseat. I want to be able to get out and walk around if necessary without causing undue notice."

Deep furrows lined Nadir's forehead as he and Bolan waited for Glasser to unlock the doors with the remote control. A second later, the beep sounded and the headlights flashed off and on.

"You are saying I will carry a shotgun with me?" Nadir asked innocently.

Bolan smiled. Even though the Hamas informant's English was fluent, he couldn't be expected to learn every slang phrase in the American version of English. "Just an expression," he told the Arab. "It means the front passenger's seat."

"But why do you call it 'riding shotgun'?" Amad asked as he opened the door and got in.

"It's a term that got started back in the Old West, when people traveled by stagecoach," the Executioner said. "The driver held the reins to the horses and sat on the left—where the steering wheel of the car is now. The man 'riding shotgun' sat to his right. With a shotgun, in case they got ambushed by bandits."

"Ah!" Nadir said, smiling. "Yes! I have seen this in American movies." He took a breath. Then, in a low, guttural voice, he said, "Throw down the strongbox!"

"You've got the idea." Bolan nodded as he got into the Mercedes behind Nadir.

"So," the informant said, twisting in his seat to continue the conversation as Glasser twisted the key and started the engine. He was grinning widely now, an expression the Executioner had not yet seen on his face. "It was the shotgun rider who saved the passengers and stagecoach line from losing all their money to the bandits?" he asked. Amad Nadir was obviously a big fan of Old West films.

Bolan buckled his seat belt and looked up. "Only in the movies," he said. "In real life, the shotgunner was the man the robbers shot first."

The smile faded from Nadir's face. He turned back around and fastened his own seat belt. "I will pray that this is like a movie, then," he said.

Bolan nodded his agreement.

But he had little hope that where they were going, and what they were about to do, could be done peacefully.

Blood was going to be shed.

DUSK WAS TURNING TO DARKNESS by the time the Mercedes reached the U.S. Embassy in Paris. Bolan ordered Glasser to circle the block, narrowing his eyes as he scrutinized every tiny detail he saw before him.

Because of the ongoing wars in Afghanistan and Iraq, the seemingly constant warfare between Israel, Lebanon, last-minute thwarted airline attacks and French anti-American sentiment, security around the U.S. Embassy was at an all-time high. U.S. Marines, decked out in full dress uniforms but bearing M-16s and sidearms, completely encircled the walls around the building. At the front gate the Executioner could see a metal detector, an X-ray machine and an explosives sensor.

Bolan watched as a car pulled into one of the few available parking spaces along the curb. A man in a black tuxedo got out, circled the automobile and opened the door for a woman wearing a brightly sequined evening gown.

"Hamas can't be planning a takeover like Iran did back in the seventies," Glasser said as he drove on. "There are too many Marines here, and unless I miss my guess, those M-16s are locked and loaded."

Bolan nodded his agreement. "A bomb isn't likely, either," he said. "The Marine K-9 dogs will have sniffed every corner of the embassy grounds several times by now." He frowned slightly as another couple in full evening dress exited their vehicle before a valet drove the car away. "Of course there's always the suicide bombers," he went on. "But they'd have to ignite at the gate—they'd never get past all the machines."

Glasser nodded from behind the steering wheel. "Most they could hope for is a few dead Marines."

As they turned the corner to circle the grounds again, Bolan noticed a parking lot across the street from the embassy. Several more couples, also wearing tuxes and evening dresses, had parked there and were headed toward the front gate.

Bolan leaned forward in the back seat. "You know what's going on here?" he asked Nadir.

The Hamas informant shook his head. "They look as if they are going to a party."

The Mercedes rolled slowly along the rear wall of the embassy grounds. "Stop and let me out, Tom," the Executioner said. "I want to find out what's going on."

Glasser tapped the brake and pulled to the curb. Bolan got out and started toward the rear delivery gate.

The young Marine stationed at the gate looked barely old enough to shave, but he wore the stripes of a sergeant on his sleeve. His eyes met the Executioner's as Bolan approached. In them, the Executioner could see that while he might still be young, he'd kill whomever he had to kill in defense of his country.

Slowly, the Executioner reached into an inside pocket of his sport coat for his phony Justice Department ID.

The Executioner opened the credential case and showed it to the young sergeant.

"Can you tell me what's going on here tonight?" Bolan asked after he'd returned the phony credentials to his coat pocket.

"The ambassador's hosting a formal dinner for all of the European UN reps," the sergeant said.

Bolan now knew why this night had been picked for the Hamas strike at the embassy. The UN, as usual, was trying to broker peace between Israel and the rest of the Middle East. And—also as usual—the diplomats were having absolutely no success at all.

If Hamas could wipe out a whole dining room full of UN representatives, especially while they were being hosted by the United States, they would not only slow down progress toward a cease-fire, but they might also succeed in escalating the current state of unrest into a full-blown global crisis.

Bolan and the young Marine sergeant stepped to the side of the gate as a white minivan, with the name and emblem of a Parisian catering service, pulled into the driveway, then stopped. The Executioner continued to ponder the situation as the driver stepped out and other Marines began searching him and the van itself. Two other Marines disappeared inside the vehicle. The Executioner heard the scraping of steel against steel as lids were lifted off serving platters to make sure they contained food rather than guns or explosives.

The Executioner felt his jaw tighten as he watched the process. An attack was coming tonight. He could feel it now, stronger than ever. He considered Hamas's goals again, and what they might stand to gain with some kind of massacre inside the embassy walls. At best, it would make the U.S. appear weak, unable even to defend even its own grounds. But in addition to that, by this time tomorrow, the story being spread across the Arab world would be that U.S. operatives had planned and carried out the assassinations *themselves.*

"Sir," the young Marine asked, breaking into the Executioner's thoughts. "May I ask why the U.S. Department of Justice is interested in all this?"

"You can ask," Bolan said, "but I can't tell you. Everything's on a need-to-know basis."

The young man's forehead wrinkled in concern, and Bolan was reminded again of just how young he looked. Almost like a little boy dressing up in his father's old uniform. "Then we should keep an eye out for trouble?" he asked Bolan.

"You should be doing that anyway," the Executioner said, then turned and walked off.

The Mercedes was a half block ahead of him, almost to the corner, where at least a dozen more Marines stood at attention. Bolan jogged to the back door of the car again. Once he was inside, he closed the door and said, "Tom, find us a place to park where we can watch the back entrance."

"What did the leatherneck have to say?" Glasser asked.

"Dinner for United Nations reps," Bolan said. "Which has to be why Hamas picked tonight." He stopped talking, thinking hard again, trying to put himself in the shoes of a Hamas leader and decide how he would carry out an attack against the heavily defended embassy.

Tom Glasser made a quick U-turn and parked along the street across from the grounds. As they watched, several more delivery trucks came and went, but not until the Marines standing guard had thoroughly checked both the men and vehicles for weapons and explosives. As they waited, Bolan closed his eyes, pondering the situation.

Bolan's mind continued to drift. Then, suddenly, he remembered an old Mafia hit man to whom he had once talked during the course of another mission. The old man was known in the underworld and to police as a crack shot with either pistol or rifle.

Which was why he always dispatched his targets with a knife. His shooting prowess provided the perfect cover.

The Executioner's eyes opened suddenly. The Marines were running tight security, and no one was going to get into the embassy with a gun, knife or bomb. The fact was, nothing that even resembled a weapon would pass through the gates unnoticed. So Hamas was going to have to carry out their plans similar to the way the World Trade Center towers had been brought down.

They'd have to carry out the mass murders in a way least suspected of them.

And suddenly Bolan knew exactly what method that was.

"Let's go," Bolan said as he threw open the backseat door.

"Where…what…?" Tom Glasser said.

By then the Executioner was on the sidewalk and had closed the door behind him. When Nadir tried to open his door, Bolan shoved it shut again. "Not you," he said. "I don't want your face burned this early in the game. Stay low and out of sight until we get back."

Bolan took off, catching up with Glasser as they crossed the street. Heading straight for the rear gate, the Executioner saw the look on the faces of the Marines as he passed. They'd seen him talking to the guard at the gate, and probably seen him flash his credentials.

That was good.

But that didn't mean he'd be welcomed inside the embassy walls with open arms. And if he overpowered the young Marine sergeant to whom he'd spoken before and bullied his way inside, he and Glasser would probably go down with a few dozen .223 rounds in their backs.

That was bad.

By the time he'd reached the gate again, most of the Marines had pulled their M-16s off their shoulders and were aiming them toward him and Glasser. Stopping in front of the gate, next to the sergeant he'd talked to before, he said, "We've got to get inside. *Now.*"

The Marine shook his head. "I'm sorry, sir," he said. "We have orders not to let anyone in who isn't on the guest list. Let me check that list and I'll—"

"Don't waste your time," Bolan said impatiently. "We aren't on it." He paused, an idea on how to get into the embassy without being killed by his own countrymen suddenly hitting him. "Who gave you your orders?" he asked as he reached into his pocket.

"Major Davenport," the Marine said.

Slowly, Bolan pulled the cell phone out of his pocket and held it high so everyone could see it. Then, after a glance at his watch and a mental calculation as to the time in Washington, D.C., he tapped in the private number to the Oval Office that the President had given him. "I hate having to pull rank on you," he said as the call bounced off dummy numbers around the world to mislead anyone trying to tap into the line. "But Major Davenport's about to be overridden."

The Man answered on the third ring. "What can I do for you, Striker?" he asked.

The Executioner didn't waste time with small talk, going straight to the subject at hand. "I'm outside our embassy in Paris where Hamas is about to kill a whole lot of important people. I don't have time to give you the details. But I need you to convince the Marines running security to let me in." He looked first to his right, then his left, seeing at least forty M-16s now aimed toward him and Glasser.

"Put whoever I need to talk to on the line," the President said.

Bolan shoved the cell phone into the hand of the young Marine sergeant. "Here," he said. "There's someone who wants to talk to you, and I suspect you'll recognize the Texas accent." He paused as the Marine took the instrument. "And it'll be something you can tell your grandchildren about some day."

The young Marine took the cell phone and pressed it to his ear. "Sergeant Maxwell here," he said. "May I ask to whom I'm speaking?"

Silence fell over them during the next several seconds. But during that time the young sergeant's eyes opened wider than saucers as his face turned red. "Yes, sir," he said into the phone. "I understand. Yes…yes…certainly sir…"

There was another short silence, then the sergeant said, "Thank you, sir. Yes, and it was nice talking to you, too." He handed the phone back to Bolan as if it was now some sacred icon.

The Executioner simply took it and dropped it back into his pocket. "Let's go," he told Glasser.

With the Kansas City SWAT commander right on his heels, the Executioner broke into a jog toward the big building beyond the gate. But he turned long enough to call over his shoulder, "Maxwell! Radio inside and tell your men stationed there not to shoot us! And have someone make sure no one eats anything yet!" He turned back and sprinted on.

"Not eat anything?" Sergeant Maxwell called back. "Why—?"

"Just *do it!*" Bolan yelled behind him.

"It's the food, right?" Glasser said as they sprinted toward the rear of the embassy building. "It's been poisoned?" They passed a small parking lot where several cars, including the minivan with the catering emblem on the side, had been parked.

"That's my take on things," the Executioner said. "Let's hope it's still cocktail hour. And the drinks and hors d'oeuvres weren't spiked, as well as the main meal. "As they ran, Bolan drew the sound-suppressed Beretta and put one round in each of the van's rear tires. "That ought to slow them down if they try to get away," he said as he returned his Beretta to his shoulder rig.

In the center of the building they found two sets of stairs. One led up, the other down. Guessing that the dining room might be in the basement, Bolan descended the steps to a glass door.

Which was locked.

The Executioner couldn't afford the time it would take to find an unlocked entrance to the building. So the Beretta served him again, with one round shattering the glass. Bolan reached through and unlocked the door from the inside. A moment later he and Glasser were inside the embassy. Faintly, in the distance, he could hear the familiar buzzing sound of a large gathering of people. Without hesitation, he ran toward the noise. Glasser followed.

The Executioner stopped for a moment as they came to a cross hallway. Again, he listened, depending on his ears to tell him which direction to go. The voices were louder now and, here and there, polite laughter could be heard.

Turning left down the hall, Bolan raced on. He glanced at the chronograph on his wrist. Europeans usually ate their evening meal much later than Americans. But would it be late enough tonight? He didn't know.

By now the hum of voices could be heard even while he

ran. He left his weapons hidden under his jacket as he pivoted into a final right-hand turn, and saw an open set of double doors at the end of a long hall. Through the doors, he could
see that the men in the tuxes and the women in sparkling evening gowns were taking seats up and down a long dining
table. Waiters in short white coats had just finished setting
salad bowls in front of the guests.

Just outside the doorway sat a bored-looking Siamese
cat—undoubtedly the American ambassador's house pet.

As he sprinted on, the Executioner saw a beautiful dark-
skinned woman in a low-cut emerald-green dress lift her fork
from the table and stab it into her salad. "No!" he yelled as
he neared the dining room. The cat saw him coming and
darted to safety around the corner and into the room.

All of the heads at the table turned his way as Bolan burst
through the doorway, drawing the Beretta as he came.

"Everyone!" the Executioner shouted. "Relax! I'm not
here to harm you. But don't eat anything! It's been poisoned!"

A tall, slender man at the end of the table closest to the Executioner suddenly stood up and dashed toward him. Reaching for the Beretta with his left hand, he threw a looping
roundhouse punch at Bolan.

The Executioner slapped the punch away with his left hand
as he shoved the Beretta back into its holster under his arm, out
of the man's reach. Then, twisting his attacker's arm behind his
back, he grabbed a handful of the man's hair with his left.

Slowly, he walked the man back to his chair and seated
him, then stepped back.

The dinner guests were now more confused than ever. Was
this big man with the quiet gun their friend or foe? Bolan repeated what he'd said earlier. But this time, he asked if anyone had eaten anything yet.

Several of the men and women admitted to partaking of the
appetizers.

"I don't think they got to the appetizers," the Executioner said. "If they had, those of you that ate them would at least be showing signs of it by now." He was about to speak again when he heard the high-pitched wail of a cat on the other side of the table.

All of the heads at the table turned to see what it was. Then a woman screamed.

Bolan hurried around the end of the table and saw the Siamese cat that had been in the doorway earlier. It was jerking wildly back and forth as a white froth mixed with blood drooled out of his mouth. Then, suddenly, it went as stiff as a board on its back, its paws curling inward into a grotesque death mold.

An inch away from the dead cat, the Executioner saw a half-eaten piece of cocktail shrimp.

**4**

Bolan turned to Glasser. "Stay here with these people," he ordered. "Hamas may have a backup plan."

The SWAT commander nodded.

Two swing doors were visible in one of the side walls of the dining room, and the Executioner had to believe they led to the kitchen. Without further ado, he sprinted that way, shouldering both doors open as he burst through them. Inside the kitchen, he saw a bewildered kitchen staff. All were dressed in white, and several had crowded around one man lying on the floor.

These would be the regular cooking staff—not the caterers that Bolan had seen searched at the gate and who had poisoned the food.

"What happened to him?" the Executioner asked, knowing the answer to the question even before he'd asked it. His eyes scanned the room for anyone who seemed out of place. Or anyone trying to slink out unnoticed.

A short stout woman, her bleached-blond hair wrapped into a tight bun and covered with a hairnet, stood up from the side of the man on the floor. "He started quivering like he was cold," she told the Executioner. "Then he started foaming at the mouth like some rabid dog or something." She glanced down. "I think he's dead now."

Bolan had no doubt about it—his arms and legs had curled inward just like the paws of the Siamese cat in the other room.

He looked back up at the stout woman. "Did he eat any of the food the caterers brought in?"

"We're not allowed to do that," the woman answered.

"I didn't ask you what the rules are," the Executioner said sharply. "People break rules all the time. What did he eat?"

"I don't know," the woman said, shrugging. "Really, I don't."

Bolan looked around the room. "Anyone here know what this guy ate right before he started spasming?"

They all shook their heads.

"Did anyone else eat anything from the caterers?" Bolan demanded. "You're not going to get fired or get into any kind of trouble if you did. In fact, admitting it now may save your very lives."

Bolan believed them as all of the heads in the room shook no. The cat's reaction to whatever poison it had ingested, as well as that of the dead man on the floor, had been almost instantaneous. If any of the other cooks or waiters had eaten anything, they'd be dead by now, too.

"Where are the caterers?" the Executioner asked.

This time, a vastly overweight man with a carefully pruned mustache and chef's hat on his head answered, "They just left a few minutes ago." He hooked a thumb over his shoulder toward a doorway. "Just stick to the main hallway and you'll find an exit to the parking lot."

Bolan nodded, then broke into a run, crossing the threshold and finding himself in a wide hallway. This would be the route for all deliveries to the embassy.

Bolan ignored the several narrow side halls that shot out to the sides as he ran. The chef had said to keep to the main hallway, and that's what he did. Finally, he saw a staircase leading up out of the subterranean level to the ground floor. Taking the steps three at a time, he pushed through another glass doorway.

Almost as soon as he emerged from the embassy, the Executioner saw two men standing behind the minivan that bore the caterer's logo. They were cursing each other in Arabic, as if each blamed the other for the pair of flattened tires. But when they saw Bolan come out of the building, both of their heads snapped toward him.

And their hands shot for the firearms hidden under their white jackets.

The man on the left was slightly taller and heavier than his partner. His hand emerged from under his jacket with a Sigarms Mauser M-2 pistol. Whether it was chambered for .45 ACP or .40 S&W, Bolan didn't know.

But that didn't make much difference at this point. Either caliber could put a man down for good with a decently placed shot.

The Executioner was determined not to let that happen.

Drawing the Beretta from under his jacket again, Bolan thumbed the selector to 3-round burst as he brought it up in front of him. The men at the van were no more than twenty yards away, so he had no need to worry about the sights. Squeezing the trigger, he directed a trio of rounds into the terrorist's white jacket.

Suddenly, the front of the jacket was pink instead of white.

The Executioner turned his attention to the other man behind the van. He was shorter and almost reed-thin. But with the Springfield Champion .45 in his hand, he was no less deadly.

Bolan turned the Beretta his way. If at all possible, he needed to keep this man alive to glean valuable information from him. Lowering his aim to the front of the man's thighs, Bolan squeezed off another 3-round burst of near silent 9 mm hollowpoint rounds.

Sometimes Lady Luck followed the Executioner around. Other times, she deserted him completely.

This was one of the latter times.

At the same microsecond during which Bolan was pulling the Beretta's trigger, the second caterer decided to go prone with his Springfield. He dived forward, with the intent of landing on his belly on the ground. He accomplished that goal.

But not before the Executioner's 9 mm rounds—meant for his knees—drilled through his face and the top of his head.

The parking lot had stayed relatively quiet since the only rounds fired were from Bolan's sound-suppressed 93-R. But now, as the Executioner hurried down the steps to where the dead bodies lay, it took on a cemeterylike silence. Quickly, he searched the men's pockets for any form of identification or other objects of interest. Besides a Fairbairn-Sykes dagger and a hideout .25-caliber Baby Browning pistol, he found nothing.

Bolan dragged both bodies out of sight between the van and the Oldsmobile parked next to it. Then, just as he was letting go of the second set of forearms, a Ford sedan that was parked on the other side of the van suddenly purred to life. It screeched its tires backing out of the parking space, then laid more rubber as it sped toward the gate.

The Executioner jumped back around the van, drawing the Desert Eagle instead of the Beretta. But by the time he was in position to shoot, the van was crashing through the exit gate. He got off only one .44 Magnum round, which flew through the Ford's back window and out the windshield, as the Marines stationed at the exit either fired into the vehicle themselves or dived out of its path, depending upon their position.

A second later, the dark sedan was gone.

Bolan holstered the Desert Eagle as air blew out of this clenched teeth. There had been Hamas men on the grounds, not just two. And the third had brought the Ford as backup transportation for any unseen situations—like flat tires.

The Executioner glanced back between the minivan and Oldsmobile, making sure the bodies of the two terrorists he'd shot were out of sight. The dignitaries at the banquet would be leaving soon, and they had no reason to see the dead men. They'd already had more excitement than they wanted, or were used to, and Bolan saw no reason to upset them further.

Bolan continued to think about the men and women who had come within a hairbreadth of being poisoned. The were politicians. Men of words, not action. And the way things stood now, neither the politicos nor their wives were going to take a bite of anything for a long time without thinking about the dead Siamese cat on the floor of the dining room.

By the time the Executioner returned to the dining hall, the guests were being protected by Tom Glasser and a dozen U.S. Marines. One man, wearing the bars of a lieutenant, stepped forward as the Executioner entered. He stood with his back as straight as a board as he said, "Okay, we got last-minute orders almost straight from the commander in chief to let you guys in. Now I find out somebody poisoned the food, I've got a dead cat on the floor, a dead man in the kitchen and I'd like some answers."

"Go out to the parking lot," the Executioner said. "You'll find a couple more dead men between the cars."

Without another word, Bolan stepped to the side of the man in front of him and hurried to where Glasser stood, talking to another member of the Marine security force. "Let's get out of here," the Executioner whispered to the SWAT man. "The threat's over, and there're going to be too many questions asked that we can't answer."

Together, they walked to the swing doors, into the kitchen and then out the same hallway Bolan had taken to catch up with the caterers.

BACK AT THE MERCEDES, Bolan and Glasser found that Amad Nadir had moved to the back seat and was slumped low. "What went on?" he asked excitedly as the two warriors got inside the car. "Everything was quiet. But you could tell things were *happening*."

Bolan got behind the wheel and stuck the key into the ignition as Glasser took the shotgun seat this time. "You saw the Ford leave, didn't you?" he said sharply. "One of them got away." As he pulled away from the curb, he had no idea where he should go. He supposed the best idea was to get a hotel room and catch up on their sleep. In the morning he'd try a fresh angle that might lead him to the Hamas-Rough Rider strike list.

Such were the thoughts on Bolan's mind when Amad Nadir answered his question. "Yes," the informant said in the back seat. "I saw Tariq leave."

The Executioner saw Glasser's head snap around as quickly as his own did. "You know the guy who was driving the Ford?" the Executioner asked.

"Of course," Nadir said. "And I am fairly sure I know where he is going."

"Why didn't you tell us this when we first got back in the car?" Bolan asked. He looked up into the rearview mirror and saw Nadir shrug. "You did not ask," he said softly. "Is this of use? I can direct you there."

The Executioner almost laughed out loud. "Yes, Amad," he said, "it's of use. So get started directing us."

Nadir guided Bolan and Glasser through the city, taking a general southwestern course until they reached the edge of the city. The stars shone brightly in the overhead sky, and a half moon helped illuminate the road toward Versailles, as well. Nine miles after leaving Paris, they were passing the site where Louis XIV had built what was often regarded as the most massive and elaborate royal residence in the world. Adjoining the magnificent structure was acre after acre of carefully groomed gardens.

Leaving the Versailles palace area, Nadir directed Bolan

into an industrial district. They began passing auto repair shops, welding contractors and similar businesses. After several twists and turns, they came to a narrow strip of blacktop that at first glance led out into an empty, open field.

"Stop here," Nadir said.

Bolan followed the direction, parking the Mercedes just to the side of the blacktop with the front of the car facing the field. He took a quick mental picture of the scene, then killed the lights. In the center of the field, all but hidden at first glance, he had seen a large, steel, barnlike building. Just to its side sat an ancient yellow M&M tractor. Parked directly in front of an overhead door leading into the barn was a car. A regular, steel entrance door stood next to the overhead entryway.

Now, with the headlights off and his eyes adjusting to the darkness, the Executioner saw that light gleamed in several windows on the side of the building facing him.

But most importantly, he saw the shadowy car.

It was a Ford. And though he couldn't see them in the dark, the Executioner knew the automobile would be peppered with a number of bullet holes.

Nadir answered the Executioner's next question before he could even ask it. "Yes," he said, "I was correct. This is where Tariq has come to hide both himself and his car."

Bolan nodded. "What's the tractor for?" he asked.

"For show," the man leaning forward in the back seat said. "To make it look as if the barn contains farm machinery."

"So what's in the barn really?" Glasser asked.

"I do not know," Nadir said. "Weapons, perhaps. I know only that it is a place where Hamas sometimes meets. And a place where they can go when they are in trouble or being sought by the law. There is an English word for it. But I cannot think of what it is."

"A safehouse," said Bolan.

"Yes!" Nadir almost shouted. "That is it. A safehouse."

For a few moments, the car was silent. Bolan stared ahead at the dark building. It might contain anything—from back-pack nukes to small arms to nothing. But one thing of which he was certain was that it contained the third man who had been at the embassy in the backup car. And even if Tariq was the only thing he found inside, it would be worth the time and effort to recon, then attack, the building.

And he might always get lucky. There might very well be computers inside the building, and on one or more of them he might find the strike list that Hamas and the Rough Riders had come up with.

Turning to his left, the Executioner saw a car wash, deserted for the night. Throwing the Mercedes into Reverse, he backed off the blacktop and back onto the street. A moment later, he was pulling the vehicle into one of the car wash stalls. "You're going to stay in the car again," he told Nadir.

The informant was only too happy to oblige.

The Executioner patted himself down, making sure the Desert Eagle, Beretta and combat knife were in place. Then he turned to Glasser and said, "Let's go."

Bolan and Glasser changed back into blacksuits. Again, Bolan noted the twin Browning .40-caliber Hi-Power pistols in the Kansas City SWAT man's double shoulder rig. Then he pulled an M-16 A-2 out of the Mercedes's trunk for himself, another for Glasser.

"Thanks," Glasser whispered, although there was really no need for such quiet this far away from the building.

Bolan nodded and closed the trunk. A moment later, he was jogging out of the car wash stall and angling toward the dark building in the adjacent field. The ground beneath his feet was loose and sandy, with patches of wild grass growing here and there. Behind him, he could hear the soft patter of Glasser's combat boots.

The night was cool, with a light breeze drifting across the

open field. The faint smell of machine oil drifted with it, reminding the Executioner they were still in an industrial area of Versailles. He was halfway across the field when the lights in the windows suddenly darkened and the overhead door in the barn began creaking open.

Bolan hit the ground on his belly, sliding several feet through the sandy soil. Glasser took one more step, then did the same, coming to a halt next to the Executioner. Together, they listened to the whine of the automatic door as it continued to rise.

The first thing they saw were two pairs of shoes. Then four legs, two torsos and two heads.

"Neither of us got a look at him," Glasser whispered. "But one of those guys has got to be Tariq."

Bolan nodded in the darkness.

The two men in the doorway continued to speak to each other until the door had fully opened. Then a man of medium build, sharp Arabic features and a mustache and goatee turned and walked back toward the Ford.

Bolan knew the men had turned out the lights in the barn in order to avoid drawing attention to the building while they pulled the Ford inside. But now, in the car's headlights, the Executioner tried to look beyond the opening. All he could see before the headlights went off again were shadows. A moment later, the door began closing once more.

Bolan waited until the door had fully closed before turning toward Glasser. "At least we know we're at the right place," he said as he pulled himself to his feet. His head jerked toward the barn again as the lights in the windows came back on. But he was close enough now to see that the illumination was light drifting through cloth.

The Hamas men had either hung tight curtains or fastened some sort of textile material over the windows. Either way, the bottom line was they didn't want anybody to see what went on inside the barn. Silently, he led Glasser in another jog up to the building. They stopped on both sides of one of the windows.

The coverings turned out to be old and dirty towels either taped or nailed to the window frames.

"I'll go right," the Executioner whispered to Glasser. "You go left. There may be a sliver at the sides, or a hole in the towel, where one of us can see in. We'll meet on the other side of the barn."

Glasser nodded and took off, walking silently toward the first window to their left as Bolan turned to go the other way.

Only one window lay between the Executioner and the front of the building where the overhead door had opened. Bolan stopped at it, doing his best to peer inside. But whoever had hung the towels over the windows had been thorough, and the oil-and-grime-streaked cloth was tight against the glass.

The Executioner moved on to the front of the building, doing his best to remain silent as he walked past the overhead door on the concrete drive. In the darkness, he stepped on several pebbles that made soft scraping sounds when pushed down by his boots. He knew the noises were too quiet for the men inside to hear. But they sounded like cannon booms in his own ears, and he stopped to listen further.

Somewhere, far in the distance, a dog barked. Otherwise, the night was silent.

The Executioner came to the regular steel door and stopped again. Slowly, holding the M-16 in his right hand, he reached for the knob and twisted it. Locked. He checked three more windows along the front of the large building, then made his way around the corner to the other side. Faintly, in the distance, he could see movement in the darkness. As he moved slowly on, the vision took the shape of a man.

A man wearing a blacksuit.

The Executioner continued, checking each window he passed. But the best look he got was a blurry image of motion where one of the towels had worn thin. It was impossible to see whether or not there were more Hamas terrorists than Tariq and the other man they'd seen through the overhead door.

Finally, Bolan came to the last window that Glasser was checking. When the Kansas City SWAT captain turned to him and shook his head, he knew Glasser hadn't had any better luck then he had. Bolan motioned for the man to follow him, then took off at a jog again. He ran around the sides of the barn Glasser had covered, then across the field and back to the Mercedes in the car wash.

Amad Nadir was waiting for them, slumped down in the backseat.

"There's something going on inside," the Executioner said as soon as both men were back in the car. "But I don't know what." He paused a moment, then added, "But whatever it is, it bears checking out further. And probably destroying."

Glasser nodded in the darkness. "It *is* Hamas, after all," he said.

"We've got several options," the Executioner said. "Option one is we shoot the lock off the front door and go in that way."

"That's gonna be loud and take a long time," Glasser said. "A long time, relatively speaking, that is."

"Which is why I don't like it," Bolan said. "Option two is to go back to the building and wait on both sides of the doors—the regular one and the overhead. When somebody opens one of them to come out, we go in."

"Which means that if more Hamas men show up, we're like spotlighted deer in their headlights," Glasser said. "There's no place to hide at the front, it'd take too long to run to the back and if we hide at the back it'd take too long to run to the front if, and when, one of the doors open."

Bolan nodded in agreement. "The third option is this," he said. "We go through the windows."

Glasser turned toward him. Even in the darkness, Bolan could see him frowning. "How do we do that?" he asked. "You saw them as well as I did. They're just single panes of glass built into the structure. They don't open."

"I didn't say anything about *opening* them first," Bolan said. "I just said we go through them." He waited, letting the thought take form in Glasser's mind.

"We crash through," the SWAT man finally said.

"Exactly." The Executioner nodded. "Simultaneously, one of us on this side, the other one on the other."

"You two are crazy," Amad Nadir said from the backseat. "Nobody in the CIA would even think of doing such a fool-hardy thing."

"Which is why America has both the CIA and us," Bolan said. His tone of voice conveyed to Nadir that he'd be wise to wait until he was spoken to again before offering an opinion.

Glasser reached up and pinched his blacksuit at the shoulder, pulling the stretchy material out, then letting it snap back into place. "Well, these things are cut resistant, right?"

"Cut *resistant*," Bolan said. "Not cut *proof.* We'll still end up with a few scratches here and there. The main thing is to protect our heads, faces and particularly our throats. If I'd known we'd be here, under these conditions, we'd have brought helmets with face masks."

"Resourcefulness is the name of the game," Glasser said. "Sometimes you've just gotta go with what you've got."

Bolan nodded. Then, turning to Nadir, he said, "Hand us our sport coats."

The CIA informant looked puzzled as he handed both men's jackets over the seat. Bolan and Glasser took them, then synchronized their watches. "You take this side," the Executioner said as he got out of the Mercedes again. "Give me thirty seconds to get around the building to the other side, then go, and go hard."

Glasser nodded his understanding. Once again, he and Bolan set off, jogging over the sandy field.

When they were halfway to the building, Bolan said, "Start counting...now." Both men glanced at the luminous dials on their chronographs as the Executioner angled off toward the rear of the barn. Passing the tractor, he made it around to the other side of the barn and stopped with fifteen seconds to spare.

Bolan took a deep breath as he wrapped his sport coat around his head, letting one sleeve fall loose to protect his throat. His face, he would tuck into his chest just before he hit the glass.

What he'd run into, or onto, once he broke through the window was anybody's guess.

Ten seconds.

The Executioner walked to the building. Quickly and carefully, he stepped off ten paces, then turned back around to face the window. Looking down at his wrist again, he waited until he had three seconds left, then took off in a sprint not dissimilar to a broad jumper at a track-and-field meet.

At the last second, the Executioner left his feet, his boots aimed at the window like the sights on a rifle. But he, himself, was the bullet and, as his chronograph clicked that last second away, his world became one of sparkling, flying chunks and shards of glass.

THE EXECUTIONER LANDED on his side inside the barn. Ripping the sport coat away from his head, he found that the towel covering the window had caught on the butt of the Beretta in his shoulder rig and cast it aside, too.

Across the huge, open structure, the Executioner could see that Tom Glasser had gotten tangled in his towel, as well. But the cloth that stuck now to the SWAT commander had covered his eyes, and the more he tried to untangle it the more encumbered he seemed to become.

As he leaped to his feet, Bolan caught quick flashes of firearms, ammunition, canisters that he suspected contained liquid explosives and other gear carefully stored in bins built into the barn's walls. Crouched low, he scanned the building for enemies.

He had little trouble finding them. And they were plentiful. The two Hamas men he had seen in the overhead door had merely been the tip of the iceberg.

But it had been little over a second since the Executioner and Glasser had crashed through their respective windows, and the shock at what was happening had not had time to wear off the terrorists. But in another second, it would. Which meant Bolan had to take down as many of the Hamas men as he could before they returned to their senses.

Surprise had been his chief advantage, and the Executioner needed to make the most of it.

One of the men inside the barn wore a carefully wrapped white turban and stood just to the side of where Tom Glasser was still trying to get the towel off his face. Like the rest of the men, he held no rifle, no doubt feeling safe inside the barn and expecting no trouble.

But he had a pistol in a flap holster on the web belt around his waist. And he went for it with both hands as the Executioner turned his M-16 that way and cut loose with a 3-round burst that unwrapped the turban and sent it flying through the air, along with blood, skull fragments and brain tissue.

Most of the other men were congregated farther forward in the barn. Some sat at tables, playing baccarat and other games of chance. Others were eating mutton that had been cooked in the makeshift kitchen along one wall. Bolan turned his rifle their way.

Several hurried shots whizzed past the Executioner as more

of the Hamas terrorists returned to reality and drew their side-arms. But panic was the mother of death, and their shots went wild. Bolan took his time, using the Quick-Kill system of rifle fire, which he had first learned as a U.S. Army Special Forces sergeant years before. It was really nothing more than the long gun version of point-shooting, and relied more on instinct and normal human response to life-and-death threats than trying on to find the sights while under the stress of being fired upon.

One of the pistoleers who had stood up from behind the tables was overweight, his huge belly stretching the thin material of a plain white T-shirt. As he tried to take aim with a Tokarev 9 mm pistol, Bolan sent a trio of 5.56 mm hollowpoints into the belly hanging over his belt. The fat man fell forward over the table, sending dice, cards and poker chips flying. But his dying carnage didn't stop there. The weight of his dead body split the table in two, with both parts flying to the sides into two other men who had been sitting at the same table.

Which was good fortune for the Executioner. They both had aimed their pistols his way, and he wasn't sure he'd have had time to swing his M-16 to both sides before they got him.

The table halves knocked the men off balance, however, and their shots flew wild. Bolan took his time now, carefully pointing his rifle at a man dressed in traditional Arab robes and sending a 3-round burst into the man's throat. Blood spurted forth with the force of a fire hose as the terrorist dropped his gun and grabbed his neck with both hands.

It did no good. He had bled out and was dead before he hit the hard-packed dirt floor inside the barn.

Bolan swung his rifle past the fat man on the floor toward the other man who had sat at the table. Out of the corner of his eye, he could see that Glasser had finally succeeded in getting the towel off his face. The Kansas City SWAT captain was returning fire at two more men who had flipped their own wooden table onto its side and taken refuge behind it. The soft-lead hollowpoint bullets in the M-16's magazine didn't seem to be penetrating the barrier, however.

The Executioner cut loose with another three rounds and took down the man on the other side of the fat body that had split the table. All three rounds hit within an inch of each other in the center-chest area, and the Hamas terrorist was as dead as the others by the time he hit the dirt.

In one smooth motion, Bolan swung the M-16 over his shoulder on its sling and drew the .44 Magnum Desert Eagle from his side. Tapping the magazine ejection button with his thumb, he let the box full of hollowpoint rounds fall to the ground. The .44 Magnum bullets might go through the table better than the 5.56 mm rounds, but this was no time to be taking chances.

Reaching to the carrier on his belt, Bolan jerked out a magazine filled with sharply pointed full-metal armor-piercing rounds and slammed it between the grips of the Desert Eagle. Then, aiming the big .44 Magnum pistol toward the table behind which the two Hamas men fired at Glasser, he tapped the trigger.

The first round out of the Desert Eagle was the hollowpoint still in the chamber. And it did pass through the table. But the wood was thick enough to throw the bullet off course, and it missed both men taking refuge there.

Not so, the armor-piercing rounds that followed.

Bolan aimed just to the left of the center of the table and pulled the trigger again. This time the armor-piercing round bore through the barrier as if it were clamped to the end of a drill press. From behind the table came a scream.

The Executioner swung the big .44 Magnum pistol back to the right and tapped the trigger once more. Another howl of agony could be heard as his second armor-piercing bullet found its mark.

Bolan holstered the .44 Magnum pistol and unslung the

M-16. Hearing fire from above, he looked up. The barn was three stories high, and while the center of the structure was open, the built-in shelves and bins that circled the building on the ground floor did the same on the upper levels, as well. A narrow plywood walkway provided access to the storage areas, and an iron rail ran its perimeter.

As his eyes skirted above him for the source of the gunfire, Bolan caught a flash picture of a bin on the second floor.

It was filled with fragmentation grenades.

Bolan's eyes came to rest on another pair of gunmen firing downward. Both stood leaning over the second-floor rail.

One of the Hamas men—clean-shaven and wearing a button-down collared shirt and khaki slacks, fell to Glasser's return fire as Bolan raised his M-16. Swinging the rifle to the right, the Executioner let the sights fall on a man in a traditional robe, the tail of his kaffiyeh hanging loose around his neck. In his hands was a lever-action Marlin .30-30. The irony of this Middle Eastern Muslim terrorist using a weapon so linked to America's Old West was not lost on the Executioner. It seemed an unlikely combination.

But then again, Bolan thought as he let his sights line up once more, from another angle, it seemed appropriate. Hamas had linked up with the Rough Riders. So why wouldn't they have had at least some exchange of weaponry between them?

The Executioner smiled grimly as he squeezed the trigger. Maybe the next time he ran into the Nazi faction of this unholy alliance, he'd find some hillbilly with a swastika on his sleeve carrying a scimitar. In any case, Bolan's 5.56 mm round caught his target squarely above the nose. For a moment the spot on the man's face made him look more Hindu than Muslim. Then residual blood gushed from the middle of the man's forehead, and he toppled over the rail to thud into the packed dirt floor.

By now, all of the men still alive in the barn had recovered from the shock of the attack and gone on the offensive. As a hailstorm of bullets flew his way, Bolan took refuge behind the only cover available—a steel support beam helping hold up the structure.

Round after round after round exploded inside the barn, striking the steel between the Executioner and his attackers and zinging back off the barrier.

Across the open area of the barn's ground floor, the Executioner could see that Glasser was behind another beam. He looked behind him and spotted a set of crude wooden steps. At the top of the stairs, a ragged hole had been cut through the plywood walkway to provide access to the upper floors. As soon as he caught Glasser's eye, he pointed to his chest, then to the stairs. Then, after pointing across the barn to the Kansas City SWAT captain, he shouldered his M-16 and mimicked firing it upward.

Nodding vigorously to make sure Bolan saw that he understood, Glasser leaned around his steel beam and began cutting loose with 3-round bursts spaced across the second and third floors of the barn.

His sudden barrage of fire caused the terrorists to move back away from the rail, out of sight, which gave the Executioner the time he needed to rise and sprint to the steps. They were divided into two parts, with a square-shaped landing at the midpoint between the packed dirt and the second floor. Once again throwing his rifle over his shoulder on its sling, the Executioner chose the sound-suppressed Beretta 93-R to lead him up the steps.

There was already more than enough mayhem going on inside the building, and the longer he could keep his upward climb a secret, the better off he'd be.

The gunfire from behind his steel beam suddenly stopped, which could only mean one of two things—either Glasser's 30-round magazine had run dry, or he'd been shot.

Bolan felt his chest lighten in relief as the M-16 began to sputter again. He continued looking upward, the Beretta in his hand and ready, as he reached the landing halfway up the stairs. Just as he turned to climb the final steps to the second floor, two men appeared in the doorway above him.

They were more surprised to see Bolan than he was to see them.

Raising the 93-R in his right hand, the Executioner flipped the selector switch to semiauto and tapped the trigger. A lone 9 mm hollowpoint round drilled into the heart of a dark-skinned man wearing a white T-shirt with something written on it in Arabic script.

Bolan couldn't read it, but it would serve as the man's epitaph.

The man in the white T-shirt came tumbling down the steps, forcing Bolan to move to the side to avoid a collision. As he did, he noticed the second terrorist—dressed in blue jeans but wearing a prayer shawl—trying to get an AK-47 off of his back. His hand had become tangled in the sling.

The man looked up, and for a moment his dark brown eyes locked to the Executioner's. In the orbs set in the man's face, Bolan saw the madness of the fanatic. Anger and hatred had eaten away at the terrorist's soul for so long it seemed to have already fled his body.

But if the man's soul hadn't already fled, it did a second later.

Bolan pulled the trigger again, and another sound-suppressed 9 mm hollowpoint round blew into the man's chest. Dropping his Russian assault rifle, he clawed at the pistol on his belt even as blood flew out of both his back and chest.

The Executioner didn't bother wasting another round on the man—he had seen where the first one hit. And before he could get his pistol out of its holster, he was tumbling down the steps along the same path his friend had taken only a moment before.

Bolan moved carefully on up to the opening to the second

floor. Below, and across the barn, he could hear Glasser still firing steady 3-round bursts from his M-16. Slowly, the Executioner began inching his head up through the hole. When he finally had an eye above the stairs, he did a quick 360-degree turn to get his bearings.

There were Hamas terrorists scattered around the second-floor railing, all firing rifles down at Glasser. But none of them was looking his way.

Slowly, the Executioner lifted his sound-suppressed 93-R. Still set for semiauto fire, he aimed just below the armpit of the closest shooter. His target was standing sideways, and as soon as Bolan's sights were lined up they created a two-point reference line to the Hamas man's heart, from the side.

The Executioner squeezed the trigger and a soft cough exited the end of the Beretta. The shooter at whom he had aimed dropped his rifle over the rail and fell to a sitting position on the floor. A second later, he was flat on his back.

Bolan's eyes skirted the entire second floor of the barn again, reevaluating his situation. Several of the other terrorists had seen the man go down. But none appeared to have noticed Bolan's head or the arm holding the Beretta that extended up from the staircase. They attributed the man's death to Glasser's fire coming from below.

The Executioner took aim at the next man, roughly ten yards on down the railing from where he still stood on the stairs. Resting his elbows on the floor just above the opening, Bolan fired once more.

The target wore a cutoff black sweatshirt and had the huge biceps and triceps of a bodybuilder. He took the Executioner's next 9 mm subsonic hollowpoint round much in the same place under the arm where the first terrorist had been shot. His well-developed muscles did nothing to slow the bullet, and he dropped back onto his side, his dead hands still clutching an AK-47.

Again, the Executioner appraised his situation. And again, he saw that none of the terrorists had yet noticed him. Good. The more men he could take out before they saw him, the better. But, sooner or later, his position would be spotted.

And at that point it would be time to change tactics.

The rest of the men on the second story were even farther down the railing. Working faster now that he knew his time of discretion was limited, Bolan put more 9 mm hollowpoint rounds through the armpits and into the hearts of another pair of terrorists. But as he pulled the trigger the second time, he looked across the vast expanse of the barn to the rail opposite where he stood.

And when he did, he saw a Hamas gunman look him straight in the eye.

Even as the terrorist swung an M-16 toward Bolan, the man opened his mouth to scream out the Executioner's position to the remaining terrorists.

He never got the chance.

Bolan turned the Beretta the man's way and pulled the trigger. The near silent round entered the man's open mouth before he could utter a word, traveled up into the lower part of his brain and blew out the back of his head.

The Executioner pulled his shooting hand back down into the stairwell hole and crouched. Again, he scanned the railing all around the building.

There were no more terrorists left on the second story of the building. But the firing above him on the third floor still continued.

It was time to climb higher.

Another set of rickety wooden steps led to the same corner on the top floor of the barn, and Bolan took them as cautiously as he had before. Glasser was still behind the steel beam. He had caught sight of the Kansas City SWAT captain several times while on the second floor as the man leaned around the steel to fire his M-16.

Glasser was pinned down, but relatively safe. Hurrying to the top floor, and getting himself killed in the process, would not help the Executioner's partner one bit. Not to mention the overall mission.

When he reached the step fourth to the top, Bolan could again poke his head up over the cut-out rectangle in the barn's plywood third floor. Edging his eyes over the ledge, he saw almost an exact replica of what he'd encountered on the floor below. A rail ran all the way around a walkway that encircled the barn. Behind the walkway were large storage areas filled with more weapons of war—rifles, hand grenades, SAMs and other small arms.

The Hamas barn was a veritable warehouse of violent death.

He had been lucky on the second floor, taking out the Hamas men before they even located his position. But the third floor of the barn was a different story. As soon as his head broke the invisible plane across the hole, a steady stream of autofire peppered the wood around him.

Bolan ducked back, dropping three more steps down the staircase as the 7.62 mm rounds from the AK-47 splintered the thin plywood around the hole.

There would be no surprise attack on this floor.

Holstering the Beretta, the Executioner jerked the M-16 off his back and flipped the selector switch to 3-round burst. The gunfire above him—however impotent—continued. He waited until it had ceased, then started to descend farther but stopped.

The Executioner's eyebrows lowered as he pondered the situation. The wise thing at this point would be to try to find another route to the third floor. And there was probably a set of steps in all four corners of the barn.

But the Hamas terrorists would be watching them now, expecting the Executioner to look for an alternate route. The route he'd just abandoned might well be the *last* place they expected to see him again.

Dropping the partially spent magazine from his rifle, the Executioner rammed a full 30-round magazine into the carriage.

Slowly, Bolan retraced his steps up the stairs until his eyes rose above the floor. The gunfire toward Glasser on the ground continued. But no more rounds were coming his way. And the attention of the Hamas men seemed fixed on the other three corners of the barn.

The Executioner made his decision in the blink of an eye. Sprinting the last few steps to the third floor, he raised the M-16 and fired.

The first 3-round burst tore through the leather jacket one of the Hamas men wore over his robe. A screech of pain and terror echoed over the gunfire as the man dropped his AK-47 and fell over the rail, toppling all three stories to the hard-packed dirt floor. Landing on his head, his neck broke, his open eyes staring upward from a head twisted a grotesque angle to the body.

The Executioner ran forward, crouching as he fired again. His next trio of 5.56 mm rounds took off the head of another Hamas man—this one clean-shaven but wearing a robe. As he pulled the trigger, the Executioner couldn't help but think of the strange mixture of modern and traditional dress that he found among the terrorists. They seemed to prefer their ancient robes and beards, but they would shave, and wear whatever helped them blend into the masses in order to accomplish their goal.

Which was spreading terror by killing innocent men, women and children.

Four more Hamas men fell to the Executioner's fire. Glasser sprayed a final 3-round burst, and then the barn took on an eerie silence as the noise suddenly died down.

The Executioner looked down over the railing and shouted, "Glasser! Clear the ground floor! I'll be down to meet you in a minute!" He broke into a run, circling the top floor of the barn and checking to make sure all of the terrorists were dead. He also eyed the bins and other containers stacked high with weaponry.

This barn had not only been a meeting place. It was a supply dump for everything from knives to surface-to-air rockets.

When he had cleared the middle floor, as well, Bolan descended the steps and found Glasser waiting for him. "You see anything that looked like an office?" he asked.

"That's a big 10-4," the SWAT man said. "Follow me." Glasser turned and jogged off toward a corner of the building.

The office area was no bigger than a second bedroom in a small house, but it was crammed full of papers and other documents—most of them in Arabic. Bolan glanced hurriedly through the stacks on the floor and a bookshelf, then turned his attention toward the desk where a computer sat.

Turning it on, the Executioner waited for the computer to warm up.

"What are we looking for?" Glasser asked.

"The list of targets Hamas and the Rough Riders plan to hit."

"But it'll be in Arabic, won't it?" Glasser asked.

"Most of it, probably," Bolan replied. "But if the list is on this computer, there's a good chance that there's an English version, too." He drew in a breath, then let it out. "The Rough Riders—at least the vast majority of them—aren't going to be able to speak or read Arabic."

Glasser nodded. "I hadn't thought of that."

As the computer continued to buzz and blink its way to life, the Executioner said, "Cover the door for me, will you? You never know when some other Hamas terrorists may show up outside."

Glasser's only answer was a nod. He exited the room to find the door they'd come in.

Finally, the computer appeared to be on. Bolan looked at the keyboard.

The letters were all in Arabic.

Pulling the cell phone from his blacksuit, he tapped in the number to Stony Man Farm. "I need the Bear," he said as soon as Barbara Price had answered. "Quick." He glanced at the doorway where Glasser had disappeared. "I don't know how much time I've got." Besides more Hamas men showing up unexpectedly, there was always the chance that one of the dead men in the building had gotten off a cell phone call for reinforcements. If that was the case, this call would have to be terminated, and terminated fast.

A second later, the Executioner was talking to Aaron "The Bear" Kurtzman. "The keyboard's in Arabic, Bear," he said into his cell phone. "I can't read a letter."

"What brand is it?" Kurtzman asked.

Bolan squinted at the logo just below the screen. "It says *Bell*."

"And the B looks almost as much like a D as a B?" Kurtzman asked.

"Yeah. With the E angled backward."

"Bells are counterfeit Dells," the computer wizard said. "Sort of the fake Rolexes of the computer industry. "I think I can walk you through it until we find the file menu."

Bolan followed the Stony Man computer genius's instructions, and a moment later a long list of documents—some in English, others in Arabic—appeared on the screen. "I've got it, I think," Bolan said.

"Good," Kurtzman said. "Pick a file in Arabic and open it."

The Executioner used the curser to do so. "Can't read a word," he said over the cell phone.

"Try another," Kurtzman said.

Bolan opened another file listed in Arabic. But this time the document was in English. It was a photostat copy of a newspaper article about a suicide bomber in Israel. He told Kurtzman.

"Now open one of the documents listed in English," Kurtzman said.

Again, Bolan followed the man's suggestion. But while the title was listed on the menu in English, the text was in Arabic.

"That's what I was afraid of," Kurtzman said, letting out a long breath.

"I don't see the reasoning behind it," Bolan said, glancing again at the doorway.

"Oh," Kurtzman said. "It's for times just like this. It's just to slow down anyone breaking into their files who doesn't speak both Arabic and English. Add to that the fact that anything important is probably in code, and you'd created a lot of busywork for people like you and me who are trying to find out what's going on inside the files."

"What do you suggest I do?" Bolan asked.

"Send the whole hard drive to me," Kurtzman said without hesitation. "Then blow the whole place up."

Again, Kurtzman took Bolan step-by-step through the process of transferring a copy of the computer's hard drive to Stony Man Farm's bank of computers. When the process was complete, Kurtzman said, "Okay, I've got it all. I'll get to work on it and get back with you."

"Great," the Executioner said. "I just hope the list is even on it. There isn't any guarantee."

"Well, we won't know until we've tried," Kurtzman said.

Bolan and the computer expert both hung up.

The Executioner jogged back across the open center area of the barn, stopping when he came to a bin filled with sticks of dynamite. Several rolls of fuses were also in the box, and he uncoiled roughly twenty feet of one and fitted it to the end of one of the sticks in the center of the pile. He could see

Glasser holding the front door next to the overhead door open with his back, and watching him.

"Get ready to run," Bolan said.

Glasser nodded his understanding.

Pulling a small waterproof tube from a pocket of his black-suit, the Executioner unscrewed the lid and pulled out a match. A second later he had struck it on the roughened end of the tube and lit the fuse.

Glasser kept his back against the door as Bolan sprinted through, then joined him as they hurried across the field to the car wash.

Amad Nadir was waiting for them again as the Executioner jumped behind the wheel of the car and stuck the key in the ignition.

The dynamite went up a second later. Then, as they backed out of the car-wash stall, the fire reached another bin of explosives and a second eruption took place.

Bolan, Glasser and Nadir were halfway back to Paris before the explosions subsided, and at least one major Hamas weapons cache had been neutralized.

But the threat from the Islamic terrorists—and their new strange bedfellows, the Rough Riders—was still as active as ever.

**5**

"Well," Tom Glasser said as the lighted outskirts of Paris appeared once again. "That was fun." He turned sideways in the passenger's seat of the Mercedes to face Bolan. "But I don't see how it's gotten us any closer to this combined Hamas-Rough Riders hit list. Or where we're supposed to go from here."

The statement was not an indictment on Glasser's part, and the Executioner didn't take it as such. "We put on a pretty good Fourth of July show for the people of Versailles," Bolan said. "Which also took out sizable amounts of weaponry, surveillance gear and other equipment. I'd call that a small success all on its own."

Glasser nodded. "Yeah," he said, "but we both know they've got plenty more toys stockpiled in other locations. This is only going to be a bump in the road for them." He turned in his seat, resting an arm over the back, and looked at Nadir. "Am I right?"

"Yes," the CIA informant confirmed. "There are Hamas weapons caches all over Europe and the Middle East, not to mention the munitions and other paraphernalia that has been shipped to the Americas and the Orient."

"Where's it all coming from?" the Executioner asked. "Iran or Syria?"

"Both," Nadir answered. "It's one of the few things the Sunnis and Shiites agree on."

"What is?" Glasser asked.

"That Israel and America must both be destroyed."

The statement brought a serious silence over the interior of the Mercedes. Bolan guided the car as traffic thickened closer to the city. "Destroying that storage facility was like slapping a bandage on a severed artery," he said. "But it's all we could do for the moment." He changed lanes and passed a pickup camper. "Besides, that's not the real value of what we just did."

"You talking about the computer?" Glasser asked.

Bolan nodded his head as he switched lanes again. "Somewhere on the hard drive I sent to Bear, I'm hoping we'll find the whole list of attack sites Hamas and the Rough Riders are targeting. As well as the big night in which the smaller assaults will culminate."

Bolan was about to continue when the cell phone in his blacksuit pocket began to vibrate. He pulled it out and flipped it open. "Striker," he said.

"I've just spot-checked the hard drive," Kurtzman's familiar voice said in Bolan's ear. "And yes, the index is in code—a code that seems to combine English and Arabic. But it wasn't that hard to decipher. It took Akira's translation software about fifteen minutes to put it all together."

The Executioner thought of Akira Tokaido, the punk-rock-looking Japanese cyber expert on Kurtzman's staff. He had forgotten that the young man had a knack for developing top-notch translation modules. Next to Kurtzman himself, there was no one better at what he did with Stony Man's magic machines.

The Executioner thought also of the code Kurtzman had just described. If it was simple, that had to mean it was meant to be used by men who spoke English but only rudimentary Arabic, and vice versa. In other words, both Hamas and the Rough Riders would need to be able to decipher it.

"The document itself," Kurtzman went on, "I suspect will be in a more sophisticated coding system than the one Akira's program figured out for the index. But before we start that, we've got to find it. And there are a lot of ways to hide a document on a hard drive."

Bolan nodded to himself. The more intricate enciphering would probably only make sense to the men at the top of Hamas and the Rough Riders. "Anything else of value?" he asked as traffic slowed and his foot moved toward the brake.

"Yeah, I think so," said the Stony Man computer whiz. "There are e-mails that I suspect are indirect referrals to this unholy union between Hamas and the Rough Riders. But nothing specific like we'd hoped—at least not yet. We may have more luck when the deciphering's finished. But like I said, if that list of strike sites you want is on this hard drive at all, it's going to take some time to search it out."

"Just tell me what you've got right now," the Executioner said.

"Well," Kurtzman said. "According to this, something's going down tomorrow. It mentions where. But not what."

"Okay," the Executioner said. "Give me the where, then."

"Chicago," Kurtzman replied. "But that's not what really caught my attention."

Bolan waited, knowing Kurtzman would tell him the rest when he was ready.

"There are a couple of places where they mention Katyusha rockets," said the wheelchair-bound computer man. "The kind Hezbollah keeps shooting into Israel." Kurtzman cleared his throat. "And there's another, seemingly unrelated reference to something called the Night of Hell. That's when the encoded words are in English. But Akira claims he came across a similar reference to an American jihad, which specifies a particular night when some gigantic strike using the combined forces of the Rough Riders and Hamas is to take place. I'm 99.9 percent certain that this Night of Hell and American jihad are the same thing."

The man in the wheelchair paused to catch his breath, then added, "We don't have the date for this night yet. Or the site, or any of the other particulars. But it appears that these smaller, single-site assaults—like the bank in Kansas City, the food poisoning at the embassy in Paris and this Katyusha rocket thing in Chicago—are all leading up to it."

He stopped talking again for a moment to let it all sink in, then said, "And I don't know if you know it or not—I know you've been up to your eyeballs in your own work—but there's been a thirty percent rise in suicide bombings, random machine-gunnings at bus and train stations and other Western-owned or -influenced sites in Israel, Europe and the U.S. And either Hamas, or the Rough Riders, or *both* have taken credit for each and every one."

"Sounds like they're leading up to something bigger to me, too," the Executioner said. "Do me a favor, will you, Bear?" He took the next exit ramp and stopped just in front of the stop sign at the cross street.

"Ask and ye shall receive, big guy," Kurtzman said.

Bolan turned under the overpass, took the access ramp and started back the way he'd come on the highway. "Give Jack a call. Tell him to fill the Lear's gas tanks and get that bird warmed up—we're on our way to the airport."

"Where are you going?" Kurtzman asked.

"The Windy City," the Executioner said. He slowed at a yellow yield sign a motorcycle passed, then pulled out into the traffic leading toward the airport. "Chicago."

"THIS KATYUSHA ROCKET DEAL Bear mentioned from the e-mails," Glasser said as Grimaldi set the Learjet down on the private plane runway at the Gary Chicago International Airport. "You think there's anything to it?"

Bolan stared out through the windshield of the Lear as the plane gradually slowed to a halt. "There certainly could be," he said. "There's plenty of old Soviet surplus weapons of all kinds floating around the black market these days. A lot were bought up by Middle Eastern countries, as Saddam Hussein proved with his old Soviet SCUDs during the first Gulf War. But Iraq's more of an *internal* problem these days. So, if Hamas has gotten their hands on some Katyushas they probably got them from Syria or Iran or both. On the other hand, they might have come secondhand from Hezbollah. We all know Syria and Iran have been supplying them for years."

"Yeah," Glasser said, as Grimaldi pulled up to an empty hangar. "But Hamas and Hezbollah aren't really the best of friends. The fact is, they hate each other."

"They do," Bolan agreed. "One group is Sunni Muslim, the other Shia. But there's at least one thing about which they both agree."

"What's that?" Glasser asked.

"They both hate America, and Israel, even more than they hate each other."

It took Glasser a few seconds to respond. But when he did, he quoted an old axiom that had been kicked around warfare since Sun Tsu had written *The Art of War.* "The enemy of my enemy is my friend."

"Exactly," Bolan said.

"And you think it's possible that they've smuggled some Katyushas into the U.S.?" Glasser asked.

"That's affirmative," the Executioner said. "Right along with the launchers. The Katyusha Multiple Rocket Launcher BM-21 can be taken apart and smuggled in piece by piece. Or if they don't have the launcher, the rockets can even be fired from a simple pipe using a car battery. Not as accurately, maybe, but they'll still blow whatever they hit to kingdom come."

Behind him, Bolan heard Glasser sit back in his seat. When he looked up into the rearview mirror he could see Amad Nadir sitting next to the new blacksuit. They had brought the Hamas informant back to the States in case they ran across any documents in Arabic. And to pick up on leads and clues that the man might snap to that an American—to whom Arabic was a second language—might not notice.

"They don't have much range, Glasser said. "Ten miles or so, isn't it?"

"To be precise 12.7," Bolan said. "But if they've got a launcher already in Chicago, they can drive it to any area of the city they want to. With the rockets covered with a tarp of some similar disguise behind the cab, it would look no different from several thousand other trucks passing through the city." He paused, took in a lung full of air through his nose and let it out through his mouth. "Pipe launching isn't as accurate, and doesn't have the range as the launcher. But no matter what they take aim at, they're going to hit something, even if their sights are off."

"I don't have any connections here in Chicago," Glasser said. "Nobody from the Arab world or Rough Riders, anyway. Do you?"

Grimaldi chuckled before Bolan could answer. "Son," the pilot told the new blacksuit, "we've got connections of some kind everywhere." The pilot turned to Bolan as he continued to guide the Learjet. "You planning on getting hold of the two guys I think you are?" he asked.

Bolan nodded his head.

"They're getting a little long in the tooth, aren't they?" Grimaldi asked.

"They aren't rookies," the Executioner agreed. "But you still won't find two better, smarter or tougher cops in the whole Chicago metropolitan area. And they tied for top honors back when they went through blacksuit training."

"Agreed," said the pilot. "Tell them hello for me, will you?"

"Will do," said the Executioner.

Grimaldi cut the engine to the Learjet and Bolan, Glasser and Amad Nadir got down out of the plane. A customs officer came walking swiftly toward them carrying a clipboard.

"You've already been cleared," he said, his face reflecting both awe and confusion. "By the President himself."

"Thanks."

"This is the first time I've ever had *that* happen in the twelve years I've been with customs," said the man with the clipboard.

"And you'll probably never have it happen again," Bolan said as he opened the luggage compartment and he, Nadir and Glasser began pulling out their luggage and equipment bags.

"There's even a rental car waiting for you in the parking lot," the customs man said. Glasser was the closest to him, so he handed the newly trained blacksuit a key ring with two car keys attached to it. "Can you tell me what's going on?" he asked as Glasser took the keys.

"You know the old joke," Glasser said. "We *could* tell you…." He let his voice trail off.

"I know, I know," the customs officer said. "But then you'd have to kill me."

"Right," Glasser said as he pulled the last bag out of the luggage compartment and Bolan slammed the door shut. "But thanks for your help."

Five minutes later, the Executioner, Amad Nadir and Tom Glasser were driving away from the airport in a new Toyota Highlander. "Where are we gonna start?" Glasser asked.

Bolan glanced up into the rearview mirror at Nadir in the back seat. The man knew no one in Chicago. But being Arab and a Muslim, he might well pick up on some nuances that Bolan and Glasser missed during their quest to find out what terror strike was about to go down in Chicago.

Tonight.

The Executioner had let Glasser drive so he'd be free to use his cell phone as they turned onto Chicago's famous Lake Shore Drive. On his right, Bolan saw the sparkling waters of Lake Michigan. Both motor yachts and sailboats could be seen in the distance as the water lapped peacefully onto the shore. Heading toward Chicago's Loop, they passed Soldier Field, then the Museum of Natural History and then the Planetarium and Aquarium.

On the right, the lake was peaceful. On the left, business was being conducted in an orderly fashion.

The Executioner couldn't help thinking that both were in direct contrast of what Hamas and the Rough Riders had planned for that evening.

Whatever *that* was.

Pulling his cell phone from the pocket of the khaki sport coat he'd changed into during the flight back to America, the Executioner tapped in the number to Stony Man Farm. He needed to talk to Shelly Cirillo and Jim Ritholz, two Chicago police officers nearing retirement. During their careers, they had served on stakeout and decoy teams, the SWAT team and had been firearms instructors.

Barbara Price answered the Executioner's call and transferred him to Kurtzman.

"You have anything new for me, Bear?" the Executioner asked.

"Uh-uh. We're still working on finding the hidden document—if there even is one."

"There's another thing I need," Bolan said. "Shelly Cirillo and Jim Ritholz. Both are Chicago PD, and you can put me in contact with them faster than if I try calling the CPD personnel office."

"Hang on a second while I hack into Chicago's files," Kurtzman said.

The man in the wheelchair had exaggerated only slightly about how quickly he could break into the Chicago PD's computers. Five seconds later, he said, "They're both currently with a counterterrorist task force that works clandestinely out of an office across the street from the Sears Building."

"Who else is on the task force?" the Executioner asked. He

could imagine territorial infighting if different agencies— particularly federal—were involved.

"Let's see…" Kurtzman said, and Bolan heard him tapping on the computer keyboard on the other end of the line. Then he said, "Two each of FBI, DEA, U.S. Customs and Border Patrol. And there's two more men but the organization they represent is left blank."

"Well, we both know what that means, then," the Executioner said.

"Yep," Kurtzman said. "CIA. They aren't supposed to be working on U.S. soil. But they are. You want the phone number to their office?"

"Yeah, give it to me," Bolan said.

Kurtzman gave him the number and hung up.

Bolan tapped the new number into the phone as Glasser slowed the Highlander to accommodate thicker traffic. "Head toward the Sears Building," the Executioner told him as he waited for the line to connect. "Jackson Boulevard exit."

Glasser nodded.

A moment later, a deep male voice answered the call to the counterterrorist task force number with a simple, "Hello?"

"I need to talk to either Cirillo or Ritholz," Bolan said into the instrument pressed against his ear.

"Who is this?" the voice croaked. "And how did you get this number?"

Bolan laughed softly. He had recognized Shelly Cirillo's hoarse voice and the Brooklyn accent. "This is Matt Cooper," he told the man. "Or Striker, as you knew me." He paused a second to let the name sink in, then said, "And I'll let you guess how I got the number."

It was Cirillo who now laughed on the other end of the line. "I suspect it was your contact who goes by the name of Bear most likely he gave it to you after he'd illegally tapped into the Chicago PD's computer network. How have you been, Striker?"

"Busy," Bolan said as Glasser took the exit to Jackson Boulevard. "I need to meet with you and your old running buddy, Ritholz."

"Well, if you've got the phone number, I suspect you know where the office is, too," Cirillo said. "Come on up."

"I don't think so," the Executioner said. "As I understand it, you've got Feds of all brands there with you. I want this kept between you, Ritholz and me and my men."

"Understandable," the Chicago detective said. "Ritholz is here with me now. And there's a coffee shop on the ground level of the Sears Building across the street." He paused for a second, then said, "How far away are you?"

"Better give us at least fifteen minutes," Bolan said. "Traffic's bad."

"It's always bad in Chicago," Cirillo said. "Jim and I'll meet you in fifteen minutes. If you aren't there, we'll wait."

"And make sure none of the other members of your squad follow you," Bolan reminded the man. "I'm sure they're all good men, but I don't need the complications that could arise by having that many agencies involved."

"Understood," Cirillo said. "Sears Building, ground-floor coffee shop, fifteen minutes," he repeated. "See you then."

"Right," the Executioner said and hung up.

Glasser had turned onto Jackson by now and was making his way slowly through the thick traffic. The expression on his face exposed a multitude of questions.

"They're both blacksuit-trained," Bolan volunteered. "Several years ago."

The Kansas City cop nodded and drove on.

It took twenty minutes rather than fifteen to reach the Sears Building. Traffic around the building was at a standstill, and parking along the street nonexistent. They had no choice but to hand the keys over to a valet wearing black slacks and a burgundy vest but, before they did, Bolan made a quick once-over of the luggage piled in the back of the vehicle.

The black ballistic nylon weapons and ammunition bags were on the bottom of the pile, hidden from view by less curiosity-provoking suitcases. The valet wasn't going to notice them, nor would anyone else who passed by the vehicle while it was parked in the underground parking lot.

Shelly Cirillo and Jim Ritholz didn't look as if they'd aged as much as most career cops during the years since the Executioner had helped train them at Stony Man Farm. They sat across from each other in a corner booth, both wearing T-shirts beneath sport coats. They smiled when they saw the Executioner walk into the coffee shop flanked by Amad Nadir and Tom Glasser. Both men stood up as Bolan led his compatriots toward the booth, and hands were shaken all around the table.

The Executioner introduced Glasser as the Kansas City SWAT commander that he was but called Nadir simply a "friend." Both Ritholz and Cirillo got the message. Smart cops never called their informants "snitches"—at least to their faces—and didn't even use words like "informant" in public.

Ritholz took a second look at Glasser and said, "Something tells me you just came from the Farm."

Glasser smiled and nodded. Bolan watched Nadir frown, not knowing what they were talking about. Good. And there would be no more mention of the fact that the other three men, and the Executioner, were bonded like brothers for life by their top-notch, and top secret, training.

Ritholz moved to the other side of the booth to sit by Cirillo and Nadir. Glasser took seats opposite them. Bolan pulled a chair away from a table just behind him and sat down at the end. A moment later, a waitress wearing a heavily starched white uniform arrived and took orders for coffee from Bolan and Glasser. Nadir, more accustomed to the strong Arabian brews, ordered a double espresso.

Ritholz was the first to speak. "I assume this isn't just a social call," he said.

Bolan shook his head.

"And may we assume it's okay to talk openly in front of everyone…including out-of-town cops and *friends?*"

This time the Executioner nodded.

The waitress appeared with their coffee and Nadir's espresso, set them in front of the men, then refilled the cups Ritholz and Cirillo already had. All conversation ceased until she had disappeared again. Then Bolan said, "What I'm about to tell you goes no further than this table. That includes the rest of your task force across the street."

"Understood," Ritholz said as Cirillo nodded his own agreement.

Quickly Bolan ran down the situation, telling the two detectives about what had happened in Paris and Versailles, then about the alliance that had been struck between Hamas and the Rough Riders and the sketchy details they had concerning a strike going down in Chicago that night. He ended the briefing with the Night of Hell, as the Rough Riders called it, and what he guessed was the same thing as the American jihad, to which Hamas had referred.

Cirillo looked up from his coffee cup, glanced at Ritholz, then said, "We've had rumors about the Rough Riders and Hamas teaming up," he said. "But they seemed too improbable to get very excited about."

"Improbable isn't the word for it," Ritholz said. "The whole idea of two terrorist groups that far apart in their beliefs getting together sounds preposterous." He paused to take a sip from his refilled coffee cup. "Hamas—like all the other Islamic-based terrorist organizations—wants a world theocracy with ayatollahs and mujadhideen running the government. The American Nazi Party—of which the Rough Riders are a part—is looking for worldwide fascism just like Hitler was after."

Bolan nodded. "That's what makes this all so dangerous," he said. "Nobody can believe it's true." He stopped talking long enough to take a drink of his own coffee. "And it's that disbelief that'll make it so effective if we don't stop it before it goes down." He set his cup back down again.

Ritholz drained his coffee cup and raised it over his head. The waitress came back, provided refills all around again, then left once more.

"So where do we fit in?" Cirillo asked. "How can we help?"

"I assume," Bolan said, "you've got *friends* like Amad here, yourself. I want you to call them in so we can talk to them."

"If we call them into our office, it's going to be nigh-on impossible to keep the other members of the task force from knowing something's going on," Ritholz said.

The Executioner nodded. "That's why I'm about to rent several hotel rooms to put them in," he said. "If I remember right, the Conrad Hilton is close by."

The two Chicago detectives nodded. "Go back toward the lake on Jackson, then turn right on Michigan Avenue," Cirillo said.

"How many men will you be calling in?" the Executioner asked.

"Three," Cirillo said. "Two Arabs with connections to Hamas and one American who's kind of on the outskirts of the Rough Riders."

"They don't know each other, I'm hoping," Glasser said.

"Of course not," Cirillo answered. "In fact our two Hamas contacts sometimes bring us reports on each other."

"Then that's perfect," Bolan said. "Bring them to the Hilton. I want to interrogate them separately, so I'll get three rooms on different floors. One of us will be in each room. Have the front desk call up so we can give the okay to them giving out our room numbers. They'll be under the names of Matt Cooper, Tom Glasser and Amad Nadir. Bring one man to each of the rooms."

Cirillo nodded. "Will do," he said. "But if our guys knew something, I think they'd have already told us."

"Maybe," Bolan said. "And maybe not. You two know as well as I do that sometimes our friends play both ends against the middle." Out of the corner of his eye, he watched Nadir for a reaction. There was none. "If that's the case, and their true loyalties lie with either Hamas or the Rough Riders, they may have chosen to omit this bit of information so the Night of Hell strike could take place." He paused for another sip of coffee. "And if they chose the strike over the money you'd have paid them for a tip-off, that means the strike is big."

Both Ritholz and Cirillo nodded in understanding as they stood up and shook hands around the table once more. "We'll have our friends meet us in the lobby of the Hilton," Cirillo said. "One of us will bring them up to the rooms when they get there."

"Bring the Hamas men to Nadir's room," Bolan said. "And the Rough Rider either to mine or Glasser's. I don't want to spook either the Arabs or the Americans with enemy-sounding names before we even get started."

Cirillo and Ritholz both nodded again.

Without another word, the Executioner turned and walked out of the coffee shop and through the lobby to the front door of the Sears Building. Glasser, Nadir, Cirillo and Ritholz followed him, with the two Chicago detectives continuing on across the street to the building that housed the task force office.

Bolan handed his parking ticket to the same valet who had parked the Highlander earlier as Glasser and Nadir stopped on both of his sides to wait. Five minutes later, the valet parked the vehicle in front of the building, got out and handed Bolan the key.

The Executioner glanced through the back window of the Highlander at the suitcases piled on top of the weapons bags. They were all in the same position he'd left them. The valet hadn't gotten nosy, and the Executioner doubled what he'd usually have tipped the man for his professionalism.

The valet's eyes opened wide as he took the bills from the Executioner. "Thank you, sir," he said, then pocketed the money and stepped back up the curb.

Bolan got behind the wheel as Glasser took the shotgun seat and Nadir got in the back.

Fifteen minutes later, they had threaded their way through the heavy Chicago traffic and were pulling up in front of the Conrad Hilton Hotel.

THE EXECUTIONER TOOK A SEAT on the bedspread and reached for the phone on the table between the two beds. Holding the receiver to his ear, he tapped in the number 1401. A moment later, Amad Nadir answered. "Yes?" the Arab informant said.

"I'm in room 307," said the Executioner. "Glasser's in 1112. Cirillo and Ritholz are downstairs." He paused to let the information sink in, then went on. "Depending on who shows up first—the Hamas or Rough Riders men—they'll be bringing them up. When you hear the knock on the door, I want you to unlock it, open it just enough to let them know they can get in and then disappear into the bathroom before they see you. Got it?"

"Yes," Nadir said. "But why?"

"Because we may need an unknown face like yours somewhere down the line," the Executioner answered.

Amad Nadir had loosened up considerably during the time he'd spent with Bolan and Glasser, and now he even felt comfortable enough with the Americans to crack a joke. "Is this because I look Arabic or because I am so handsome?" he asked in a deadpan voice.

Bolan chuckled. "I'll let you decide that for yourself. Cirillo or Ritholz—whichever one brings their man up—will call me and I'll come down to interrogate them. Any questions?"

"No," Nadir said. "It is all simple enough."

Bolan pushed the button to end the call, then let up on it again. As soon as he heard the dial tone, he punched in the numerals 1112. When Glasser answered, he gave the Kansas City SWAT captain similar instructions. But Glasser didn't question why he should stay out of sight in the bathroom. He knew that there was no way for Bolan to interrogate the informants without exposing his face to them. But there was a cardinal rule—particularly among undercover cops—that you never burned an operative's face when you didn't need to.

Besides, either Ritholz or Cirillo would also be in the room with the man Glasser knew as Matt Cooper, and there was another rule that more than two interrogators intimidated the subject, which promoted exaggeration or even downright lying just to please them. The recent blacksuit graduate did have one question, however.

"What do I do if the snitch needs to take a leak?" he asked.

"That's what the shower and the shower curtains are there for," Bolan answered.

Glasser laughed. "Stupid me," he said. "Here I was all along thinking they were so you could take a shower."

"Anything else?" Bolan asked.

"Uh-uh," Glasser said. "I guess I'll see you when I see you."

Bolan dropped the receiver back into the cradle. Twisting on the bed, he lay back against the headboard and crossed his arms behind his neck. Waiting, with nothing to do, was always the hardest part of any operation, and it was especially difficult and even painful for a man of action like the Executioner. But it was unavoidable. It was going to take some time for Cirillo and Ritholz to round up their snitches and get them to the Conrad Hilton, and there was nothing he could do to quicken the process. These pauses in physical activity were a part of every mission, and Bolan had found the best way to get through them was to use them to organize his thoughts.

So he did so now.

So far, the assaults fell into two categories: foreign and domestic. The foreign attacks had been carried out by foreigners—Hamas. The domestic strikes had been conducted by homegrown terrorists—the Rough Riders. The only evidence of any connection between the two groups was the word of Amad Nadir and the references to the Night of Hell and American jihad from the e-mails on the computer in Versailles.

Bolan pulled his arms down from over his head and stood up, walking past the room's table and chairs to the window and pulling back the curtain. Even from only three stories up, he had a good view of Lake Michigan, and he watched the sailboats and motorcraft move smoothly through the water. Again, his mind couldn't help but contrast the peaceful scene he saw before him with the rocket attack he expected sometime that night. If the references to Katyusha rockets in Chicago that Kurtzman had found in the e-mails were true, it was the first solid connection between the American and Arabic terrorists.

The Rough Riders weren't likely to have come up with Katyushas on their own. They would have to have obtained them from the Middle East.

The Executioner shut the curtain, walked to the sink and began unwrapping the paper around a water glass. Could that be the only connection between the two groups? Trading equipment? Maybe the Rough Riders had sent Hamas some kind of American weapons in return for the rockets.

Bolan had just taken a drink of water when the phone rang. Setting down his glass, he lifted the receiver and said, "Yeah?"

"It's Cirillo," said the voice with the Brooklyn accent on the other end, sounding slightly out of place on this hotel phone in Chicago. In the background, Bolan could hear bits and pieces of conversation and other lobby noises. "One of our *rough and rowdy* friends just walked in. I'm taking him up to Glasser's room."

"Affirmative," Bolan said. It was clear that the American Rough Rider informant had been the first to arrive, but Cirillo didn't want to mention the terrorist organization by name with all of the people coming and going around him.

"I'll see you there," said the Executioner, dropping the receiver back into the cradle on the table.

Quickly checking the sound-suppressed Beretta in his shoulder rig, the Desert Eagle on his hip, the combat knife and the rest of his equipment, the Executioner slid his arms into the khaki sport coat he had hung over the back of a chair at the table by the window.

He pulled back the curtain and took a final glance through the glass to the peacefulness of the lake. He doubted that the Rough Riders planned to shoot their Katyushas into the water, that would not accomplish the terror and destruction they'd want.

No, the targets would be somewhere else within the metropolitan area of Chicago. Some place where hundreds, perhaps thousands, of people were likely to have gathered.

Some place where those hundreds or thousands of people would die.

The Executioner glanced at his watch. It was almost five o'clock in the afternoon. Rush hour on the streets and thoroughfares.

He had to find out where the Katyusha launch sites were, and he had to find out fast. Hurrying to the door, he opened it, stepped through and let it swing shut behind him as he walked briskly to the elevator.

As soon as he was inside the car, he reached out and pushed the button for the fourteenth floor.

**6**

Silence fell over the hotel room on the eleventh floor of the Conrad Hilton as the man who had been introduced to Bolan simply by his code name—Omar—finished speaking.

Already, in room 1401—two floors above them—the Executioner had spoken with Jamal, the other Hamas informant. Jamal had revealed that he had overheard talk about giving one BM-21 launcher and several Katyusha rockets to some American group that wasn't actually part of the Hamas. But that was all he knew.

Bolan believed him. Jamal didn't have enough sense to come in out of the rain, and the Hamas cell leaders in the United States certainly weren't going to entrust any top secret information to a man that stupid. What the Executioner suspected he saw before him in Jamal was a future suicide bomber. It was the only reason he could think of that might explain why Hamas even kept him around. In a quiet aside in the hotel's bathroom, out of Jamal's earshot, Bolan asked Ritholz why Jamal was on their payroll.

"We've got him because, stupid or not," Ritholz had said, "he's one of the only links to Hamas we've come up with. Sometimes you gotta take what's given to you."

The Executioner knew the truth of that statement.

Gus, the Rough Riders informant, was smarter. He was also of a different species of informant than Jamal. He'd been more or less tricked into joining the Rough Riders with false statements about their goals and purposes. Gus had been told that the Rough Riders were nothing more than an offshoot of the American Nazi Party, which had done away with the fascist approach and wanted a true democracy in which everyone had an equal chance. Gus had agreed that the most persecuted minority group on Earth today was middle-class white men. When the Rough Riders told Gus they had no intention of ever using violence in any form, he had swallowed the bait.

And by the time he'd learned the truth, he was in too deep to get out; he'd have been killed by the Rough Riders. So he had gone to the police, and ended up staying with the Nazi extremists and passing on everything he knew to Cirillo and Ritholz.

By the time Bolan reached Glasser's room, Gus had already reported all of the information he had about the Katyusha rockets. There was apparently only one BM-21 involved instead of several, and they would therefore need to find only one launch site. Gus had also confirmed the fact that there was definitely some kind of affiliation—at least a temporary one—between the Rough Riders and Hamas.

But the Executioner reminded himself that even one full salvo of Katyushas from the mobile launch truck would fire the equivalent of four Iraqi-style SCUD missiles. Gus also knew that the multiple rocket launcher had been smuggled into the U.S. in pieces, then assembled somewhere in the Chicago area.

While he had no idea where the launch site was, Gus knew the target—Soldier Field, where a Billy Graham Crusade, conducted by the famous retired evangelist's son, Franklin, was being held. The stadium could hold more than one hundred thousand people.

And a full house was expected. Hamas, or any other Islamic terrorist group, could not ask for a more populated Christian "infidel" target than that.

But according to Gus, the Katyusha rockets on the lone launcher were each equipped with VX chemical warheads. As well as the people at Soldier Field who would be killed by the rockets' explosions themselves, this nerve gas would spread for miles in the wind, killing thousands more innocent men, women and children and bringing lifelong physical disabilities to those whose lives it didn't fully claim.

If the Katyushas were allowed to launch and explode in Soldier Field, the Executioner estimated that close to a half-million residents could be affected. Chicago wasn't called the Windy City for nothing.

Bolan continued to stare at Omar, who sat across the table from him. The Executioner had been suspicious of the man since Cirillo had first walked him through the door. Omar had been in the room for fifteen minutes now, and so far a lot of words had come out of his mouth.

But very few of them were of assistance to the mission at hand.

"I've asked you this several times already, Omar," the Executioner said. "We already know the target. Now, I want the launch site."

Omar looked down at the table in front of him. "I regret that I must answer you the same way I have each time you asked before," Omar said. "I do not know where they plan to launch." He paused long enough to pull a gold cigarette case out of an inside pocket of his jacket and said, "Do you mind if I smoke?"

Bolan took note of the fact that the Hamas informant's hand was shaking as he held the cigarette case. That, combined with the downward glance before finally answering the Executioner's question, suggested that he was lying. Such body language was not a certainty by any means, but it was a strong indicators of deception.

"Yeah, we do mind if you smoke," Cirillo said. "This is a no-smoking room. There aren't even any ashtrays."

"But I am needing a cigarette," Omar pressed. "It will help relax me so I may answer your questions more efficiently."

Bolan didn't waste the opening. In any interrogation, the interrogator tried to find his subject's weakness and then exploit it. The Executioner knew that the craving for nicotine could be as strong and seized the opportunity. "You just keep talking, my friend. The sooner you tell us what we want to know, the sooner we'll get you some place where you can smoke." He reached out, took the gold cigarette case from Omar's hand, snapped it shut and dropped it back into the side pocket of the informant's yellow jacket.

"Now," Bolan said without breaking stride, "maybe you really don't know the location of the launch site. But if that's the case, you know somebody in the Chicago Hamas cell who does. And who you can contact." He watched Omar squirm uneasily in his chair.

"Of course I do know such men," Omar said, leaning back and crossing his legs. "But they would not tell me, and they would wonder why I asked. They would then suspect me on everything about which I was curious."

The Executioner not only didn't like the garish man sitting across from him, he was quickly losing patience. He glanced down at his wrist and saw it was almost seven o'clock. The Katyusha strike could be going down at anytime now.

It might already be too late to stop it. They were running out of time, and the Executioner knew it. Jamal had been too stupid to be of any value. Gus, the Rough Rider informant, had only been able to give them the target, and that intel was useless without the launch site. As the anger continued to build within him, Bolan stared at Omar.

It was time for a change in tactics.

"Would you be willing to take a polygraph test on all this?" the Executioner asked Omar.

"A lie detector test?" He smirked, then looked dramatically around the room. "I do not see the proper instrument."

"Oh, it's here all right," Bolan said. "But it's a different kind of lie detector instrument." He stood up and stepped around the table, stopping a foot or so away from Omar. Slowly, so the man could watch every move, he drew the huge .44 Magnum Desert Eagle from the holster on his belt.

As Omar's eyes widened at both the sight and size of the big pistol, the Executioner shoved the barrel against Omar's lips. "Open your mouth," he demanded.

"What—?" Omar started to say.

The informant's lips parted just enough for Bolan to shove the Desert Eagle's barrel between them, and past the man's teeth. The Executioner stopped the forward progress of the gun barrel just before the gag reflex and continued to speak in a low, threatening voice. "Do you understand how this polygraph works now?" the Executioner asked.

With terror-filled eyes, Omar nodded slowly.

Bolan gave him a second, then clicked the safety off the big pistol.

The click sounded as loud as a hand grenade in the quiet room.

"Now, I'm going to ask you again," the Executioner said. "Who do you know that we could go ask about the launch site?"

"It is true what I said," Omar mumbled around the gun. "All of the Hamas men who know where the launch site is are already there. They are waiting for the stadium to fill up."

Bolan tightened his grip on the Desert Eagle.

The movement wasn't lost on Omar. "Wait!" he said. "Do not shoot! It does not matter that they are already there!"

"Why not?" Bolan asked.

"Because I know where the launch site is myself!" Omar mumbled again. Suddenly, tears streamed from his eyes and he began to sob.

Bolan pulled the Desert Eagle out of the double agent's

mouth and wiped the saliva off the barrel on Omar's bright yellow sport coat. Then he let the gun fall to the end of his arm at his side. "Get up," he said. "You're going to take us to the launch site yourself."

Omar continued to cry but nodded.

"What time do they plan to launch the rockets?" the Executioner asked as he pulled the man to his feet.

"The service at Soldier Field starts at eight o'clock." Omar sniveled. "They are going to wait until between eight-thirty and nine in order to get any latecomers."

The Executioner glanced at the chronograph on his wrist. It was almost eight o'clock now. "Then we'd better hurry," he told Omar as he pushed the man toward the door.

The Executioner opened the door and pushed Omar through. Turning back toward Cirillo, he said, "Go get Glasser and Ritholz and meet us down front. I'll take Omar and get the Highlander."

Bolan grabbed the back of the informant's bright yellow sport coat at the nape and hurried toward the elevators.

THE EXECUTIONER TURNED OFF Lake Shore Drive just before they reached the Adler Planetarium, then glanced to the man seated next to him in the Highlander. "Which way now?" he demanded.

"Toward the Museum of Natural History," Omar said, his voice still bearing an irritating, sniveling quality to it.

Slowing to just under the speed limit on the side street, Bolan glanced up into the rearview mirror as they passed through an area of light industrial businesses mixed in with ancient houses. In the darkness, he could just make out the faces of Ritholz, Cirillo and Amad Nadir crammed into the Highlander's backseat. Farther back, he could see Glasser sitting sideways atop their equipment bags and other luggage in the very rear of the vehicle.

The Executioner looked back to Nadir, and the sight made him frown.

Bolan had not liked "burning" Nadir's face to Omar. But considering the time restraints under which they were working, he'd had no choice. It had been something of a surprise meeting for both men.

"Turn here," Omar said. "Turn to the right."

Bolan followed the man's directions and almost immediately saw the BM-21 Multiple Rocket Launcher parked in front of the darkened windows of some kind of small business. It was less than a block away, and in the streetlights he could see the soiled brown tarp covering the entire rear portion of the vehicle. Although it was invisible beneath the cloth, the Executioner could tell that the tarp was held in its rectangular position by some sort of inner frame.

"That is it!" Omar said, ducking low behind the dashboard so his face would not be seen.

The men in the backseat knew that a man behind the wheel of the Highlander, with three men in the back and no one riding shotgun, was bound to draw suspicion.

Cirillo, Ritholz and Amad Nadir dipped down behind the seat in front of them, too. Glasser, in the far back, had disappeared, as well.

Bolan kept his speed steady, watching out of the corner of his eye as he drove past the camouflaged rocket launcher. The only thing even remotely remarkable to the naked eye about it was the fact that it stood at a slightly strange angle away from the curb. But that angle had not come from a sloppy parking job.

The missiles under the tarp were aimed directly at Soldier Field, a few miles away.

Two men stood outside the BM-21, leaning against the tarp and smoking cigarettes as they talked. They gave the Highlander only a cursory glance as it passed by. Bolan saw two more men in the cab as he drove on. They, too, paid him little attention.

The Executioner turned right at the next corner, drove two more blocks and pulled the Highlander over in front of a sign that read House of Vacuum. A large picture of a Hoover vacuum cleaner had been painted next to the words. He raised his wrist and looked at the time—8:27.

Omar had said the rockets might be launched at any time between eight-thirty and nine.

Turning toward the back, the Executioner rested his right arm on the top of the seat. "Glasser, can you hear me back there?" he asked.

"I hear you" came the voice from the rear of the Highlander.

"Okay, guys," Bolan said. "We've got to assume they've got that thing primed and ready to launch at the push of a button," he said. "Which means we can't go charging in like the cavalry."

Three darkened heads just behind him, and a fourth in the rear of the vehicle, nodded their understanding.

"Somehow we've got to get right on top of them without raising their suspicions."

"You have any thoughts on how to do that?" Ritholz asked.

"Yeah," the Executioner said. "I do." He extended his arm into the back. "Let me borrow your handcuff key," he told Ritholz.

The Chicago detective frowned, but he reached into his pocket, came up with a key ring and handed it to Bolan.

"Turn sideways, Omar," the Executioner ordered.

The informant did as he was told, and the Executioner took the handcuffs off his wrists.

"Now listen, and listen well," the Executioner said. "They've got cell phones." It was a statement rather than a question.

"I do not know if they have cell—" Omar started to say.

Bolan backhanded him across the face and knocked him back against the door. A short, raspy sound of pain sputtered from the man's lips. "I told you to listen, not talk," the Executioner said. "You're going to call them and tell them you were sent to patrol the perimeter and you caught a plainclothes Chicago police officer. Tell them you're bringing him in to them."

Omar was through protesting. When Bolan reached into his pocket, then handed the man his cell phone, he simply took it and began tapping in the numbers.

"And remember, Omar," the Executioner said, "while most of us don't speak Arabic, Amad does."

Omar nodded.

A moment later, someone answered the call and the man in the bright yellow sport coat began speaking. Bolan couldn't understand the words, so he watched Nadir's reaction to the brief conversation. It lasted less than thirty seconds, then Omar handed the phone back to the Executioner.

"They are suspicious," he said.

"Of course they're suspicious," Bolan said. "They'd be fools if they weren't. No one told them anything about a perimeter patrol in advance, and catching a plainclothes Chicago cop sounds almost ludicrous." He leaned to the side and drew the Desert Eagle from his hip. "But with suspicion comes curiosity and confusion, and curiosity and confusion cause hesitation." Dropping the magazine from the big .44 Magnum, he pulled back the slide and ejected the chambered round. "And hesitation is all we need, Omar." Pocketing both the magazine and the round from the chamber, he handed the Hamas informant the unloaded gun and saw the shocked look on his face.

When Bolan got out of the Highlander, the first thing he noticed was the wind. It had to be blowing close to thirty miles per hour. Which meant the VX, once it left Soldier Field, would spread across the famous Chicago Loop, through the downtown area and then cover a great deal of the rest of the metropolis, as well.

As he walked around to the Highlander's passenger's side, the second thing that caught the Executioner's attention was the faint sound of distant organ music being amplified through a large sound system. While he couldn't make out the words, Bolan recognized the tune. "How Great Thou Art" was a Billy Graham standard. For most of the Christian evangelist's career, it had been sung by George Beverly Shea.

Tonight, Bolan knew, a younger singer would be at the microphone. But, just as the wind had brought to the Executioner's mind how quickly the VX would spread, the song reminded him of how many people were a hairbreadth from dying at nearby Soldier Field.

Opening the passenger's door, Bolan pulled Omar out, then stuck his head back inside the vehicle. "One of you get behind the wheel," Bolan said. "Give us a couple of minutes, then drive to the corner—as close as you can get without being seen from the launcher." He stepped back and connected the handcuff teeth to the clamps on the largest settings, then slipped them over his hands in front of him.

Glasser had opened the Highlander's hatchback, exited the vehicle and taken the driver's seat. "You gonna be shooting that sound-suppressed Beretta?" he asked.

Bolan nodded.

"Then how will we know when to come in?" the Kansas City cop asked.

"If you hear gunfire, you'll know it's not from me and I need you," Bolan said.

Glasser nodded. "And if we *don't* hear gunfire, it'll mean you got them all yourself," he said.

"Either that," said the Executioner, "or I'm dead." Without another word he shut the door, grabbed Omar's arm with both of his loosely shackled hands and took off at a jog.

JUST BEFORE THEY REACHED the corner past which they could be seen from the rocket launcher, Bolan and Omar slowed to a walk. "Take my arm like you're bringing me in," the Executioner ordered.

Omar hesitated.

"Take it!" the Executioner whispered into the traitorous informant's ear.

Omar grabbed his arm.

"Now," said the Executioner. "Hold the gun on me like you mean it." Without waiting for the other man to comply, he grabbed the Desert Eagle's barrel and brought it, along with Omar's arm and hand, up against his neck. "Now, let's go. And you'd better make it look real. If not, you'll be the first one I shoot."

The two men turned the corner under a streetlight, and Bolan knew that the men in and around the BM-21 missile launcher were getting a good look at them. He could only hope that the whole charade looked convincing enough to buy him a few more seconds of indecision. The controls for launching the missiles would be inside the cab of the truck, which meant he had to get close quickly now.

Close enough to kill both men inside the cab before either could activate the launch system.

The murmur of the men's voices carried toward the Executioner on the wind as he and Omar walked on. The words were too low to make out, but they held a questioning lilt. Most sounded like Arabic, but the Executioner was surprised to hear English, too.

As they neared the BM-21, Bolan saw that the two men smoking cigarettes outside of the truck both wore light blue work coveralls that blended in with the truck. Clearly Rough Riders rather than Hamas terrorists. Both were light-skinned with Caucasian features—one of the men, who sported a short, carefully trimmed goatee and mustache, dropped his cigarette to the pavement and ground it out with the heel of his heavy-soled work shoe. Then he looked up and called out in an American Southern drawl, "Omar, what the hell's goin' on?"

The Executioner had already been convinced several times over that there was a working relationship between Hamas and the Rough Riders, but each new step he took seemed to confirm that fact more concretely. There were two Rough Riders outside the truck. And the Arabic he had just heard spoken had been more muted, telling him that the other pair of men inside the cab of the mobile launcher were Hamas.

The Rough Riders knew Omar by name, which told Bolan that Omar was deeper into the Hamas hierarchy than he had wanted to let on.

"Answer him," Bolan whispered to the man holding his unloaded Desert Eagle.

"Just what I told Imad over the phone, Bobby Jim," Omar called out. "I have captured a Chicago police officer. He did not have time to use his radio."

Bolan had to hand it to Omar. He knew how to make lies sound convincing. Now the men from Hamas and the Rough Riders wouldn't rush the launch by worrying about backup coming to save their plainclothesman.

However, a second later, just one step from the open driver's window of the BM-21, Omar suddenly pushed Bolan away from him, stepped back and screamed, "He is CIA! CIA! And my gun is empty! Kill him!"

While Omar was not strong enough to push the Executioner far, his sudden turncoat tactic came as a surprise and caused Bolan to stumble forward a step. Letting the handcuffs fall from his wrists cost him another second and slowed his draw of the sound-suppressed Beretta under his left arm.

By the time he had unholstered the machine pistol, both Rough Riders had drawn pistols.

The Executioner dropped to his knees as both guns ex-

ploded, spitting lead just over his head. Behind him he heard
a shriek of pain and terror, and knew that Omar had taken the
rounds meant for him. Raising the 9 mm pistol in his hand,
he thumbed the 93-R's selector switch to 3-round burst and
sent a trio of semijacketed hollowpoint rounds through the
coverall zipper in the middle of Bobby Jim's chest.

The Rough Rider dropped the dark black automatic pistol
he'd jerked from his pocket, opened his mouth and spewed
out what looked like at least a pint of crimson blood. Then he
fell forward onto his face.

The other American, who had remained nameless, would
continue to do so for the rest of his life—which wasn't long.
As he lowered the aim of the 1911 Government Model .45 in
his fist, Bolan sent another short burst of fire his way. The Executioner's first round struck the man's gun hand and sent the
pistol flying through the air before drilling into his torso. The
nameless man fell forward on top of his partner.

Bolan leaped to his feet, his eyes darting to the window into
the launcher's cab. He had planned to take out the two men
inside first—before dealing with the men in the coveralls. But
Omar's sudden treachery had forced him to change that plan.

And now, he saw that both men were leaning forward,
fumbling with controls on the dashboard.

The Executioner brought up the Beretta just as the Highlander came around the corner, tires squealing so loudly they
threatened to blow. Aiming at the back of the head of the man
in the driver's seat, Bolan switched the selector switch to semiauto and put one round into the man's skull. He fell forward,
what was left of his head coming to rest on top of the dashboard.

The man's body blocked the Executioner's view of the control panel, and he couldn't tell if the missiles had been pro-
grammed to launch or not. But before he moved the body to find
out, something had to be done about the other man in the cab.

Taking a step to the side, the Executioner saw that the man

in the passenger seat of the cab held both of his hands in the air, empty. But in the pale light that filtered into the truck, Bolan saw a smile on the man's face. The Beretta aimed at the curling lips, the Executioner walked forward.

The Highlander screeched to a halt next to the BM-21 just as Bolan reached the open window. The man still alive inside the launcher was definitely Arabic.

"English?" Bolan said.

The man shook his head and continued to grin. *"Allah akhbar,"* he said. *God is great.*

"Hold your fire!" the Executioner ordered the other men as they piled out of the truck brandishing weapons. "Nadir! Come here!"

The CIA informant hurried to the Executioner's side.

"Ask him why he's smiling like that," Bolan said, although he feared he already knew the answer.

Amad Nadir and the Hamas man inside the cab exchanged a few words, then Nadir turned to Bolan. "It is because they had time to set the launch system in place," he said. "The missiles will take off in less than a minute now."

"Ask him if there's any way to stop it," Bolan said.

Nadir did as he was asked. Bolan watched the man inside the truck shake his head as his smile widened.

Nadir knew Bolan had seen the answer so he had no need to translate. "He is probably lying," he said. "But I do not think we have time to force the truth from him."

"No," the Executioner said. "We don't." He opened the driver's door and saw that the two Arabs wore the same light blue coveralls as their American allies. Reaching in, he grabbed a handful of the thick cloth at the dead driver's back and jerked the body out and onto the pavement. Then, stepping up into the cab, he dragged the other man across the bench seat by the throat.

The smile finally disappeared from the Hamas terrorist's face as he coughed and choked for breath.

Bolan dropped the man on top of his dead friend, then took a seat behind the wheel. In addition to the regular features that would be found on any similar truck, this dashboard contained one panel that was obviously meant for operating the launch system.

The problem was, Bolan had no idea how it worked. The only two things he recognized were what looked like a vertical angle determinator and a timer that was quickly counting off the final seconds before the launch.

Shooting a look outside the truck at the Hamas man, the Executioner saw that Glasser and Cirillo had pulled him to his feet and handcuffed him. But the smile was back on his face as he awaited the inevitable launch of the Katyusha rockets with the VX warheads.

The Executioner glanced back at the timer. Twenty-nine seconds remained. Not enough time to beat any information out of the Hamas man. And if he held a gun to his head and threatened to shoot him, the fanatic was likely to welcome the prospect of becoming a martyr.

There was only one possible solution to the problem, and he now had less than twenty seconds to put it into play.

Looking down at the truck's ignition, Bolan saw that the keys were in it. Twisting them, the mobile launcher roared to life. Throwing the truck into gear, he eased it away from the curb into the middle of the street as the rest of the men parted to get out of his way.

Bolan glanced at the timer again. Twelve seconds.

Throwing the transmission into Reverse, the Executioner angled the BM-21 to face Lake Shore Drive and Lake Michigan beyond. He knew that the vertical angle would be at precisely the right setting to drop the rockets into Soldier Field, and that angle was dependent on precisely how far away the stadium was. Unfortunately, Bolan didn't have that information. And he had no time to get it. If he left it as it was, the warheads might fall short and hit some other building along Lake Shore Drive.

Six seconds.

Punching the numbers in the box just to the side of the screen, Bolan saw the small black silhouette of a rocket begin to raise its nose. When it was at a forty-five-degree angle, the Executioner released the control button and leaned back.

He was still in the cab when the rockets took off, shredding through the tarp that had concealed them. The Katyushas dragged pieces of the aluminum frame and heavy canvas several hundred feet into the air before dropping them and heading toward Lake Michigan.

Bolan jumped out of the mobile launcher and practically dived into the passenger's seat of the Highlander, where the rest of the men had already assembled. Omar's death during the first few seconds after the Executioner had abandoned his clandestine approach to the BM-21 had left a seat open. The smiling Arab who had ridden shotgun in the truck cab was now handcuffed and squeezed between Cirillo and Ritholz in the back seat. Glasser was behind the wheel, and this time it was Nadir who had squeezed into the small luggage area at the rear of the vehicle.

The Kansas City SWAT commander took the shortest route back to Lake Shore Drive, and they emerged from the neighborhood just in time to see several tiny flashes of light far across the water. Soft popping sounds drifted back to land from the distant explosions. Glasser pulled to the side of the road and stopped the Highlander.

Bolan and the rest of the men watched as the glow continued in the distance. Under ideal conditions, at their forty-five-degree-angle settings, the Katyusha rockets would have traveled close to thirteen miles. But since they were flying through a crosswind, the Executioner guessed it would be closer to eleven.

But eleven was fine. The rockets had still exploded far enough away from land for the VX to dissipate long before it encountered the shore.

"Man," Ritholz said, "I feel like I just ran a marathon wearing cinder-block shoes." He paused, then said, "What now?"

Bolan turned in his seat and stared at the somber face of the Hamas man who had smiled so easily only moments before. "I think it's time we had a little talk with our new friend," he said. "Your task force have a safehouse or some similar place where we won't be bothered?"

"Got several," Cirillo said, leaning forward in his seat. He turned and smiled at the Hamas man next to him. "And at least one where there's nobody to hear noises like screams."

The smiling man's face fell into fear.

He knew more English than he'd let on.

**7**

The words painted on the glass door that led from the reception area to the hall read Davis Concrete, Inc. But no concrete construction of any kind had ever come out of the small office complex.

In the back office, Benjamin Franklin Davis leaned back in his desk chair, crossed his arms behind his head and grinned at the American flag in the corner of the room. Hamas could call their campaign the American jihad if they wanted, but it truly was going to be the Night of Hell.

Not only hell to the current government and the lazy, disinterested voters who had allowed America to fall into its current state of disgrace, but hell to the Islamic religious fanatics who thought they were on the same team as the Rough Riders, too.

Nasab and his Hamas religious dupes didn't know it yet, but Davis had cut another deal with Hezbollah. And before Hamas learned about his Hezbollah connection, most of them would have taken a bullet in the back of their heads.

Honor among thieves? Davis thought to himself. Maybe some. But never among terrorists.

He reminded himself that the Night of Hell was more of a symbolic, rather than destructive, strike. But while America was still spinning with panic, he would send out his Rough Riders dressed as American soldiers and Marines and have them mow down as many visible minorities as they could find.

And that was perhaps the most beautiful thing about his whole plan; these mass murders would all be blamed on U.S. servicemen who the public would suspect had gone wild in their quest to restore order within the country.

Davis reached forward and picked up the phone. None of this would happen overnight, he thought as he lifted the receiver to his ear. But eventually America would truly be for true Americans. It would be a nation of white-skinned Aryans, and he would restore them to their rightful position of power.

But first, Davis thought as he tapped in the intercom numbers to Eleanor's desk just outside the door, he had to make sure the Night of Hell was successful. The man waiting in the outer office to speak with him would play a vital part in that plan.

The voice of an elderly woman answered Davis's interoffice page. "Yes, sir?" she said.

"Send in my guest, Eleanor," Davis told the woman.

"Yes, sir," Eleanor said, and Davis heard a click and dropped his own phone back into its cradle.

A moment later, the door opened and Eleanor's gray-blue hair, rolled into its usual tight bun, appeared. She was the widow of a former high-ranking officer in the American Nazi Party, and although she looked as sweet as someone's own grandmother, she was as dangerous as any Rough Rider he had in his pack. If he suddenly told her to cut the throat of the man she now ushered into his office, the small, razor-honed Hitler Youth knife—an original, not a copy—she still kept in her purse would be out and slicing through his neck before the Hezbollah man even knew what had happened.

But she smiled sweetly now as she stepped back and let the dark-skinned man in the flowing white robe and long, unkempt beard into Davis's office.

"Hello, Mr. Davis." The Hezbollah man said. He didn't offer to shake hands.

Davis breathed a silent sigh of relief as he nodded toward

the leather armchair directly in front of his desk and said, "Ghassan. It is good to see you. Won't you sit down?"

The man called Ghassan nodded, walked farther into the room and sat in the chair.

Davis nodded to Eleanor and the elderly lady left. The gray-blue bun disappeared as the weighted office door swung itself shut again.

"I trust your flight was comfortable?" Davis said. He had sent one of the Rough Rider pilots all the way to Iran to pick Ghassan up and fly him to the U.S. They had entered the country clandestinely, flying low under the radar.

"It was fine," Ghassan said in British-accented English. "And I trust we are still on schedule?"

"Everything is working out well," Davis said. "I simply wanted to go over the final plans with you personally. This is a one-shot deal—our only chance, maybe—to accomplish what we both want."

"Yes," Ghassan said, nodding. "If we are not successful, it will be a long time before we get another such chance."

Davis agreed, then began going over the plan. "My men will go in first, dressed in camouflage fatigues and looking more or less like U.S. regulars. That should throw the Secret Service for a loop—at least for a few seconds. Time enough, anyway, for Ibrahim Nasab and his Hamas men—who'll be dressed in traditional Islamic clothing—to follow behind them. The camou fatigues, and their robes, should also help differentiate my men from Nasab's and the Secret Service guards."

Ghassan nodded. "And my Hezbollah troops, accompanied by a few dozen Taliban who have taken refuge with us in Iran, will follow Hamas, unknown to them," he said. "We will be wearing robes, as well, but we will have red sashes tied around our arms as armbands. And we will shoot everyone else wearing a robe while doing our best to avoid killing your men in camouflage BDUs."

"Sounds pretty simple when we put it that way, doesn't it?" Davis said.

"It may *sound* simple," Ghassan said, "but it is not." He stopped for a second, then went on. "You realize there is a high probability that stray shots will mean that my Shias will kill some of your Rough Riders, as well as the Sunnis? And when the men from Hamas see their comrades falling, their first instinct will tell them it is the Americans in the BDUs doing the killing, not more men dressed like them with the same beards and dark skin."

"My men will know there are risks involved before the fighting begins," Davis acknowledged. "*Big* risks. But they'll be willing to die for what they believe in if it comes to that."

Ghassan frowned. "You speak in what I believe is called the future tense," he said. "Your men 'will know' and they 'will be willing to die.' Does that mean they do not know that Hezbollah will be following them into the strike site yet?"

Davis shifted in his seat. "That's exactly what it means," he said. "They know that Hamas will be following them, and that they're to turn on the Sunnis as soon as the site is secured. But I've seen no reason so far to tell them about you yet. It doesn't pay to give them too much time to think about it. But don't worry—I'll make sure they know about you and the red armbands right before the strike."

Ghassan stared at him with piercing brown eyes. "We operate similarly," he said. "But are you sure your men will be willing to take the chance of being accidentally killed by us?"

"They will," Davis said confidently. "We think a little differently than you do. We don't use suicide bombers and the like. But that doesn't mean we aren't willing to lay down our lives for what we believe."

Ghassan shook his head. "I fail to see the difference," he said. "But I suppose—at least in the Western mind—there is one."

"How about your men?" Davis asked. "How are they going to feel about killing Hamas troops, fellow Muslims?"

Ghassan looked at the Rough Riders' leader as if he had suddenly grown a second head. "The Hamas men are not true Muslims," he said. "They are Sunni. We are Shia." He stopped talking as if that was all the explanation anyone could possibly need.

"Well," Davis said. "To paraphrase your own earlier comment, I suppose there's some difference in the Middle Eastern mind."

Several seconds of silence went by, then Davis said, "We have one other problem, and I suppose we should get it out in the open right now and deal with it."

The penetrating brown eyes stayed on Davis's face as Ghassan said, "Indeed. And that problem is that eventually one of us must kill off the other."

Davis nodded slowly. "The key word is *eventually.* Right now we have a common enemy. Two common enemies, actually—the U.S. government and Hamas. We can work together on them. And who knows?" He paused to make sure Ghassan was taking in every word. "Somewhere down the line, we may come to some unforseen agreement that allows both of us to coexist peacefully."

"We will never swear swastikas and become atheists," Ghassan said simply.

"And we aren't going to drop to our knees on a prayer rug five times a day and hope we're facing East, toward Mecca, either."

When Davis saw the fire in Ghassan's eyes again, he softened his last statement by saying, "But the future is always unclear, Ghassan. Who knows what God, or Allah, might come up with to help us live together peacefully?"

"Allah willing," Ghassan said, "it will happen."

"Yes," Davis said, although he believed in no god. "God

willing." He stood up and Ghassan followed his lead, rising to his own feet. "We have you booked into a nearby hotel," Davis said. "I trust you will approve of the accommodations."

"I need nothing but a place to sleep, pray and read my Koran," Ghassan said. "In the past, I have spent many months living in caves along the Pakistani and Afghan border. I am sure the accommodations will be fine."

Davis came around the side of the desk and led the way to the office door, opening it. He let Ghassan go first, then followed him into the reception area. Eleanor was busy at the computer keyboard, and a clean-shaved young man sat against the wall. He wore a burr haircut and a navy blue suit and tie as he rose from his chair.

"Please escort our friend to the hotel, Terry," Davis said.

The young man nodded.

Ghassan turned to Davis, and the situation and timing again called for a handshake. It was awkward, but the two men avoided it.

"Goodbye," Davis said simply.

"Goodbye," Ghassan replied, his dark brown eyes drilling holes through the Rough Riders' leader.

Davis returned to his office as the two men left for the elevator. But instead of going to his desk, he walked to the window. From the high floor where his office was located, he could see the Senate Building, the Washington Monument and even the White House in the distance. It made him smile.

Soon, those historical buildings would once again stand for what they had been intended to stand for—a white man's democracy. With none of the lesser races around to cause problems, commit crimes and drain the country of welfare and unemployment funds.

Clasping his hands behind his back, Davis continued to stare out over the city, but his mind returned to that final incisive look he had seen in Ghassan's eyes as he left.

The Hezbollah man wanted to kill him. He could barely control himself.

Davis grinned at the glass in front of him. Ghassan would never get the chance. Because there was a very special part of the Night of Hell that the Rough Riders' leader had neglected to tell his Shia ally.

After Hezbollah and their Taliban allies went in to kill the Hamas men, a second wave of Rough Riders would attack the site. Uniting with the camouflage-clad men who had gone in first, they would catch both the Hezbollah and Hamas men in a cross fire.

The victory would belong to the Rough Riders alone. And while Davis was too pragmatic to believe it would actually mean the downfall of the American government, it would be quite a feather in the cap of the Rough Riders and the American Nazi Party, as well as ridding the world of many of the top Arab terrorists at the same time.

Davis returned to his desk, his mind focusing on the recent Hamas terrorist attacks that had gone awry. It seemed that a very small band of men—some claimed only two—had some inkling of what was going down. Both dressed in some kind of stretchy black combat uniforms at times, and one of the men was described as a warrior with skills just this side of Superman.

Though the thought of these two men made Davis uneasy, they could not possibly make any difference, even if they learned the particulars of the Night of Hell.

Davis lifted the phone and tapped in the number to the safehouse where Ibrahim Nasab and some of his Hamas men were staying. It was time to finalize plans with him, as well. But as he waited, the anxiety he had felt about the two mysterious Americans came over him again. Nasab's voice, however, took his mind away from the problem.

"Hello?" the Hamas leader said.

"Hello, my friend," Davis said, and again he soothed his mind with one simple fact: two men, no matter how good they were, could not possibly make a difference in a plan as large as his Night of Hell.

THE SAFEHOUSE TO WHICH Cirillo and Ritholz had taken them was in the Chicago suburb of Evanston, home of Northwestern University. And even at night, it had the look and feel of a long-time college town. Ivy grew up the sides of buildings well over a hundred years old, and the houses in the neighborhoods just off campus were small, obviously built with students in mind.

The safehouse itself, however, was a good two miles from the campus, standing unobtrusively in a residential section of more recent construction. To Bolan, it looked as if the structure—and all the surrounding houses—was of early 1960s vintage. That had been the height of the cold war between the United States and the Soviet Union, and it wouldn't have surprised the Executioner one bit if there was a fallout shelter in the basement of every one of them.

Pulling the Highlander into the driveway, Glasser got out, opened the garage door, then returned to the vehicle. A moment later, the Kansas City SWAT commander had pulled the vehicle inside and closed the door.

Bolan and Glasser got out. The Executioner found the door from the garage to the house unlocked and opened it, waiting while Cirillo and Ritholz pulled the handcuffed, belly-chained and leg-ironed Hamas man through the doorway. Glasser went in as a light came on inside what looked like a laundry room, then Nadir started in.

The Executioner stopped him momentarily. "Go on into the living room or some other part of the house and wait," he told the informant. "This guy's seen your face, but it was under stress. He might or might not remember it. But if he doesn't, there's no point in giving him a chance to memorize it."

Nadir chuckled, deep in his chest. "Ah," he said. "Once again I am too handsome for this kind of work." Then, turning serious, he added, "I understand. Besides, there are already too many of us for a successful interrogation."

"Right," Bolan agreed. "I'll be sending Glasser in to keep you company in a minute of so," he said.

Nadir walked on inside the house and Bolan stepped in behind him, pulling the door closed as he came. He was indeed in a laundry room, complete with washer and dryer. But it didn't look as if any dirty clothes had seen the room in some time. The fact was, a thin layer of dust covered the tops of both appliances.

The laundry room led into the kitchen, which opened to a family room. Doors led to both a living room and a hall the Executioner assumed would take him to bedrooms. By the time he got into the kitchen, Ritholz and Cirillo had seated the Hamas man in one of the kitchen-table chairs, facing outward. Sidling up to Glasser, Bolan whispered, "We're too heavy in here."

Glasser knew what he meant. Without any words of protest, he followed Nadir through the door to the living room.

Bolan stared at the captured enemy in the kitchen chair for a moment. Had the VX-capped Katyusha rockets been what the Rough Riders called the Night of Hell and Hamas had code-named the American jihad? They would have easily killed over a hundred thousand people, minimum. But something inside the Executioner told him no. The Executioner knew that whatever the Night of Hell was, it was even bigger than the failed rocket attack. He looked up to see a large, plain-faced kitchen clock mounted on the wall above the refrigerator. The clock told him it was just after 10:00 p.m.

At least it didn't look like tonight was the night. Whatever it was, if it had gone off, they'd have heard about it by now. The Executioner also doubted it would be scheduled on the same evening as the Katyusha rocket launching at Soldier Field.

Why terrorize America on only one night when you could stretch it into two?

Or more?

As Ritholz and Cirillo pulled two more chairs from beneath the kitchen table, Bolan took up a standing position right in front of the Hamas terrorist. "What's your name?" he demanded.

"Ramzi."

"Ramzi what?" the Executioner asked.

"Ramzi is enough," the man said. "I will answer nothing further." His chin shot out in defiance.

Ritholz looked over at Bolan. "I think our friend Ramzi here, whose last name he claims to be Isenof, is a little confused as to who's in charge here."

Cirillo nodded his agreement, then picked up on his partner's play on words in regard to what Ramzi had told them about his last name. Looking the captured terrorist squarely in the eye, he said, "Mr. Isenof, I'd strongly suggest you start talking before out big friend here—" he indicated Bolan with a shrug "—gets warmed up." He looked at the floor and shook his head sadly. "Believe me, once he gets started there's absolutely *nothing* we can do to stop him."

Bolan remained silent. But Ramzi said, "This is America. You police have rules you must adhere to."

Ritholz glanced at Bolan, then looked back at Ramzi. "He's not police," he said in the same sad, fatalistic tone of voice that Cirillo had used.

When Ramzi didn't reply, Bolan let a long sigh escape his lips. "Well," he said, shaking his head as he looked up at Ritholz and Cirillo on both of Ramzi's sides. "It looks like I'll have to do this the hard way."

"It appears so," Cirillo said.

Ritholz nodded. "It's a shame, though," he said. "There won't be much of him left when you're finished."

Ritholz and Cirillo were both seasoned interrogators,

and they had snapped to the Executioner's battle plan immediately. It was a version of the time-honored "good cop, bad cop" routine in which one detective came on hard and mean, then let his partner pretend to be sympathetic to the subject.

"Go ahead and try with him while I get ready," the Executioner said. "Maybe he'll wise up and spare himself some body parts." As he turned away from the table toward the kitchen cabinets, he saw Ramzi's defiant chin retract slightly.

Bolan had never believed in torture to gain information from his enemies. For one thing, he considered it immoral. If a man had to be killed, you just killed him and went on about your business. Causing more suffering than was necessary went against the Executioner's grain.

But there was another reason why Bolan never used torture—it was impractical. Physical pain made people talk, but it didn't necessarily make them tell the truth. It was far more likely to make them say whatever they thought their torturers wanted to hear in order to stop the pain.

The *threat* of torture, however, was a different story, and Bolan had put it to good use on many occasions. Making preparations—especially those which the subject couldn't quite understand—left a man's imagination free to roam. The fear of pain just got bigger and bigger until it became a psychological and emotional pain all unto itself.

"Okay, Ramzi," Bolan heard Cirillo say behind him. "Who gave you the orders to launch the rockets tonight?"

"My name is Ramzi," Ramzi said again.

Bolan opened two drawers and closed them, then found a large butcher knife and a paring blade in the third. Taking both knives out, he held them up in the kitchen light, inspecting them closely and making sure Ramzi got a good look at them, too. Nodding as if satisfied, he set them down on the counter where they'd remain in the Hamas man's view.

Out of the corner of his eye, he saw Ramzi staring at the knives, his expression one of perplexity.

"What's the Night of Hell?" Ritholz asked the man sitting between him and his partner.

"My name is…Ramzi" came out of Ramzi's mouth again. But the tone held a little less defiance this time.

Bolan dropped to one knee and opened the door to a lower cabinet. Inside, he found a variety of pots and pans. Selecting the smallest, he took it out by the handle, then slapped the pan itself against the palm of his other hand several times. Tossing it up onto the counter next to the knives, the noise it made as it settled on the plastic top had a disconcerting effect in the quiet room.

Ramzi shifted uncomfortably in his chair.

"What's the Night of Hell?" Ritholz asked again.

This time, Ramzi didn't bother to repeat his name.

Bolan pulled the largest pot he could find out of the cabinet, then rose to his feet. On his way to the sink, he passed the electric stove and stopped long enough to turn on one of the top burners.

"Tell you what," Cirillo said. "You tell us anything you want to tell us besides your name. We'll start there."

Again, Ramzi made no reply.

As the pot began to fill in the sink, the Executioner dug through more drawers. In one he found more kitchen utensils and pulled out an old-fashioned can opener-corkscrew combination tool. Turning back toward the table, he frowned down at his arm as he pressed the can opener into his forearm and pried up slightly. Then, pulling out the corkscrew, he held it in front of first his right eye, then his left. Nodding to himself, he dropped the combo-utensil next to the knives and small pot.

"Oh, shit," Ritholz said, turning his attention Bolan's way. "He found a corkscrew. You know what that means, Shelly."

"Indeed I do, Jim," Cirillo said.

By now, the large pot was three-fourths of the way full. Bolan lifted it from the sink and carried it to the stove. The burner he had turned on a few minutes earlier glowed bright orange as he set the pot on top of it.

"Damn shame to go through all this again," Cirillo said. "But don't forget, Jim. It's your turn to clean up."

Bolan stood with his back against the cabinet as the water heated. Then, suddenly as if an afterthought had caught his attention, he turned back and opened the cabinet beneath the sink. Pulling out a roll of paper towels, he set them on the counter. Then, glancing up at Ramzi and frowning, he reached in for another roll.

"What is he doing?" Ramzi shouted. "What are those for?"

"They're for the cleanup we were talking about," Cirillo said.

Bolan lifted a sponge from the cabinet top next to the sink, held it up for all to see, then soaked it with water from the tap. Squeezing out the excess moisture, he set the damp sponge next to the paper towels.

Ramzi gasped.

"Feel like talking at all yet, Ramzi?" Ritholz asked.

When Bolan turned back, he saw that Ramzi had closed his eyes and was mumbling some unintelligible prayer from his lips.

The Executioner opened the refrigerator. In addition to half-eaten hamburgers and other fast food, he saw an unopened two-liter bottle of soda pop. Pulling it out, he turned to Ritholz and Cirillo. "You don't have any smaller bottles?" he asked.

"Nope," Cirillo said. "But that size'll work. I've used them. Try it."

Bolan broke the seal and twisted off the cap. Closing his left nostril with a finger, he held the bottle's neck up to his nose. "A little larger than I like," he said as he recapped the bottle. "But you're right. It'll do the trick."

Ramzi had been watching through half-closed eyes. Now they opened wide in his head, seeming to take up half his face. "No!" he screamed.

Bolan just stared at him. Shaking up a bottle of pop and then shooting it up into the sinuses had long been a Mexican *federale* form of interrogation torture. There were few ways to create as much pain without leaving marks or killing the subject. The "soda pop" approach could be dragged out as long as the interrogators wished, and it looked as if Ramzi had either seen it or at least heard about it.

By now the water was boiling on the stove. Bolan had seen a pair of oven mitts in one of the drawers, and now he pulled them out and put them on his hands. Looking down at the various instruments on the cabinet, he lifted the can opener-corkscrew and said, "I think I'll start with this." Holding it by the very end, he dipped the sharp edge down into the boiling water and held it there.

Ritholz looked across to Ramzi and shook his head. "You poor bastard," he said. "This isn't going to take very long with him starting with that."

Cirillo nodded, then shook his head. "Horrible way to go, though," he said. Then, grinning as if he couldn't keep himself from reminding his partner that it was his turn to do the cleanup, he added, "And more work for you when it's over."

This time, Ritholz just shot him a dirty look.

Bolan pulled the heated can opener out of the water, looked at it for a second, then turned and started toward the table.

"No!" Ramzi screamed again. "Stop! I will talk! I will answer any questions you have for me!"

Bolan halted halfway to the table. Then, turning back, he returned the can opener to the counter and dropped the oven mitts next to them. "I'll leave the water boiling just in case you change your mind or I think you're lying to me," he said. He walked quickly around the table and got the fourth chair

from under it, lifted it high over the heads of the Hamas man
and the two Chicago cops, then shuffled his way past them to
set the chair down directly in front of Ramzi.

"What…what were you going to do with the can opener?"
Ramzi asked.

"You'll never know," the Executioner said. "Just keep in mind
that I can still do it if I don't think you're telling me the truth."

"I will tell you all I know," Ramzi said, his voice shaking.

"Get started."

The Hamas man did.


THE CHICAGO COUNTERTERRORIST task force wasn't the only
group that had safehouses hidden around the city.

It appeared that Hamas did, too. Unfortunately, Ramzi was
aware of only one. But, almost ironically, it was less than six
blocks from where Bolan, Glasser, Ritholz, Cirillo and Amad
Nadir were holding Ramzi at that very moment.

The Executioner took Ramzi with him in the front seat of
the Highlander while Glasser and Nadir climbed into the
backseat. Bolan had noticed a dark red, nearly new Toyota
Tundra pickup parked along the curb when he'd first turned
into the driveway earlier, and now he learned that it was one
of the many low-visibility vehicles that the task force used.

Not knowing whom they might capture alive when they
reached their destination, the Executioner had Cirillo and Ritholz follow the Highlander in the Tundra. It had only a small
half seat in back, but two men could be squeezed into the area
if necessary. And such seating arrangements also freed up
more room in the Highlander should they need it.

Ramzi directed Bolan through a residential area that gradually become less affluent. When they crossed a major four-
lane thoroughfare, the neighborhood suddenly turned from
middle-class to blue collar, with houses that, while still in
good repair and well-kept, were at least fifty years old.

As they drove, Bolan pulled out his cell phone and tapped in the number to Stony Man Farm.

"Hello, Striker," Price answered.

"Let me speak to Bear," the Executioner said.

A click sounded in his ear. A second later, Kurtzman answered. "I was just about to call *you*," he said. "What's new on your end?"

"More of the same," Bolan said. "We're heading toward a Hamas safehouse at the moment. You had any luck with the computer?"

"Negative, Striker," said the Stony Man computer genius. "I'm convinced neither the list of strikes nor this Night of Hell is on this hard drive. Or if it is, it was hidden by someone a lot more computer-savvy than me."

"We both know such a person doesn't exist," the Executioner said. "If you haven't found it, it's not there." He lifted his foot from the accelerator and moved it to the brake, stopping at a stop sign. "Anything else of interest going on?"

"You'd better believe it," Kurtzman said. "That's why I was getting ready to call you. A lot of things are breaking, and breaking fast." The computer wizard stopped long enough to take a deep breath, then went on. "Every member of the U.S. Senate and half of the House of Representatives have gotten anthrax mail."

"You're kidding," Bolan said, frowning. "That again?"

"Yep," the computer man said. "It's all over the news."

"Anything else?" Bolan asked.

"Oh, yeah," Kurtzman came back again. "There've been several cases of food poisonings around the country."

"Sounds like what happened at the American Embassy in Paris," Bolan said.

"It does, except for the fact that they're using a different MO. They appear to be going around to supermarkets and injecting fresh fruits and vegetables with something."

"Do you know what that something is?" Bolan asked as he turned a corner in the direction Ramzi's pointing finger indicated.

"Not yet. It just started. No lab results back. But there are eleven dead bodies scattered all over the U.S. map. And as soon as the news goes public—which it will have to do just to protect the people—fresh fruits and vegetables are going to begin rotting away on the grocery store shelves."

Bolan nodded to himself. Poisoning the food supply was not only a great device to instill terror in the hearts of the people but it played hell with the American economy, too. "Anything else I should know?"

"One more thing," Kurtzman said. "The Border Patrol is currently handling over twice their usual number of illegal aliens at the Mexican border. But here's the rub—only about sixty percent speak any Spanish at all."

"Let me guess," the Executioner said. "The other forty percent speak Arabic."

"Right on the nose, big guy. And there have even been other illegals of Arab descent caught coming down from Canada. But here's the biggest news of all. The Coast Guard snatched a hundred-foot yacht trying to off-load several dozen men on the Virginia coast. And every last one of them was from one Arab country or another."

Bolan paused for a second. "For every illegal who gets caught, you've got to figure twenty or more got through and into the country," he finally said.

"Don't I know it, big guy," Kurtzman said.

"They're leading up to it, Bear. This Night of Hell or American jihad or whatever you want to call it."

"Oh, yeah. No doubt there."

"Okay, Bear, the Executioner said. "You've got my number if anything else comes up. Call me. If I don't answer, it's because I'm too busy shooting either Arab or American Nazi terrorists."

"I'll leave a message and you can return the call."

"Right," Bolan said. "Over and out, Bear."

"Over and out, big guy."

The Executioner dropped the phone back into his pocket. Continuing to let Ramzi direct him, he turned onto Iowa Street and slowed as they passed a split-level dwelling with the numerals 714 tacked to the house next to the front door.

"That is it," Ramzi said, ducking nervously. "And they have been planning something big. What exactly, I do not know."

Bolan studied the house as he drove by. Its shingle siding was painted a dull, bluish gray. A detached garage stood just behind it, to the side, at the end of the driveway. Judging by the number of vehicles parked in the driveway and on the curb, the place had to be full. On the other hand, Hamas might keep a whole fleet of cars and pickups there, using different ones at various times in order to maintain a low profile.

In any case, the Executioner would have to assume that the split-level was full of armed men when they attacked in a few minutes. It was okay to hope for the best.

But you had to prepare for the worst.

Driving on to the end of the block, the Executioner glanced up in the rearview mirror to make sure Ritholz and Cirillo were still behind him. The Tundra was there, and Bolan pulled out his cell phone and tapped in Cirillo's number.

A moment later, the Chicago cop said, "Yeah, Cooper?"

"Were you guys aware of this place before?" the Executioner asked.

"Uh-uh," Cirillo said. "First we've seen of it."

"Stay with us," Bolan said, then drove on, leaving the cell line open. Two blocks later he came to what looked like a grade school. Perhaps an acre of sandy land, spotted by clumps of wild grass here and there, served as a playground.

In the corner farthest from the school building stood a baseball backstop, but there were no baselines or infield or outfield specifically designated.

The Executioner pulled into a parking space beneath a streetlamp at the side of the school and stopped, leaving the Highlander's engine running. A second later, Ritholz pulled the Toyota pickup in next to him and rolled down his window.

"Glasser and I'll take the front door," Bolan told the detectives in the Tundra. "You guys go around back."

Ritholz nodded. "What do you plan to do with them?" he asked the Executioner, indicating Nadir and Ramzi.

Bolan twisted in his seat and eyed Ramzi first. He was still bound in handcuffs, a belly chain and leg irons. He could hobble off into the darkness while they were inside the house if he wasn't guarded, but he wasn't going anywhere fast. Still, the Executioner didn't want to leave any of his blacksuit-trained personnel in the car with him. They were likely to be vastly outnumbered by terrorists, and every experienced gun would be needed.

Turning farther, the Executioner's eyes fell on Nadir. The man was a paid informant of the CIA. Did that mean he could be trusted? Not necessarily. On the other hand, Nadir had already proved his loyalty several times during this mission.

Bolan's instincts told him to trust the informant. And, over the years, those gut feelings had proved every bit as reliable as physical evidence.

"Amad," he said to the man in the back seat, "reach over your shoulder and get the black bag on top."

In the illumination from the street lamp flowing into the Highlander, the Executioner saw mild confusion on the CIA informant's face. But the man did as he'd been told, turning back to drop the bag in his lap.

"Now unzip it," Bolan said.

Nadir did so.

"Somewhere in there, you'll find a black nylon pistol rug. Get it out."

Nadir fumbled through the black bag, finally coming up with yet another zippered covering.

"Unzip it, too," the Executioner said, and again Nadir followed his orders unquestioningly.

A second later, the informant pulled out a huge, X-frame, 500 Smith & Wesson Magnum 5-shot revolver with black rubber Pachmayer grips and a four-inch compensated barrel. Staring at the massive weapon in awe, Nadir said, "Did you have no hundred-pound cannons available for me?"

Bolan ignored the joke. This wasn't a time for merriment. "If our buddy here—" he nodded toward Ramzi at his side again "—tries to get away, or tries anything else, one round should be all it takes to change his mind. Forever."

Nadir pushed the latch on the side of the gigantic revolver and swung out the cylinder. Tapping the ejection rod lightly with a forefinger, he removed one of the gargantuan cartridges.

"It's a 440-grain semiwadcutter," the Executioner said, staring deeply into Ramzi's frightened eyes. "It'll bring down an elephant—and you're not an elephant. Do I need to say more?"

Ramzi shook his head vigorously back and forth. "I will sit here patiently and not even move until you return," he said in a trembling voice.

Bolan turned back to the window as Nadir pushed the cylinder back into the X-frame.

"You want to just leave the vehicles here?" Ritholz asked him.

"Good a place as any," the Executioner said. He opened the door and got out. Glasser did the same from the backseat behind him as Ritholz and Cirillo exited their vehicle beneath the light of the street lamp. Bolan threw a quick glance back inside the Highlander and saw Nadir holding the compensated barrel of the 500 S&W Magnum pistol against the back of Ramzi's head. He walked to the tail of the vehicle, opened the hatchback and reached into another of the equipment bags. A moment later, both he and Glasser gripped M-16s in their fists.

From somewhere in the pickup, Ritholz and Cirillo had come up with long arms of their own. Cirillo bore a Winchester 1200 pump-action 12-gauge with a Choate folding stock and extended magazine, and Ritholz held a Heckler & Koch 94.

The HK-94 was the civilian version of the company's famous MP-5. It had a sixteen-inch barrel to make it legal, and fired semiauto only. But the trigger pull was so short it could deliver more rapid rounds than many full-auto submachine guns.

Both Chicago task force members were well armed for what lay ahead.

"Everyone ready?" the Executioner asked.

The heads of the other men bobbed up and down in the darkness.

"Then let's go," Bolan said, and took off at a jog back toward the Hamas safehouse.

**8**

It took only a minute or so for Bolan and the rest of the men to run back to the split-level Hamas house. When they got there, the Executioner led them quickly out of sight to the side of the dwelling. Staring at a set of windows along the ground, it became obvious that the house contained a large subterranean area.

When they had assembled in the darkness, the Executioner said, "Glasser and I'll go in the front. Jim, you and Shelly take the back. My guess is there's a back staircase leading into the basement. Clear any rooms you come to on the way to those stairs, then go down and secure the underground floor." He paused, turning to stare at the darkened house again, guessing again at its probable layout. "We've also got to keep in mind that there may be more than one staircase leading up to the next two levels. Glasser and I'll take the front steps. If it turns out there's another set in the rear, come up it after the basement is taken care of. If not, circle around and follow us up." He paused again. "Everybody understand?"

"Yes," came the reply from the three men.

Bolan lifted his wrist to look at his watch. "Glasser and I'll give you two thirty seconds to get into position. Starting…now."

Ritholz and Cirillo turned away from Bolan and Glasser. As quietly as possible, Cirillo opened the latch of a wooden, waist-high gate and pushed the ancient, screeching wood open.

Bolan felt himself cringe slightly at the sound, and he couldn't help wondering if it was loud enough to be heard inside the house. But if this was truly a Hamas safehouse, there would be members of the terrorist group coming and going frequently. The noise wouldn't necessarily alert the men inside that intruders were about to enter.

Leading Glasser, the Executioner kept his back close to the house as he rounded the corner and returned to the front. Sliding sideways behind a row of short, well-trimmed bushes, he made his way to the porch. The three steps that led up to the door were in front of the bushes, so he bent his knees low, then leaped straight up, his feet coming down on the concrete.

Turning back around, he grasped Glasser's outstretched hand and pulled the Kansas City SWAT commander up behind him.

The Executioner glanced down at his watch. Cirillo and Ritholz still had ten seconds before their half-minute head start was up. But he had barely dropped his arm again when he heard an explosion come from the rear of the dwelling.

Cirillo's Winchester 12-gauge.

A split second later there was a short burst of what sounded like 9 mm rounds exiting a carbine barrel.

The Chicago cops had evidently encountered Hamas men in the backyard before they could even enter the house. If the screeching gate hadn't alerted the terrorists inside, the gunfire surely had.

Bolan lifted a leg and drove his foot into the front door. The frame split as the dead bolt cracked the jamb. The door swung open on its hinges to reveal a room packed with Hamas terrorists.

And every last one of them was diving for a rifle or trying to draw a pistol from a holster or waistband.

Bolan flipped his M-16's selector switch to full-auto and pulled the trigger back, sending a steady stream of 5.56 mm

NATO rounds into the crowd. He was blocking the doorway, but Glasser had learned his blacksuit lessons well back at Stony Man Farm, and the Kansas City SWAT commander knelt at the Executioner's side, firing his own full-auto barrage of bullets beneath Bolan's arms.

Clouds of crimson flew about the room as the bullets indiscriminately took out terrorists, who screamed, shouted and gasped as their lives drained away and they fell to the floor.

Bolan stepped on into the living room as the bolt of his rifle locked open. He tapped the button to eject the empty magazine. Less than a second later, his well-practiced hand had replaced the empty with a full 30-round box mag, the bolt had slid home, chambering a round, and he was firing again.

More than half the men had fallen during Bolan's and Glasser's initial salvo, but those who had escaped that onslaught now reached their own weapons. Dropping to a knee, the Executioner took partial concealment behind the arm of an overstuffed chair next to the door. He dodged the first return fire from an AK-47 in the hands of a Hamas man with a huge drooping mustache. The fact was, the man bore a striking resemblance to the former Iraqi leader.

Which certainly didn't earn him any points with either Bolan or Glasser.

Flipping the selector switch to 3-round-burst mode, Bolan tapped the trigger and sent a trio of rounds flying toward the man's hairy upper lip. The mustache disappeared along with the top of the terrorist's head, and the Saddam Hussein lookalike tumbled awkwardly back into the wall before sliding down to a sitting position in death.

To his side, Bolan saw that Glasser had entered the house behind him and taken up another kneeling position directly in front of the stairs. The Kansas City SWAT commander was firing his own M-16, but the angle of the barrel told the Executioner that he was aiming toward the second level of the house. A moment later, as if to prove the point, another AK-47 came tumbling down the steps.

Then a dead body, wearing the strange combination of a polo shirt, khaki slacks and a kaffiyeh, followed the rifle, rolling down from the second floor to a halt on top of the weapon he had just dropped.

Another volley of fire came toward Bolan, but this time it had the sharp cracking sounds of a short-barreled weapon. He dived to his side, landing on a small end table and knocking a lamp off to the side. Rolling off the table, Bolan landed back on the floor on his feet and saw that the assault was coming from a Hamas man with a Glock 18. The machine pistol continued to spit death right up until the time the Executioner pulled the trigger again.

Another trio of 5.56 mm rounds burst forth from Bolan's M-16. All three struck the man within an inch of each other, directly in the middle of his chest. The man with the Glock wore a white shirt, but as his heart exploded, the front became instantly red.

Then he, too, fell to the pile of dead men on the floor.

Bolan took out three more Hamas terrorists with three more bursts before return fire forced him to dive toward the door again. As he rolled, he saw Glasser down another of the Hamas gunners. Coming up on one knee, the Executioner pulled the trigger back toward the guard again and sent another hailstorm into a terrorist in a blue suit, complete with necktie. The first round caught the man in the Windsor knot he'd tied just below his throat. The second hit the throat itself, and the third climbed on up to strike him squarely between the eyes.

Suddenly, the living room was quiet and the Executioner realized that all of the men who had been there when he'd kicked in the door were now dead. But now, with the explosions dying down in his ears, Bolan could hear the gunfire coming from the back of the house.

The Executioner knew the old saying about the best plans going out the window as soon as the first shot was fired, but that didn't mean that a trained warrior panicked. Often, it simply meant that a plan had to be changed, or at least altered, due to unforseen circumstances once the battle had begun.

And this was one of those times.

Glasser was busy again, firing up the steps toward the middle level of the house. "Tom!" the Executioner shouted. "Can you hold them where they are for now?"

Glasser fired again, and another Hamas body came tumbling down the steps. "Go on!" he yelled back.

Bolan had to jump over the dead bodies as he made his way through the living room toward the back of the house. He entered a dining area. Empty. But through a doorway on the side wall he could see into the kitchen.

Two men stood at the window, both firing out into the backyard. One was shouldering an AK-47. The other held a Beretta 93-R almost identical to Bolan's. The only difference was that if had no sound suppressor screwed to the barrel.

As he watched silently, both men fired, ducked low to avoid return fire, then rose to fire again.

What was happening was more than obvious to the Executioner. Cirillo and Ritholz had encountered sentries posted in the backyard and been forced into starting the battle early. That had alerted the terrorists in the house, and now the two Chicago cops were pinned down behind some kind of cover.

Shifting the M-16 to his left hand, the Executioner drew his own Beretta from his shoulder rig. Flipping the selector switch to semiauto, he carefully lined up the sights on the back of the head of the man shooting the AK-47. A lone 9 mm hollowpoint round coughed almost silently from the barrel. The metallic grind of the slide going back, then forward again to chamber another round was louder than the cartridge exploding.

The man with the Russian Kalashnikov-designed rifle fell

forward, his head, neck and shoulders coming to rest for a moment in the large sink. Then the deadweight of his lower body gave way to gravity, and he slumped out of the sink to sprawl awkwardly on his side on the tile floor.

The Hamas terrorist with the 93-R had started to turn as the Executioner swung his weapon the short distance between the two men. But his left side was all he managed to get toward Bolan as the Executioner squeezed the trigger once again. Another semijacketed, subsonic 9 mm round spit from the sound suppressor, and a small red dot immediately appeared in the terrorist's temple. At almost the same time, a wave of blood, brain and other body fluids blew out of the other side of his head.

Bolan holstered the Beretta again, then crept silently into the kitchen, the M-16 held low and close to his body in case anyone was hiding out of his field of sight. But when he stepped through the doorway, he saw that the man with the AK-47 and the one with the 93-R were the only occupants.

And they were way beyond causing any more trouble. At least in this lifetime.

Crouching, the Executioner crept into the kitchen toward the window. He kept one eye on the stairs, which, as he had predicted, led from the kitchen down into the basement. He stepped over the body of the man who had wielded the AK-47 and grabbed a crumpled, damp dish towel from the top of the cabinet. Draping the towel over the barrel of his M-16, he slowly let it rise into the air.

The towel drew one shot from Ritholz's H&K, then the shooting stopped. Still moving slowly, the Executioner kept the towel in full view as he rose up in the kitchen light so he'd be seen through the window.

Looking out through the glass, all he could see was blackness. It became obvious that the Hamas men has simply been firing blindly into the dark, hoping to hit whoever was firing back at them. And another thing had become obvious to the Executioner since he'd made his way to the kitchen, and it brought a hard smile to his face now.

Both Ritholz and Cirillo were still alive. He'd heard both shotgun and carbine fire.

Knowing he was a perfect target in the kitchen light, the Executioner slowly extended an empty hand and waved toward himself.

A second later, he was unlocking the back door for the two Chicago cops.

No words were necessary as the two men entered the kitchen. Bolan had kept watch in his peripheral vision on the stairs leading down to the basement, but no one had yet appeared. In bold contrast, he could hear the blasts of any number of automatic rifles and pistols coming from the front of the living room. Motioning Ritholz and Cirillo to continue on to the basement, he retraced his steps back through the dining room, then the living room, toward where Glasser now lay in a prone position, still firing up the stairs.

The bodies of three more Hamas men—making a total of five—had come rolling down the steps. Glasser had piled them on top of each other and was using them as cover.

A lull in the explosions came as Bolan neared the human fort. Glasser glanced his way. A second later, the Executioner had dived behind the bodies and lay next to the Kansas City SWAT commander on the carpet.

"They're getting smarter," Glasser whispered. "Not exposing themselves like these guys." His eyes indicated the dead men behind which they'd taken cover. "They just twist their weapons around the corners at the top of the steps and fire blindly down, hoping they'll hit me."

"Sooner or later, they will," Bolan said.

Glasser nodded. "The law of averages gets stacked a little higher against me with each bullet," he said. Then, nodding toward the stack of bodies in front of them, he added, "No pun intended."

Bolan set his M-16 down between them and dropped his final two extra magazines next to it. "Take these," he said. "You may need them."

Glasser frowned, trying to figure out what Bolan was doing.

The Executioner reached under his right arm and pulled out a fully loaded 9 mm magazine. Dumping the one from the Beretta—from which he'd used two rounds on the men in the kitchen—he replaced it in the shoulder-rig pouch and crammed the full load between the Beretta's grips.

Transferring the sound-suppressed weapon to his left hand, he rolled to his side and drew the Desert Eagle with his right.

Glasser had finally snapped to what the Executioner was up to, and he took the extra M-16 magazines and slipped them into his waistband. "You a hundred percent sure about this?"

"No," the Executioner said, "but I'm hardly ever a hundred percent sure. The bottom line is that sometimes you just have to take the best of a whole bunch of bad ideas, and go with what you've got." Turning toward Glasser, he added, "Cover me as best you can."

Glasser nodded. "You've got it."

Bolan waited, watching as two hands holding an AK-47 suddenly appeared at the top of the steps to his right. The hands held the rifle backward, with a thumb on the trigger. As he waited, the thumb moved backward and sent a wild spray of 7.62 mm rounds down the steps to drill into the dead bodies in front of them.

When the magazine ran dry, the hands quickly jerked the rifle out of sight again.

Bolan had risen from behind the dead men as soon as the AK-47's bolt locked open, and now he took the steps two at a time, the Desert Eagle in his right hand, the Beretta in his left. He was halfway to the top when another of the Russian assault rifles appeared around the corner to his left.

Raising the Beretta, the Executioner sent a 3-round burst at the rifle. As least one of the rounds hit home, sending a loud clanking sound back down the stairs. Another 9 mm round had to have hit one of the shooter's hands or arms, because as they jerked the weapon back out of sight, Bolan heard a scream and saw a flash of cherry-red blood fly up into the air.

The Executioner turned his sights toward the corner of the wall itself, and another trio of rounds spit from the suppressor. He saw the holes where the bullets hit the old plaster-and-lath wall, and knew that the hollowpoints would have filled with the material, essentially becoming hard-nosed rounds.

All the better for the penetration he needed.

As he continued up the steps, Bolan heard another scream from behind the wall to his left. He was about to fire again when the AK-47 to his right appeared once more.

Ignoring the rifle and the arms that held it, the Executioner aimed the Desert Eagle at the corner of the wall—behind which the body wielding the Kalashnikov had to be. The massive .44 Magnum Desert Eagle's hollowpoint rounds needed no help from the plaster and lath to blast through the two walls that met to form the corner, and Bolan heard yet another screech of horror as at least one of the big slugs hit home.

By now, the Executioner had reached the top of the steps and he crouched low, the Desert Eagle pointing toward his right, the Beretta to his left. But to his left, he saw nothing but a small alcove that hung over the living room. It was empty.

Except for the dead Hamas man who lay, eyes wide open, staring at the ceiling for all eternity.

To his right, the Executioner saw three open doors. One led to what looked like the master bedroom. Another appeared to be a smaller bedroom, and directly across from it in this split-level dwelling was a bathroom.

He could see no Hamas men.

But the Executioner knew they were there.

From the landing where he now stood, another set of steps led up toward the top floor of the house. With the M-16 held in front of him at the ready, Bolan glanced back down to the lower floor, then waved Glasser on up after him. Two floors below, from the basement, it sounded as if World War III had begun. Shotgun, carbine and automatic rifle fire blazed away as if the basement were the gate to hell itself.

Glasser reached the split-level landing and returned the Executioner's M-16 and extra mags. Bolan pointed him toward the bathroom. Then, as Glasser pressed the stock of his M-16 against his shoulder, the barrel aimed down at a forty-five-degree angle, the Executioner did the same toward the larger of the two bedrooms.

He didn't have to enter the room before the next gunfight began.

As he stepped into the doorway, two men—both wearing white turbans and equally white T-shirts—rose from behind the bed. One had a long, unkempt beard as he aimed a British Sten submachine gun over the bedspread.

The other had trimmed his whiskers into a more fashionable goatee and mustache. And he had obviously been caught unprepared for a gunfight.

He held only a long, wickedly curved scimitar in his hands.

The terrorist with the unruly beard got off a nervous and hurried volley of shots that passed high over the Executioner's head into the ceiling. Bolan raised the barrel of his M-16 to chest level, concentrated on the man's face and pulled the trigger.

A lone round drove its way through the nose beneath the turban, and the Hamas man fell back and away from the bed.

By then the man with the scimitar had leaped up onto the bed. *"Allah akhbar!"* he screamed as he lifted the long sword blade over his head with both hands. Then, using the bed springs like a trampoline, he dived toward the Executioner.

Bolan turned his rifle to the man while he was still in the air. Switching the selector switch back to full-auto, he hammered a half-dozen rounds into the man's torso.

The man with the scimitar and goatee died in the air, but his body continued to fly forward. Bolan had to step aside to avoid it.

The Executioner moved on into the bedroom. Dropping to one knee, he aimed the M-16 under the bed as his eyes searched beneath the box springs for anyone who might be hiding there. Then, suddenly, it felt as if the hair on the back of his neck stood up.

Lifting his head back away from the bed and up, he turned to see a robed man with long black hair bringing a Skorpion machine pistol into play. Bolan had no idea where the man had come from—he had either snuck up the stairs behind them or come out of the other bedroom while Glasser was busy clearing the bathroom.

Not that it mattered much at this point—the long-haired man was intent on killing the Executioner.

As the Skorpion continued toward him, the Executioner flipped the barrel of the M-16 upward and shot from the hip. A 3-round burst exploded from the rifle, with the first round striking the man in the upper thigh. Bolan corrected his aim, raising the barrel slightly so that the second and third rounds caught the man center chest.

The long-haired terrorist's eyelids peeled back farther than Bolan would have thought humanly possible. The brown-dotted white orbs stared at the Executioner in shock. The man opened his mouth as if to speak, but instead of words, a wave of deep red blood flooded from between his lips.

Then he fell to the floor.

Bolan heard the telltale roar of automatic 5.56 mm rounds

from the other side of one of the bedroom walls, and knew that Glasser was under attack. But the distinctive sounds told him something good, too.

The Kansas City SWAT commander was still alive.

Moving swiftly to the closed closet door, the Executioner gripped the M-16 in his right hand and reached for the knob with his left. Then, taking a long stride to his side, he threw open the door and aimed his assault rifle one-handed into the closet.

All the Executioner could see were clothes hanging on hangers from a rod, but as he watched, rifle rounds exploded from behind them, making the clothing jump and sending ragged pieces of cloth sailing out into the bedroom.

The rounds had been aimed straight ahead—toward the spot where anyone opening the door *should* have stood—which was why the Executioner hadn't, and why he was now able to send his own steady stream of fire back into the clothing until the magazine ran dry.

In less than a second, he had dropped the empty magazine and inserted a new one.

Bolan frowned as he peered into the closet. The clothes were now in complete disorder, with the ragged sleeves of jackets and torn trouser legs hanging in front of the hangers. Lint and scraps of cotton, wool and other materials still floated in the air.

But was the man—or men—who had fired the initial volley from behind the clothing dead? There was only one way to know.

As he moved toward the hangers, the Executioner suddenly spotted a patch of what looked like light brown skin in the mess of clothing. Keeping the M-16 aimed at the hangers, he reached through the torn garments and felt a wrist.

Bolan used all of the muscles in his shoulder and arm to yank the Hamas man out through the clothes and into the bedroom. When he let go of the wrist, the man fell to the floor with multiple entry and exit holes spotting his body. He had been dead seconds after Bolan had pulled the trigger. Only the hangers and clothes had kept him on his feet.

The Executioner reached out and grabbed the bar that held the hangers. With a mighty tug he jerked, and the screws that mounted the bar to the wall were stripped out. The bar and all of the hangers fell forward out of the closet into one huge, tangled pile on the floor.

The M-16 still aimed through the opening, Bolan watched a second Hamas terrorist fall to the floor. Two of the terrorists had hidden in the bedroom closet, but now, the room was cleared.

Wasting no more time in the bedroom, the Executioner reached the landing in time to meet up with Glasser, who was just coming out of the smaller bedroom. "Bathroom was clear," the Kansas City SWAT commander said. "I've neutralized another one in the smaller bedroom."

Bolan nodded. "Then it's time to hit the top floor."

The Executioner led the way up the darkened steps, noting several posters on the wall. One featured the *Star Wars* cast. Another pictured Arnold Schwartzenegger as *Conan the Barbarian,* and yet another showed Sylvester Stallone, complete with headband and knife, as *Rambo.*

The Executioner didn't know who had occupied the house before Hamas moved in, but whomever it had been, they'd had a little boy. And this top level of the house had been his bedroom.

When they reached the top of the steps, Bolan turned to Glasser and held a finger to his lips. Pointing two fingers at the SWAT man, he then pointed to the left. After tapping his chest with the same two fingers, he pointed to the right.

Glasser got the message.

Bolan turned toward the open door. Below, he could still hear sporadic shotgun and other fire, dulled by the distance and the floors and ceilings between them. As soon as he and Glasser had cleared this top level, they'd be able to hurry back down and help Cirillo and Ritholz if they still needed it. But right now, they had their own work cut out for them.

Bolan stepped into the bedroom and moved to the right to let Glasser in. Quickly, he surveyed the room. Only one bed stood just to his left, but bare mattresses were strewed all over the floor. It reminded the Executioner of his years fighting the Mafia, when the heat would be on and they'd all hole up in some secret apartment and sleep on similar bedding. The practice was even called "going to the mattresses."

The ceiling was highest on the side of the room where he and the SWAT commander stood, but it tapered downward as it moved to the opposite side, finally stopping at around six feet.

Cabinets, closets, drawers and other storage receptacles had been built into the opposite wall, making use of what would otherwise been wasted space in the split-level house.

The drawers could be ignored for now, as they were too small to hide a human being, but each of the cabinets and closets would have to be checked.

For the second time since entering the house, the Executioner found it wise to change his battle plan. Grabbing Glasser by the arm, he kept the wall with the cabinets and closets in the corner of his eye. "I want you to work the doors," he whispered to the Kansas City SWAT commander. "Stand to the left of the doors, reach across them and swing them back as fast as you can. I'll stand slightly to the side to keep you out of my line of fire. But make sure you don't inadvertently get in front of any of the doors. You do, and they don't get you from inside the closet, I'm likely to hit you from outside. Got it?"

Glasser nodded. Then, without further ado, he slung his M-16 over his shoulder and drew one of his Colt Commander .45ACP pistols and gripped it in his right hand.

Bolan heard the click of the safety coming off as Glasser moved silently across the bare wooden floor, heading for the far left end of the opposite wall. He had to stoop slightly as the ceiling gradually lowered, and by the time he stood next to the first door, he'd bent slightly at the waist. With his back to the wall, he reached across the full-length closet door in the corner, then looked back at Bolan.

The Executioner raised his M-16 and aimed it at the door. He nodded his readiness.

Glasser twisted the doorknob and jerked the door open toward him, staying behind it but aiming his .45 through the crack between the door and the frame.

Bolan focused his eyes into the closet, which was pitch-dark.

But no fire came out at him, either.

Sliding silently forward, Bolan kept the M-16 trained inside the closet. Once he was close enough, he could see a long string hanging from the ceiling. Pulling it turned on a bare light bulb above his head and revealed stacks of blankets, sheets, pillows and more clothing—both civilian and military BDU style. He remembered the man in the blue suit from downstairs.

Hamas obviously had a multitude of operations going on at the same time, and each required a slightly different costume to deceive the honest people around them. Well, it looked as if they were well stocked for any occasion, be it "ball" or "brawl."

Pulling a small laser flashlight from his pocket, the Executioner attached it to the mounting on his M-16.

Glasser moved swiftly to the next door, which was a cabinet rising only halfway to the ceiling. After another glance to the Executioner and another nod, he pulled on the cabinet knob and stepped back again.

This time, light was no problem as the flashlight lit up the small cubicle. What came as a surprise, however, was the fact that a Hamas man had somehow squeezed himself into the tight opening and now squinted back at the bright glare of the flashlight. His face was a mask of horror.

Bolan and Glasser had been as quiet as possible since reaching the top level of the house, and their silence had evidently paid off. While the man squeezed into the tight cabinet held a Russian Tokarev in his hand, his arms were crossed in front of him and the pistol was aimed to the side.

He'd had no idea that the Executioner and the Kansas City SWAT commander were even in the top bedroom.

Letting the flashlight work as his sighting system, Bolan held the trigger back and sent a spray of lead into the man's cramped body. Blood shot back out of the cabinet. The Executioner let up on the trigger and nodded toward Glasser.

The Kansas City SWAT man simply closed the cabinet door again, sealing the Hamas terrorist behind it with a soft click. He moved to the next door—another half cabinet.

The Executioner was primed and ready as the door swung back on its hinges. While the first man who had contorted himself into hiding in the storage space had received no warning of their presence, the blasts from Bolan's M-16 would have alerted anyone else hiding in the room.

They'd be ready.

Ready to *kill*.

But as the cabinet door came back and the flashlight illuminated the small area, all the Executioner could see were several empty shelves, a cracked plastic tape dispenser on the floor and a child's large picture book. The book leaned against the wall, and Bolan could easily read the title. It was a child's version of *1001 Arabian Nights,* which seemed more than appropriate.

Bolan wondered briefly if the little boy who had occupied the room before the terrorists moved in had forgotten the book, or simply grown out of it and abandoned it. But he had no time to dwell on such thoughts because by now Glasser was moving on to the next cabinet door.

Bolan glanced up slightly, taking in the whole wall at once. There were three more of the smaller cabinet doors, then another full-size closet at the far right end. There might or might not be armed Hamas men behind each and every one of them, but he would have to assume that there was. To do anything else could be signing his, and Glasser's, death warrants.

The next cabinet door Glasser opened revealed another empty storage space. When he moved on to the one after that, the Kansas City SWAT commander had barely touched the knob when the door came flying back toward him as if by itself.

The man cramped inside the small storage space gripped an Uzi submachine gun in his right hand, but in the tight space of the storage area he was unable to bring his left around to help support the weapon. He got off a short string of wild shots before Bolan drilled a 3-round burst into the short beard that covered his face.

Death caused the man's body to relax, and he tumbled half out of the cabinet to land on his belly.

The last cabinet door before the closet opened on its own now, and a gunner wearing a cutoff sweatshirt, blue jeans and white-and-gray athletic shoes extended his empty hands out of the opening. He rattled off something in Arabic that neither Bolan nor Glasser could understand, then began scooting out of the opening.

"You speak English?" the Executioner called out to him.

"Yes!" said the man, now kneeling in front of the open cabinet door. His raised hands shook violently. "I speak English. And I wish to surrender."

But it was not to be.

Before Bolan or Glasser could respond, the full-sized closet door at the right of the room, next to the man, flew back to bang against the wall. Another of the traditionalists wearing a long, untrimmed beard, robe and kaffiyeh emerged holding an old Thompson submachine gun.

Bolan raised his M-16 that way, but it was not the Executioner who was the man's primary target—it was the surrendering man on his knees. Before Bolan could fire, the Hamas terrorist had pumped a short burst of fire almost directly down into the top of his former ally's head.

The head of the surrendering man exploded like a pumpkin struck with a baseball bat.

But at the same time, Bolan squeezed the trigger of his M-16 and sent a similar number of 5.56 mm hollowpoint rounds through the terrorist's robe to break into fragments as soon as they entered the man's body. The kaffiyeh fell off of the terrorist's head as he jerked back and forth with every round that hit him, as if he were performing some outlandish final dance of death.

Then he fell to the floor.

Bolan's M-16 was still raised, and it was a good thing it was. For behind the man in the kaffiyeh, the Executioner now saw a second man who had been hiding in the same closet. He, too, wore a traditional robe, but his head was topped by a brown-and-black checkered *shemagh*. The long cloth had been wrapped over his head, then around his face just under the nose as if he were on a camel in the middle of the desert, fighting a sandstorm.

But as he raised the American-made M-16 in his hands toward Bolan, the *shemagh* fell away from his face and the Executioner saw his reason for wearing it as he did.

A long, ugly scar, starting an inch above his left eyebrow and extending diagonally across the bridge of his nose, then on down his right jaw, showed a vivid red in the light of the Executioner's flashlight-sighted M-16. The scar had come either from a knife or a sword. Bolan was guessing knife.

If a full-sized sword been used, the man's head would have been separated into two halves.

Bolan pulled the trigger, sending a final burst of fire into the closet. When he finally let up on the trigger, the scar on the terrorist's face was gone, along with the rest of the man's face.

As the echoes from the gunfire died down, Bolan again heard the dull roars of the other firefight going on two floors below them. He could still hear the distinctive discharge of Cirillo's shotgun and the softer plink of Ritholz's long-barreled Heckler & Koch 94.

Evidently, Cirillo had brought plenty of extra shotgun shells and Ritholz had enough 30-round 9 mm magazines. But that wasn't what worried the Executioner.

A lot of time had gone by since he'd left the two Chicago cops on their way down into the basement. By now, the gunfight should have been over. One way or another.

Something was wrong or they wouldn't still be firing. They'd have either killed the Hamas men in the basement, or been killed themselves.

As he turned toward Glasser, Bolan saw that the Kansas City SWAT commander had dropped to his knees and was checking under the lone bed in the room. When he jumped back to his feet, Bolan knew no more terrorists were hidden there. It was the last possible place in the uppermost bedroom where they could have been.

Which meant it was time to go back down to the basement and find out what was going on.

Turning his back to the SWAT man, Bolan sprinted out of the bedroom, down the steps past the posters still on the wall, to the landing with the bathroom and other two bedrooms. He paused there for a moment, listening to make certain no one had come up the steps leading down since they'd left that floor. Satisfied that the level was still deserted, the Executioner bounded on down the steps to the living room with Glasser at his heels.

The two men had to hurdle the dead terrorists scattered across the carpet as they made their way back through the living and dining rooms to the kitchen.

Stopping just before the door to the kitchen, Bolan ejected the partially spent magazine from his rifle and rammed home the last full one he had on him into the carriage. A round was already chambered, so there was no need to worry about that. Then, cautiously, he stepped off the carpet onto the tile between the dining room and the steps down to the basement.

He immediately saw what the problem was. Ritholz and Cirillo had never made it down to the basement. They still stood on both sides of the entrance to the steps, occasionally leaning around the corners to fire quickly downward, then jumping back to avoid return fire.

Both Chicago detectives looked up as Bolan and Glasser entered the room. "They got the jump on us," Cirillo said. "Knew we were coming down."

"I was halfway down the steps before we realized it," Ritholz said. He tapped the right shoulder of his sport coat with his left hand. The padding had been shot out and the shoulder area of the jacket was in complete tatters. "This is all it got me."

"You hurt?" Bolan said.

Ritholz shook his head. "Didn't even touch the skin. Besides, as my old football coach used to say, 'It ain't near my heart.'"

"So give me a quick rundown on what's down there," the Executioner said. Almost as soon as the words had left his mouth, automatic fire roared up the steps to strike the kitchen wall behind them. As soon as it stopped, Cirillo leaned around the corner, the barrel of his Winchester shotgun aimed downward. After firing a load of 12-gauge buckshot, he pumped another shell into the chamber, then fired again before jumping back to cover once more.

"We don't know how many are down there," Ritholz said above the roaring in all of the men's ears. "But they've got the stairs well covered, as you can see."

In the corner of his eye, Bolan saw Glasser frown. "And if

there's a phone down there, or one of them has a cell phone, they may have already put out calls for reinforcements." Instinctively, the Kansas City SWAT commander looked back over his shoulder to see if something might be creeping up on him from the rear.

"This the only staircase leading down?" Bolan asked.

"The only one inside the house," Cirillo said. "Outside—where we first got into this fiasco with the lookouts—it looked like there were some steps leading down to what was probably a door into this same room." He indicated the basement with a sideward nod.

Bolan turned to Glasser, waiting as Cirillo fired another double blast of buckshot down the staircase, then said, "You take the steps outside."

"Where will you be?" Glasser asked.

"You remember those windows half-sunken in the ground where we stopped to regroup?"

"Yeah," said the Kansas City SWAT commander. "They had to lead into this basement." He stopped talking long enough to glance at the Executioner's wide shoulders. "But you think you can get through one of them?"

"It'll be tight," Bolan said. "But, yeah, I think so." He handed his M-16 to Glasser and added, "This'll just be in the way, though. Strap it across your back as a backup. I'll use my pistols."

Glasser looked skeptical as he took Bolan's rifle.

"What do you want us to do?" Ritholz asked.

"Exactly what you've been doing," said the Executioner. "I don't want the guys downstairs to notice any change up here at all. Got it?"

"Ten-four," Ritholz said. He ejected the magazine from his H&K and pulled another from his jacket pocket.

Bolan and Glasser both exited the door from the kitchen to the back yard and dropped down the three steps that led to the grass. The concrete stairs leading on down to the basement were directly to the right, and the Executioner stopped Glasser as the man was about to descend them. "Give me thirty seconds to get into position," he whispered. "Then kick in the door and come in."

Glasser nodded in the moonlight.

Bolan walked swiftly to the same screeching gate through which Cirillo and Ritholz had entered the backyard earlier, but this time, he waited until the roar of one of Cirillo's shotgun shells exploded in order to cover the noise. As soon as he was through the gate, he jogged to the side window nearest the front of the house.

A window well had been dug in front of the glass to allow for light to enter the basement during the day, and the Executioner had roughly two feet of space in which to maneuver. Stepping down into the well, he tried to crouch low enough to get his head and shoulders in front of him. Impossible.

The Executioner rose back up, then sat down on the ledge with his feet still in the window well. The wells might have been designed to let light in, but in order for that to work they had to be cleaned every decade or so. The Hamas men appeared not to have bothered washing the windows. They might have been sloppy. On the other hand, it might just be their way of keeping prying eyes from seeing into the house.

Leaning forward again, Bolan reached down into the window well next to his feet. Countless leaves had blown into the hole, and most were damp. Grasping several large ones in his hand, he used them to wipe away a tiny corner of the grime on the glass. Then he pressed his eye to the hole and looked inside.

From his vantage point, the Executioner could see at least two dozen men, all armed with assault rifles. Most also had pistols on their belts. The vast majority were dressed in OD green BDU pants and blouses, and a few wore U.S. Marine "covers" on their heads.

These would be the assault teams, Bolan realized as he straightened again. Hamas's "best of the best" with small arms, and responsible for the random shootings and assassinations for which the organization was responsible.

The Executioner glanced at his watch. He had five seconds left before Glasser came in the back door. And if he wasn't there to help the man, Glasser was likely to be dead in another five seconds.

Quickly, Bolan again tried to bend low enough to press his shoulders against the glass. And again, he found it impossible. That meant the only way he would be able to enter the basement would be to sit where he was, kick the glass out with both feet, then slide down into the well and through the window.

And that didn't even take into consideration the fact that unless he wanted to be cut to shreds by the glass that would remain around the sides and in the corners of the windows, he'd have to clear it away somehow.

Four separate steps instead of the one he'd hoped for. And each step would take at least a second to *perform*—if everything went smoothly. And during those four or more seconds, he'd be like a duck floating by in a shooting gallery.

The problems didn't stop there. The Executioner knew he'd need both of his hands free to push himself through the tiny opening once the glass was broken out, which meant he have to leave his Beretta or Desert Eagle holstered until he was inside the basement and on the floor.

Another second, maybe two.

Far more than enough time for the Hamas terrorists to react to the surprise of his appearance at the window and kill him.

Several times over.

There was no other choice, Bolan told himself as he prepared for his entry. There wasn't even enough time to get back to Glasser and change the plan.

With a deep breath, the Executioner kicked out with both feet and felt the glass shatter beneath the soles of his shoes.

At almost the same time, he heard Glasser's foot kicking in the back door to the basement.

**9**

The Executioner's feet went through the glass, but several razor-edged shards remained around the sides.

Running the Desert Eagle's barrel quickly around the entire window frame, he cleared the opening of the larger pieces of broken glass. There were still enough tiny shards to scratch through his jacket and pants and lacerate his flesh when he began working his way, feetfirst, through the hole. But minor injuries such as that were to be expected.

Holstering the Desert Eagle, the Executioner dropped back to a sitting position on the edge of the window well. Gunfire—far more than he'd heard earlier when Ritholz and Cirillo had been their only target at the top of the steps—exploded as he extended his legs through the window, then scooted forward. During the split second during which he was in this position, and blind to what was going on in the basement, his mind pictured two dozen AK-47s aimed at his legs.

Bolan pushed the image out of his brain. It would do no good, and would just get in the way of his entry into the basement.

Wriggling his body back and forth, Bolan felt the sting of the sharp glass ripping at his arms, legs, chest and back. He ignored the pain much in the same way he'd ignored the vision of the AK-47s readying themselves to blow off his legs. Extending both hands behind him, he pushed with every fiber of muscle in his arms and shoulders. At the same time, he felt the vibrations as an unknown number of rounds struck the wall next to him.

This was the most vulnerable position he'd be in during the entry, so he wasted no time. Pushing against the concrete side of the window well behind him, his shoulder suddenly gave way and his body shot through the opening.

Still in the air, the Executioner reached for the Desert Eagle. By the time he landed on the carpeted floor, he had the big .44 Magnum pistol in his hand. Bringing it up to a point-shooting position, he cut loose with a double-tap of rounds that exploded the chest of a man in OD green BDUs. The man was less than ten feet away, and as he fell forward in death, his arms extended, he practically handed the Executioner his Russian rifle.

Bolan grabbed the AK-47 and holstered the Desert Eagle. As he checked to make sure the safety was off, he caught a glimpse of Glasser on the other side of the room. The Kansas City SWAT commander had made it through the outside door to the basement but was now pinned down behind a couch. But he was still firing, and it looked as if he'd taken out the two men who'd been shooting up the steps at Cirillo and Ritholz, as well as at least one other man.

The Executioner felt blood dripping down his back. The cuts from the glass were deep—he could tell that from similar wounds he'd experienced in the past. But they didn't appear to have severed any arteries or major vessels. This was, however, no time to be thinking about superficial injuries. He still had work to do and now he swung the AK-47 slightly to target a man in green-and-brown-camouflage fatigues.

The Hamas terrorist had a puzzled look on his face, as if he still couldn't believe that a man had just come crashing through the basement window. That bewilderment didn't make him any less dangerous as he attempted to raise a heavy Bren automatic rifle.

The weight of the weapon saved the Executioner's life.

Bolan pulled the trigger on his lighter Kalashnikov and sent three 7.62 mm rounds at the man. One hit the Bren as it rose in the air, causing sparks to fly from the steel out of which the big rifle was constructed. The other two rounds ducked under the Bren to drill through the Hamas terrorist's chest.

Return fire from somewhere across the room forced Bolan to dive forward, beneath a table-tennis table that stood off to the side of the basement. The table had been blocked from his vision when he'd looked through the hole in the dirt-covered glass, but he had not been surprised to see it as soon as he'd landed inside the basement. These Hamas men spent days in isolation in this safehouse, and they needed recreation and particularly *competitive* recreation. These men were, first and foremost, killers. And if they stayed in the these cramped quarters very long, those murderous instincts would emerge against anyone nearby.

In other words, they'd start killing each other.

But table tennis was also a way to hone the fighters' reflexes for other pursuits, and was used as a method of cross-training by athletes, martial artists and warriors the world over. The table, however, offered no cover, and precious little concealment from the Hamas gunmen who still vastly outnumbered Bolan and Glasser. At least one of the terrorists realized this and began spraying the top of the thin table with rounds. But as soon as he'd drilled holes through the corner of the table to the Executioner's right, Bolan rolled that way. From there, he heard the blasts and saw the holes appearing to his left as the Hamas man tried to cover all his bases.

Looking up, however, Bolan could see the man through one

of the sharp, ragged bullet holes. Wearing khaki BDUs and an OD-green T-shirt, the terrorist was still firing along the opposite edge of the table.

Raising his own AK-47, Bolan angled it toward the man's chest, then directed a steady stream of 7.62 mm stingers into the man.

The holes penetrated the thin green metal at an angle, the sharp fragments the rounds left in their wake pointing directly at the Hamas man. Through the bullet holes, the Executioner could still see the man's face.

A mixed expression of surprise and horror came over the Hamas terrorist. His faded green T-shirt turned black with blood, he dropped his rifle, looked down at his chest, then reached up slowly and covered the wounds with both hands.

Bolan saw no need to waste more ammunition on him. A split second later, the Hamas man fell forward onto the table, causing it to collapse.

The bottom of the table came down hard on the Executioner's shoulders, and he felt his skin tear again as one of the sharp edges around the bullet holes sliced into his upper arm. But like the other cuts he'd already sustained, this one was minor compared to the other dangers he was facing.

The Executioner pulled the magazine from his AK-47 and saw that only two rounds remained. Counting the one in the chamber, that made three. When he came out from under the table, he would need far more shots than that if he intended to stay alive. If he switched the selector to semiauto, he could take out a maximum of three men. And there were far more than three Hamas men still standing. After the third shot, he'd have to change weapons.

And the time that took—however brief—might well be all that was needed for another of the Hamas terrorists to kill him.

Bolan had already pushed the odds to their limit when

he'd come through the window. He'd be better off just starting off this next battle series with his handguns.

Dropping the AK-47, the Executioner drew the Desert Eagle in his right hand, the Beretta 93-R in his left.

Then he rolled out from beneath the collapsed table.

BENJAMIN DAVIS SAT behind his desk. The only light on in the office was a small lamp on a table in the corner. Eleanor had gone home for the day hours ago, but he had stayed, waiting for the phone call to come.

Things were coming to a head now. The following night, his master plan would begin, and it would change the world forever.

Davis opened the bottom right-hand drawer of his desk and pulled out a silver aluminum box. Setting it in front of him, he turned the rollers of the built-in combination lock until they were lined up the way he wanted them. Then he flipped the two latches and opened the lid.

Even in the dim lighting, the nickel silver revolver gleamed.

Davis took out the Colt Single Action Army revolver carefully, holding it by the grips. They were made of mother of pearl, and the head of a longhorn steer had been laboriously hand-carved into the right side of the curved handle.

Holding the gun up in the light, Davis studied it closely. There was holster wear on the nickel finish where the barrel had rubbed against leather during the three decades his great-grandfather, Hank Davis, had been a lawman in Texas. But for close to a hundred years now, the gun had not been carried—at least on a regular basis. Davis's grandfather had been a shopkeeper, and had kept the Colt hidden beneath the cash register at his store. His father had inherited the single-action weapon, and kept it in a drawer until he passed away and it became his son's.

Except for his great-grandfather, Davis suspected he had the most respect for the revolver. It was sometimes called the "Gun that won the West," and the head of the American Nazi Party's Rough Riders branch knew it to be true. But America had forgotten that along with the Colt Single Action Army revolver, it had taken a good deal of righteous blood to win this country. In today's world, the average citizen was willing to give up freedom for safety against terrorist organizations like Hamas and Hezbollah. And as Benjamin Franklin Davis's namesake had once said, anyone willing to sacrifice freedom for safety deserved neither.

The phone on Davis's desk finally rang. With the Colt still in his right hand, he lifted the receiver with his left and said, "Hello."

"Hello," Ibrahim Nasab's heavily accented voice said. "How do we stand?"

"We're in good standing," Davis said. "No, I'd say *great* standing. Our men will start moving into position tomorrow afternoon."

"I am worried," the Hamas leader said.

"About what?" Davis asked. With his free hand out to his side and his index finger inside the trigger guard, he twirled the Colt in a series of fancy spins.

"The same thing that has worried me for days now. This apparent rogue element of U.S agents, or whatever it is. There have been more attacks on my men, and it seems now that their number has swollen from one or two men to at least four. Do you know who they are?"

"No," Davis said, "and I've got men planted in almost every branch of the federal law-enforcement community. Nobody seems to know who they are." He cleared his throat. "But there's no reason to sweat it. They're operating on a very small scale. They can't have any idea of what's about to go down tomorrow night, or they'd be taking a more direct route to both you and me."

A long sigh came from the other end of the line. "I suppose you are right," Nasab finally said. "But I have already lost many good men to what you call their small scale."

"I've lost men, too," Davis was quick to add.

"Yes, and that is what worries me even more," Ibrahim Nasab said. "Since they are attacking both Hamas and your Rough Riders, it is more than obvious that they know we have united."

"It could just be chance," Davis said, knowing it wasn't.

"It is *not* chance," Nasab insisted, "and we both know it."

"Okay, whoever they are, whoever they represent, they've somehow found out that Hamas and the Rough Riders have linked up together." Davis twirled the Colt again, watching its nickel silver finish sparkle in the lamplight and the light drifting in through the window from outside the office. "So what?" he continued. "They aren't going to have time to learn anything more before tomorrow night, and after that, it'll be too late. Besides, after tomorrow night, we'll be *advertising* who was behind the strike."

"I suppose you are right," Nasab said. "I would sleep better tonight, though, if these men were not around."

"Well, try to relax," Davis said. "Take my word for it—we've got nothing to worry about. We're about to shake America, and the world in general, right down to the bone." Before Nasab could speak again, he said, "Where are you now?"

"New York," Nasab answered.

"Any trouble on your flight from Saudi?"

The Hamas leader laughed out loud. "No," he said. "It was just as you claimed it would be. The airline personnel, security, customs and immigration people were so worried they'd offend me that they barely gave me a second look." He stopped and laughed again. "There was an elderly American woman—I'd say seventy years old at least—right ahead of me. She was traveling with two grandchildren. I found out later that security detained her for over an hour."

The story brought a mixture of mirth and anger to Davis's

chest. "It's been a long time since this country has operated on common sense," he finally said. "On the other hand, I've got to say, 'three cheers for political correctness.' It's got a great deal to do with our ability to go forth with our own plan."

Nasab continued to chuckle. "I praise Allah for every well-meaning, ignorant and confused American you have in your country," he said. "Without their naïveté we could not operate at all."

"When will you be getting in?" Davis asked. "To Washington, I mean?"

"I have already rented a car," Nasab said. "I will begin the drive as soon as we hang up. I will find some out-of-the-way motel in which to spend the night, then come to your office tomorrow afternoon."

"Great," Davis said, delighted to learn that the Arab was not expecting to stay at his house. "I'll expect you then. Fact is, we can watch the fireworks through my window."

"Agreed," Nasab said. "Is there anything else I should know before tomorrow?"

Davis couldn't help grinning to himself. Just that Hezbollah and more of my Rough Riders will be shooting your men in the backs, he thought. But of course he didn't say it. What he did say was, "No, it's pretty simple, really. My men will go in first, followed by yours. We'll vastly outnumber the guards on duty, and kill them and any other personnel we find on-site." He paused for a second, then finished the speech with, "The local cops may well get word of what's going on and be on the scene by the time both of our parties exit the building. But my Rough Riders—dressed in Army BDUs—should confuse the hell out of them. They'll think some U.S. military unit has already rounded up your guys in the robes, and when we all turn on them it'll be like a Chicago slaughterhouse."

"It is unfortunate that we have no nuclear weapon to leave behind," Nasab said.

"Maybe for you it is," Davis said. "But we could never out-run a nuke's range—especially if there are more cops than we anticipate when we leave." He waited a second and listened to Nasab breathing on the other end. Then he said, "And like I told you before, I hate to disappoint you, but we Americans don't cotton to suicide missions."

"Cotton to…what?" Nasab said.

"It's an American expression," Davis said, somewhat impatiently. It was bad enough having to team up with for-eigners like Nasab. Worse when you had to stop several times during a conversation because he hadn't learned the nuances of what was someday destined to be the language of the entire world. "It just means we don't do suicide bombings."

"Then I will see you tomorrow," Nasab said.

"Right," Davis said. "Just keep in mind that our best weapon is just like it was with the World Trade Center and Pentagon."

"What do you mean?" Nasab asked. "They are totally dif-ferent types of attacks."

"Yes, but they hold one thing in common," Davis said.

"What?"

"They're both low-tech, and that's not what the U.S. is looking for these days. They're expecting nukes and bio-chemical agents, not superior fire and manpower. Particu-larly on their own soil and even more particularly on the very *heart* of their own soil." He chuckled softly. "What we have planned is so preposterous that no one's even considered it a possibility. They're totally unprepared for such an attack."

"I understand," Nasab said, and then the two men hung up at the same time.

Davis started to replace the nickel-plated Colt in the safety box, then stopped. Instead, he reached into the box and pulled out five lead-nosed .45 Colt cartridges. Opening the loading gate on the right side of the wheel gun, he pulled the hammer back to the first click to release the cylinder lock. Then, one by one, he dropped the rounds into the gun, making sure the hammer was finally lowered onto the one chamber he'd left empty.

Single-action revolvers of this vintage had not made use of a transfer bar and were prone to discharge if dropped on the hammer. A lot of men in the nineteenth century had found that out the hard way.

Opening the bottom drawer again, Davis reached in and pulled out a weather-beaten leather holster. Family legend said that the holster was the original one carried by Davis's great-grandfather, and Davis had no reason to doubt it. The logo on the back read H. H. Heiser, Maker, Denver, Colo. Below the logo was the number 720.

Davis stood up. Unbuckling his belt, he threaded the holster on until it hung at his side, rebuckled the belt, then dropped the shiny pistol into the leather. His sport coat hung over the back of his chair and he slipped his arms into it.

The tail of the jacket fell over the Colt and holster, easily concealing it.

Davis turned off the lamp on the table and used the light coming in through the window to find his way out of the office toward Eleanor's desk. Stepping out into the hall, he turned back and inserted his key in the door, locking it.

The following night would mark the beginning of a new attitude in the U.S. The average citizen would finally realize that the only road to freedom was muddy—made of dirt that had been wet by the blood of patriots.

And he would go down in history as one of those patriots.

Davis patted the revolver beneath his coat as he punched the button for the elevator. The feel of the gun made him smile.

It seemed only fitting that this symbol of an America-past, a *better* America, be with him during tomorrow night's actions.

The elevator doors swung open and Davis got on.

A QUIET 3-ROUND BURST from the Beretta was followed by a roaring double tap of .44 Magnum rounds from the Desert Eagle. Then came another trio of sound-suppressed 9 mm bullets from the 93-R.

By now Ritholz and Cirillo had made their way down the steps to join Bolan and Glasser, and the explosions from a 12-gauge shotgun, a Heckler & Koch 94 and an M-16 joined in with the Executioner's pistol rounds.

Suddenly, the last Hamas man standing was on the ground.

Bolan's eyes skirted from right to left, then back again, his handguns still up and ready for any apparently dead body that might suddenly come back to life. None did.

The Executioner's teeth tightened so firmly that his jaw began to ache. He had counted on taking at least one of these men alive in order to learn more about the Night of Hell. It had not worked out that way.

Glasser realized they had worked themselves to a halt on a dead-end street at almost the same time. "What now?" he asked the Executioner as he slung his rifle over his shoulder.

Glasser, Ritholz and Cirillo all looked to Bolan at the same time.

The Executioner's eyes searched the room again before settling on a desk in the corner of the room. No, he realized as he focused on the table and chair again, not a desk. A computer hutch.

Complete with computer.

Bolan hurried toward the computer and took a seat. "You guys cover my back in case any more of these clowns show up," he told the three blacksuit-trained cops. "We'll see if this hard drive has any more intel on it than the other computer did."

Glasser took up a position facing the back door through which he'd just come. Cirillo lifted his shotgun toward the steps leading up into the kitchen while Ritholz kept an eye on the windows with his H&K 94 aimed the same way.

Bolan turned the computer on. As soon as it had warmed up, he tapped the number to Stony Man Farm into his cell phone.

"The Bear. Quick, Barb," he said as soon as Price answered.

Price wasted no time answering, and a second later Aaron Kurtzman was on the line. "Yes, Striker," Kurtzman said.

"We just took down a Hamas safehouse in Chicago," the Executioner said, "and I'm sitting in front of a computer."

"What kind of computer is it?" Kurtzman asked.

Bolan glanced at the logo in front of him. "Dell," he said. "Inspiron 8600 model."

"Ah," Kurtzman said. "They're easy." He guided the Executioner through the steps that sent a copy of the computer's entire hard drive to Stony Man Farm.

"Have you got the data yet?" Bolan asked after a brief pause.

"Yeah," Kurtzman said. "Just finished. You want to wait while I check to see what's on it? We've got enough other information to feed into my computers that I can scan the whole hard drive pretty fast."

Bolan glanced around the room. The neighbors in this quiet neighborhood were bound to have heard the gunfire. Even now, black-and-white police cars should be speeding toward 714 W. Iowa. "Okay, but hurry, Bear. The cops'll be here any minute and even though I've got two of their own with me, I don't want to get bogged down in questions and paperwork."

"No sweat," Kurtzman said. "I've already done it— scanned it while you were talking. Sorry, old buddy. There's absolutely nothing about a Night of Hell or American jihad on the hard drive."

"If it's *hidden* on the hard drive somehow," the Executioner said, "like we thought it might be on the other computer, how long will it take you to check?"

"About the same length of time as before," Kurtzman said. "To cover every nook and cranny, anyway."

Bolan's hands clenched into fists. Then, suddenly, he had a thought. "What if they anticipated a potential raid like this, Bear? If you thought there was a possibility of your Stony Man computers falling into the wrong hands, what would you do?"

"I'd erase everything from the hard drive," Kurtzman said. "Just like they've done here."

"But first you'd—"

"Right," Kurtzman agreed. "First, I'd burn everything on CDs."

Bolan had anticipated that answer and was now jerking open all of the drawers and cabinets built into the computer hutch.

He found a CD in the cabinet just above the screen. The CD case on the very top bore a white label. Using a red pen, someone had designated it "N. o. H." He read the label to Kurtzman, who said, "I'd say we've struck gold, Striker. You don't get much closer to Night of Hell without spelling out the whole words. So stick her in the slot and send her my way."

Bolan followed the computer man's directions and did just that. A moment later, Kurtzman said, "Okay, I've got it."

"What's it say?" Bolan asked. "Just give me the highlights."

"The combined forces of the American Nazi Party Rough Riders and Hamas are planning to take over the White House and kill the President."

Few things in life surprised the Executioner anymore—he had seen too much already. But for he next few seconds, he was speechless. Then he said, "How do they plan to do *that,* Bear?"

"According to this, by using the oldest strategy in the world," Kurtzman replied. "Sheer manpower."

"They've got that many men?" Bolan asked.

"According to this disk, thousands when you combine the native-born Nazis and all of the Hamas terrorists who've been sneaking across the border for the last couple of years."

"We'll have to get the President out of there," Bolan said. "When's this supposed to go down?"

"Tomorrow night," Kurtzman said. "And of course we'll get the President out—along with all of the other noncombatants on duty at the White House. But think of the morale victory this is going to bring to terrorists the world over. The most powerful nation in the world can't even defend its own seat of power?"

"The defeat for Americans will be just as devastating as the victory for the terrorists," said Bolan said. "So what we've got to do is find a way to stop this attack before they even get on the White House grounds."

"According to this disk again," Kurtzman said, "all of the different cells of Hamas and the Rough Riders won't meet up until a minute or two before they invade. That'll keep the President from calling in extra troops in time to stop them. Until that moment, the different cells don't even know where each other are—let alone *us* knowing how to find them."

"Then we'll just have to stop them at the fence," Bolan said.

"I don't know how you expect to do that," Kurtzman replied.

"I do," the Executioner said.

Even under the extreme weight of the predicament, Aaron Kurtzman couldn't help belting out a hearty laugh. "I never doubted that for a minute."

TENDING THE ROSE GARDEN and the trees and shrubbery that grew in the other areas of the White House grounds was a never-ending chore, so none of the laborers working the next day so much as batted an eye when several men riding mini-excavaters began making their way around the inside of the fence, digging a three-foot trench in the ground. By noon, they had covered the entire eighteen acres within which decisions were made that affected the entire planet.

Bolan was escorted inside the East Wing by a Secret Service special agent who pointed him toward a small bedroom, then took up a crossed-arm position with his back against the hall wall as the Executioner shut the door behind him.

On the bed, Bolan saw the blacksuit. Beneath it, out of sight, were his Beretta 93-R and Desert Eagle. He suspected the agent outside in the hall would faint dead away if he knew this man—who was receiving such special, and unexplained, treatment—was in possession of such firepower this close to the President.

Bolan chuckled softly as he slipped out of the khaki shirt and pants he'd worn to help dig the trench. Walking into the bathroom, he turned on the shower. He smiled as he stepped under the hard, hot jet spray, remembering the words of one of the other groundskeepers he'd overheard in reference to the trench he'd been digging.

"Probably another one of those weirdo planting schemes the first lady dreamed up," the man had said as he and another worker stared at the trench.

Bolan finished washing his body and poured shampoo onto his hair. In a way, the worker had been right.

Come nightfall, the trench would be planted full. Just not with anything he or his fellow groundskeepers imagined.

When he had finished his shower, the Executioner turned off the water, grabbed a towel from the rack and dried himself. Moving back into the bedroom, he slipped first into his blacksuit, then the shoulder rig for his Beretta and buckled the nylon web belt carrying the Desert Eagle and other equipment around his waist. The low-profile blue blazer and gray slacks he'd brought along with him to the White House were a size too large in order to fit over his guns and other gear.

Bolan had used his combat knife to cut out the right-hand pocket of the slacks, however, which allowed him to reach through the hole and gain access to his big .44 Magnum pistol. The sound-suppressed Beretta could be reached, as well, if he used what was often called the Superman draw. Hidden under his shirt, he would have to rip away the buttons with both hands before he could get to it. But if he needed it that fast, a few missing buttons wouldn't be too high of a priority.

The Secret Service agent was talking into the mouthpiece connected to a headset when Bolan emerged from the bedroom again. "Yes, sir," the agent said. "Right." He looked up at the Executioner. "He's here right now, sir. We're on our way."

Without another word, the Secret Service man said, "Follow me, please." Then he led the Executioner down several long halls, past the East Room, then the Blue, Green and Red rooms and up to the Oval Office.

As soon as he was ushered inside, The President of the United States rose from behind his desk and gripped the Executioner's hand. "Thanks for coming," he said, purposefully not using any name or appellation.

Bolan returned the firm handshake. "It's what I do," he said. He followed the President and they took seats across from each other on matching antique divans.

The Executioner got straight to the point. "Mr. President," he said. "I think we have all the bases covered, but word has come down the pipe that you intend to stay here tonight. I have to tell you I'd feel a lot better if you were at Camp David, or on Air Force One, or even in a Super 8 Motel someplace on the interstate. Anyplace else."

The Man smiled. "And I'm sure that's exactly where my predecessor would have been under these circumstances," he said. "He was a great one for stirring up hornets' nests and then escaping before he got stung." He shifted slightly on the divan and crossed his legs.

Bolan noted that he wore black ostrich-skin cowboy boots with his charcoal-gray suit.

"But did you forget what state I came from?" the President asked, smiling.

"No, sir," said the Executioner. "Texas."

"Correct," the Man said. "And there's nothing a Texan likes better than a good old-fashioned brawl. At least when he knows he's on the right side."

"Well," Bolan said, "this is about as big as brawls can get, which means a lot of things could go wrong."

"You have to think of this from a political point of view, too," the President said. "How would it look to the public if the President ran away from his own house? Would any of them ever feel secure in their own homes after that? And I won't hide in the downstairs bunker, either."

Bolan had to admit the Man had a point. "How about a compromise?" he said.

"Of what kind?" the President asked.

"How about you have Marine One twirling its blades from the time the attack begins until it's over? Then, if things look bad, you can lift off in the chopper at any time."

The President rose and extended his hand. "You've got a deal," he said.

"Not yet," the Executioner said. "There's one more part to it."

The President laughed softly. "You're starting to sound like a politician," he said. "Tacking things onto bills at the last second so no one'll have time to fight you."

Bolan chuckled. "It's not *that* bad, sir," he said. "It's just that if you stay, then I stay with you. Consider me your personal bodyguard for the evening."

"My Secret Service detail will want to be in on this," the President said. "And they're good men. I don't want to shut them out."

Bolan nodded his understanding. "We won't shut them out," he said. "Just make sure they know I'm in charge."

They shook hands yet again. No more words were necessary.

**10**

The White House grounds didn't seem like a lot of land to protect. Not unless a person considered the fact that several thousand terrorists planned on attacking it at the same time.

Of at least one thing, the Executioner was certain. The simple iron fence, even with spikes at the top of each bar, wasn't going to keep them out. Particularly when at least half of them were Islamic, and considered what they were doing to be a holy act that would send them straight to Paradise if they were killed. These enemies—at least the ones from Hamas—didn't care if they lived or died.

And such men were the most dangerous in the world.

Darkness had just fallen over Washington, D.C., when what appeared to the public to be nothing more than a power outage occurred. All of the lights in the White House, and for blocks around it, went suddenly black, leaving the area in almost total darkness beneath the tiny fingernail clipping of moon that could be seen in the sky. But while the men, women and children in their homes and offices lit candles, switched on flashlights and settled in to wait for the electricity to be restored, a great deal of activity was going on inside the White House fence.

First, the 101st and 82nd Airborne Divisions of the U.S. Army were landing on the grounds after performing HALO—High Altitude Low Opening—parachute jumps beneath black canopies that were invisible in the darkness. As soon as he had hit the ground, each man gathered up his chute and raced to the section of the fence to which he'd been assigned. Not only were they dressed in black, white and gray camouflage fatigues that blended in with the White House surroundings, but also they had brought with them complete ghillie suits.

While the Airborne units were donning their ghillie suits and preparing to drop down into the trench that now circled the grounds, more men fell from the sky. These were detachments from Delta Force, the Green Berets, the U.S. Navy SEALs and Marine recon units and were assigned to guard every entrance—be it door or window—to the White House.

By the time they had set up, the Airborne units in the trenches looked more like rows of recently planted bushes than professional fighting men standing practically shoulder to shoulder. And the half joking, half serious, statement that passed along throughout Delta Force and the other special units was, "It's okay to shoot into the bushes—unless they're holding M-16s."

From the darkened Oval Office, the Executioner watched through infrared binoculars as the U.S. troops assembled to defend their President and all he represented. From the CD Bolan had found at the Hamas safehouse, they had learned that a detachment of around five hundred Rough Riders, dressed in U.S. Army fatigues, would attempt to breach the fences first. They would be followed by another five hundred Hamas terrorists, dressed in traditional Islamic robes.

That made a total of one thousand enemy combatants preparing to attack the very center of the free world.

But one slight discrepancy had bothered both Bolan and Kurtzman ever since they'd first translated the encoded plan. In certain places, the text on the disk used the word "thousands" not "one thousand," and that variant—which might have been nothing more than a typo—had not left the Executioner's mind since.

Bolan's gut told him there was more to this attack tonight

than the one thousand mixed terrorists specifically mentioned on the CD. And since the CD from which they'd gotten that intel they had come from a Hamas computer, he had to assume that Benjamin Franklin Davis—and the Rough Riders—were behind whatever it was that he, Kurtzman and Hamas didn't know about yet.

All along, Bolan had known that this alliance between two terrorist organizations as directly opposed to each other in philosophy couldn't last long. As soon as possible after they'd reached their common goal, both groups would be trying to figure out how to destroy the other one.

There was some kind of double-cross between Hamas and the Rough Riders going down tonight in addition to the direct attack on the White House. Exactly what it was, Bolan didn't know. But he intended to find out.

Bolan scanned the portion of the fence he could see through the binoculars again. With all of the ghillie suits extending up and out of the trench he and the other groundskeepers had dug that morning, it looked as if a new hedge had been planted just behind the plants that grew closer to the spiked iron bars. And the men in the leafy green-and-brown outfits were as well disciplined as any troops in the world. The only movement within the trenches were the leaves swaying in the gentle breeze that blew across the grounds.

The men's M-16s were also out of sight, hidden somewhere in the phony foliage.

The electricity suddenly came back on and Bolan hurried to the light switch by the door, flipping it off. "No use pressing our luck," he told the President. "Besides, I'll be able to see out the windows better this way. But I'd appreciate it if you'd stay away from those windows, sir."

One of the Secret Service attached to the President's personal-protection team opened the door to the hall and stuck his head in. "Lights back on in here?" he asked.

The President said, "Yes, Al. Thanks for checking. You've got my family out of here, right?"

"Yes, sir, Mr. President," Al replied. "By now they should be settling in at Camp David. And I hate to keep bugging you about it, sir, but I'd feel a lot better if you'd let us chopper you off to join them."

Ever since Hal Brognola had contacted the President and told him what Bolan had learned about the forthcoming attack on the White House, the President had been doing his best not to make his Secret Service bodyguards feel that they'd been forced into taking a backseat to Bolan. The personal-protection team, however, was made up of intelligent men, and they weren't being fooled.

The President moved toward his desk. "It's important that we defeat these men tonight, Al," he said as he stopped next to his chair. "But it's just as important that the American public sees that their leader can't be run out of his home." He bent at the waist and slid open a bottom drawer in his desk. "I want to be able to walk out onto the veranda as soon as this battle's over and hold a press conference. And I want every dead terrorist body possible to fall on the *other* side of the fence to show the world that they can't even get on the White House lawn to take a leak."

"Sir, I fully understand that," the Secret Service agent said. "But we could have you back here, out of the chopper and on the ground, sixty seconds after the last shot is fired. It would look like you'd been here the whole time."

The Man looked up. "I don't *lie* to the people who elected me, either, Al," he said. "You're confusing me with my predecessor."

The Secret Service Agent named Al turned red for a moment. Then he said, "Sir, I'm just worried for your safety—which is what my job is all about. Isn't there some kind of compromise we can make?"

Bolan watched as the Man pulled a plain-looking 1911 Government Model .45 out of the drawer. The only adornment that wasn't standard GI issue—before the .45 had been replaced by the Beretta 92—was a set of ivory grips. The seal of the State of Texas was imbedded in the ivory.

Pulling back the tail of his suit coat, the President pushed the barrel of the pistol down behind his belt and slacks, next to his kidney. "Yes, Al, there is a compromise we can make. But we've already made it."

Al frowned, confused.

"I'm up here in my office instead of down there in the trenches where I'd prefer to be," the President said, then turned his back to the door to end the conversation.

Bolan turned back to the window, trying not to grin. The Man's home state of Texas was still a place where young men grew up shooting guns and hunting, and it produced some of the best soldiers around. They also knew the intricacies of their weapons, and before the President's coat had fallen back over his .45, the Executioner had noted that the gun was cocked and locked. The hammer was back with the thumb safety on.

Finally, since he was facing away from the room and out the window, the Executioner allowed himself to smile. But when he looked up into the glass, he saw the President looking at his reflection.

The Man was smiling back at him.

BENJAMIN FRANKLIN DAVIS was sometimes amazed at how many Nazi sympathizers were wealthy. And equally amazed at how generous they could be with their wealth.

Using secret contributions that had gone directly to his Rough Riders—completely bypassing the American Nazi Party—Davis had rented or purchased low-income housing all around the White House. These dwellings had served as safehouses for his men, but tonight, they would play a different role.

They would become the gathering places from which his men would launch their initial attack on the White House. A detachment of five hundred Rough Riders would converge on the grounds all at once, breach the fence with aluminum ladders and mow down the Secret Service guards using sheer manpower. Then a special detachment of one hundred would enter the building and search out the President, vice president, their families or any other notable persons who might be present.

And kill them, too.

The other four hundred Rough Riders would remain outside for what was scheduled to occur next.

From other secret safehouses, Ibrahim Nasab and his Hamas terrorists would be the next to come over the fences and enter the fray. They would be on the lookout for any uniformed or plainclothes Secret Service men who might have hidden and survived the Rough Rider attack.

The third set of safehouses—primarily warehouses and other buildings that Hamas knew nothing about—would serve as meeting places for Ghassan's Hezbollah troops who would surprise Hamas from the rear. The Hezbollah Shia Muslims would wear red armbands to differentiate them from their rival Sunni Hamas men when they began killing them.

But that was hardly the end of Davis's elaborate plan. A second wave of Rough Riders already grouped in a large storage building several miles away would begin moving toward the White House in a variety of vehicles as soon as the first shot was fired. Davis had timed the drive several times, and they should arrive during the hottest part of the battle in which Hamas was taking rounds from Hezbollah on one side, and from the first detachment of Rough Riders on the other.

The second wave's job was to surprise Hezbollah the way they had surprised Hamas. They'd storm in and shoot everyone with a dark face wearing robes—red armbands or not. Between his first and second detachments of Rough Riders, Davis would have all of the Muslim terrorists caught in a cross fire.

The fight shouldn't take more than about five minutes after that. And, with any luck, there wouldn't be a Muslim terrorist left standing on the White House lawn. Then, as one united front, the Rough Riders—now some two thousand strong—would enter the White House itself to join the initial hundred men who had broken off earlier. The Rough Riders would occupy the White House, something that had not been done since the British set it afire during the War of 1812.

Davis smiled. The morale effect on America would be devastating. The average citizen would be forced to take notice of just how weak the country had allowed itself to become. And a new wind of change would blow across the country. A wind within which the word "Nazi" was no longer hated but revered.

This new America, of course, would need a new leader.

President Davis? Benjamin Franklin Davis thought. No, that sounded too much like Jefferson Davis, the President of the Confederacy. And the Confederacy had *lost*.

He planned to win.

Davis looked at his watch, then pulled his cell phone from the pocket of his gray Brooks Brothers suit. He caught a glimpse of himself in a window and liked what he saw.

As he stared at his reflection, the conference call was answered. One by one, two dozen voices from with the safehouses closest to the White House said, "Hello?"

"Gentlemen," Davis said. "This is General Davis." He paused dramatically, then more breathed than spoke. "It is time to proceed."

FROM HIS VANTAGE POINT at the window in the Oval Office, the Executioner saw them coming—dozens of men wearing

BDUs in dozens of small groups, double-timing it down side streets toward Pennsylvania Avenue. Since a machine-gun attack by a madman several years earlier, the Secret Service had blocked off the street directly in front of the White House. Uniformed guards stood at small guard shacks at both ends of the block. Their numbers had been tripled for this evening.

Still, many of these uniformed Secret Service men would give their lives for their country tonight as the Rough Riders stormed by them, guns blazing. They knew that. Yet every one of them had volunteered for the duty.

Bolan had chosen what many soldiers would have considered a strange weapon for the sniper work he was about to perform—a lever-action Marlin .45-70 with a Burris scope. Most lever-action rifles were not as tightly constructed as those of the bolt-action variety, and therefore less accurate. But this particular Marlin had been worked over by John "Cowboy" Kissinger, Stony Man Farm's ace gunsmith and weapons expert. The tolerances had been minimized to the point where the Marlin could hold its own with any bolt-action rifle in the world.

And the lever action was a speedier way to chamber new rounds after each shot.

The Executioner had opened the window as soon as he saw the first Rough Riders jogging down the streets in the semidarkness. Now he extended the Marlin's barrel through the opening as he dropped to one knee. Working the lever, he chambered a round and waited for the Rough Riders to get within range.

Bolan felt a presence at his side and looked up to see the President standing next to him. The man had his .45 out in his hand with his thumb on the safety. "You don't have an extra rifle somewhere, do you?" he asked the Executioner.

Bolan shook his head. "No sir," he said. "And I'd really appreciate it if you'd get back from this window. After the second shot, they're going to be able to pinpoint my location and some of their bullets are going to start flying up this way."

"Dammit," the Man said. "They're attacking my country. My White House. I feel like I need to drop at least a few of the bastards myself."

Bolan chuckled softly as he let the crosshairs of the Burris scope drop on a Rough Rider leading a pack of men about to reach the guard houses. "I know you'd like to do that, sir," he said. "But the fact is, you're the President, and you're too valuable to the country to take a chance of losing."

"Well," said the Man, "I'm also the commander in chief of the armed forces. What would you do if I ordered you to give me that rifle and get out of my way?"

Bolan didn't hesitate with his answer. "With all due respect, sir, I'd mutiny, overpower you and then duct tape you to the chair behind your desk," he said, then ended the speech with yet another, "sir."

The President let out a roar of laughter. "I believe you'd do just that," he said. "Okay." He moved back away from the window again and shoved the .45 back in his belt.

As soon as the lead Rough Rider entered his range, the Executioner gently squeezed the trigger. The Marlin's short barrel spit out a huge wadcutter that practically cut the Rough Rider in two.

It was the first shot of the battle. But now, the war was on.

Below, the Rough Riders now raised their weapons—a wide variety of assault rifles, submachine guns and short-barreled 12-gauge shotguns with extended magazines—and opened fire. The guards around the shacks had taken cover as soon as Bolan's shot rang out, and now they returned fire. But the sheer number of men in the BDUs meant they were overrun. Some of the guards died, as they had known they might. Others escaped death only because the Rough Riders primary mission was to get past them, not kill them.

It seemed now that Rough Riders appeared from every direction on Pennsylvania Avenue, emerging from the darkness and firing as they stormed their way toward the fence. Some of the men carried lightweight aluminum ladders that would obviously be used to leap over the iron fence, and a quick mental image of Santa Anna's Mexican troops at the Alamo passed through the Executioner's mind.

Santa Anna's men had used quickly constructed wooden ladders, but the basic strategy behind overcoming the Alamo walls and the White House fence hadn't changed in nearly two hundred years.

Bolan lowered his aim and glanced through the scope at the "bushes" inside the fence. They had not yet moved— more proof that the Airborne units were among the most highly disciplined fighting men in the world.

Nor did any of the ghillie suits move at all until the dozens of ladders had been leaned up against the other side of the fence. Then, the "leafy bushes" stood up with the synchronization of a chorus line.

All around the eighteen-acre White House grounds, the defenders began firing at the same time, taking out the first the men who had already started up the aluminum ladders, then firing between the bars in the fence to get at the Rough Riders still waiting their turns to climb over the spikes. And they didn't stop their hailstorm of lead until the dozen or so ladders the Executioner could see had fallen to the ground next to the dead American-grown terrorists.

Bolan had already worked the lever on his Marlin, taking out the first man to reach the top of the fence with another giant wadcutter. Just before, and just after he fired, he had heard the pepper of the smaller 5.56 mm and 7.62 mm automatic rifles below as both the U.S. troops and the Rough Riders began shooting at each other from between the iron fence bars. In between rounds, he heard the duller roar of rounds being fired on the other sides of the White House.

Just as Bolan had suspected they would do, the Rough

Riders were leaving no stones unturned. They were attacking the White House from all angles.

One man succeeded in dropping over the fence and somehow escaped the rounds that whizzed past him as he raced toward the White House. Bolan lowered his point of aim and his third shot struck the man squarely in the nose. The Rough Rider stopped dead in his tracks as if he'd suddenly run into an invisible brick wall. His head disintegrated, and blood shot up from his carotid arteries as if propelled by a fire hose.

So far, this was the only man to have breached the fence and Bolan remembered the important words the President had spoken concerning the public's reaction to the ability of America's enemies to force their way onto the White House grounds. Pulling his cell phone from a pocket in his blacksuit—he had earlier shed the outer garments that concealed it—he tapped in Tom Glasser's number.

Bolan didn't bother to identify himself. "As soon as things die down a little, toss that worthless carcass back over the fence. At least before the news people get here."

"Consider it done," Glasser said. "Whoa!" Glasser suddenly shouted. "Here comes that second wave of Hamas we learned about on the CD. They're dressed in robes with rifles and scimitars, and about half of them look like Indian Ocean pirates who ought to have black eye patches and daggers between their teeth."

"How many of them?" the Executioner asked.

"Hard to tell," Glasser said amid the explosions coming over his transmitter as well as through the window of the White House itself. "But I'd say that the five hundred noted on the CD was pretty accurate." The Kansas City SWAT commander paused long enough to cut loose with his own stream of fire, then came back on. "What's weird is the fact that they seem to be shooting at least as many of the Rough Riders outside the fence as our Airborne personnel are from the inside, in the trenches."

Bolan studied the situation through the scope. Glasser was right. He could come to no conclusion except that the Hamas terrorists were now deliberately eliminating their former allies.

The Executioner had suspected a double cross on the part of Davis's Rough Riders since he'd first found the CD at the Hamas safehouse on Iowa. But was there a double-double cross going on? Did Hamas have its own agenda that included eliminating the Rough Riders in a rear ambush like he appeared to be seeing now?

Maybe. And if so, all the better. The more jihadists and American Nazis who took out each other, the better chance the true Americans had in defending the White House.

Bolan heard a door open behind him and whirled from his kneeling position at the window. But all he saw was the tall, lanky Secret Service man and a couple of other faces he recognized from the presidential detail entering the room. All three of the men, however, had pulled Heckler & Koch MP-5 subguns from the briefcases he'd seen in their hands earlier, and had them pointed down at the floor, ready for use.

"Sir," said Al, the leader of the protection team, "there are at least a thousand of the enemy who have just arrived on the scene. That means that, even with the men who've already been taken down, we're now facing over twice the number of assailants we'd counted on."

"And your point is, Al?" the Man asked.

"My point is that if they keep pulling armed suicide-mission fighters out of their hats like magicians producing rabbits, sooner or later they're going to get you."

The President nodded toward Bolan. "Not with him around, they aren't."

As soon as the thousand men had appeared, the Executioner had been itching to get down onto the ground, nearer the fence, and join in the battle from a shorter distance. So now he took advantage of the situation to turn back toward the President. "He's right, sir. I like to think I'm fairly good at what I do, but I'm not perfect by any means." He paused for a second while the President frowned. "And the more men who arrive, the less good I can do you up here."

Turning to a tall, broad-shouldered agent holding one of the MP-5s, he reached out and took the man's submachine gun, as well as three extra 30-round magazines.

In turn, he handed the agent his lever-action Marlin.

"Thanks," the broad-shouldered man said sarcastically. "What do you want me to do now? Circle the wagons? Go hold up a stagecoach?"

"I did all right with it," he said. "Give it a try yourself."

Then, without further ado, Bolan raced out of the room and down the steps.

As HE SAT IN ONE of the overstuffed leather armchairs that had been pulled across the carpet of Davis's office to give them comfortable seats during the show, Ibrahim Nasab felt the anger boiling up inside of him.

Things were not going as planned.

Davis offered Nasab a cigar from a red cherry humidor and the Hamas man took it, stuck the end into his mouth, and then lit it with a gold lighter that Davis also produced. That was one of the advantages of being a Sunni instead of Shia Muslim, Nasab thought as he puffed away to get the tobacco lit evenly. The Sunnis had dropped many of the 5th and 6th Century rules which men seeking power for themselves had come up with in order to gain that power.

In today's twenty-first century, Nasab saw no future in pretending they were still living in the iron age.

Davis took his seat. Nasab watched him from the corner of his eye. Although his face barely reflected it, the Hamas leader could see that the head of the Rough Riders was as perturbed as he was. Nasab had planned for his backup Hamas men to take advantage of the pathway cleared by the Rough Riders, mowing down the surprised Americans as they swarmed through the White House like killer bees. But that pathway had never quite opened up, and from as high as they were in Davis's office complex, it appeared that the Rough Riders were killing as many Hamas men as they were White House guards.

And those bushes that had suddenly risen three feet into the air all around the White House grounds. Their "limbs" were firing assault rifles at both Nasab's and Davis's men.

But when Nasab suddenly saw the third front of men in robes appear—a contingent nearly twice as large as the Rough Riders and Hamas men already engaged in battle—he vaulted to his feet out of the chair as if from a rocket. "Who are they?" he demanded. "Who are the men wearing the red armbands?"

"Not that it'll matter much to you," Davis replied, "but they're some other friends of mine. From Hezbollah."

Nasab stared out the window, watching this new round in the bloodbath going on below them, and what had happened suddenly became evident. Davis had not only formed an alliance with Hamas—an alliance that he never met to honor—but had also cut a side deal with Hezbollah to destroy Hamas.

Much in the same way Nasab had instructed his own men to wipe out the Rough Riders from the rear as soon as they had entered the White House grounds.

The sudden knowledge that he had been outwitted at his own game caused Ibrahim Nasab to whirl angrily toward Davis. The first thing he saw as he turned was the huge smile on Davis's face.

The second thing he saw was the nickel-plated revolver in the Rough Rider leader's hand.

And the last thing he saw was a blinding white-and-orange light.

WITH HIS MARLIN now replaced by the Heckler & Koch 9 mm submachine gun, the Executioner raced down a set of steps toward the ground floor. When he reached the doorway leading out of the stairwell into one of the building's many lobbies, he suddenly found himself face-to-face with the business end of an M-16.

Bolan stopped and looked past the weapon to the man holding it. He wore the insignia of the U.S. Army's Delta Force on the sleeves of his uniform blouse.

"Do you know who I am?" the Executioner asked bluntly.

"Not exactly," the Delta Force soldier said, "but we got your description, as well as the descriptions of several other top-secret operatives who'd be either inside or outside the building. If those descriptions are correct, that would make you the leader of the bunch."

"It's correct," Bolan said. "Now, if you'll excuse me…" He moved to the side of the Delta Force man and started to step around him.

"I've got to ask where you're going," said the young man, growing increasingly nervous as he realized—although Bolan's blacksuit was completely sterile of markings—that he was in the presence of a much higher-ranking officer.

"Out to join the fight," the Executioner said. Then, gently, he pushed the Delta Force man to the side and stepped out into the lobby.

Here, he was met by at least two special forces men from every branch of the armed services. But these men were older, and the Executioner even recognized a few of the faces he'd worked with in the past. They let him through with nothing more than a nod.

Finally exiting the building toward the Rose Garden, Bolan saw that perhaps half of the beautiful multicolored flowers had been shot away. He used what remained of the shrubs for cover as he moved closer toward the front fence. Again he could hear the roar of gunfire coming from behind him and to the sides of the grounds.

He had sent Shelly Cirillo and Jim Ritholz to the far back fence where he couldn't see, or help, them. He could only pray that they'd be all right when this attack was finally over.

By now a half-dozen more Rough Riders, and an equal number of Arab terrorists had made it over the White House fence. They had been stopped almost immediately, however, by fire from the ghillie-suited men in the trenches.

So much for the President's wishes that none of the enemy make it onto the grounds. The Man was going to have to compromise at least a little. Or else lie. And Bolan knew this President meant it when he said he refused to mislead the American public.

The Executioner spotted Tom Glasser hunkered down in a trench to the side of the White House and headed that way. He dived headfirst into the long hole a second before a blast of 7.62 mm rifle fire had a chance to blow holes in his chest. "What've you got here?" Bolan asked.

Glasser shook his head. "I don't know for sure," he said. "But if you'll put those binoculars up to your eyes, I think you'll see a whole shitload of robed and bearded men amassing behind that brick building two blocks down." The Kansas City SWAT commander looked up and down the trench. "And they've been hitting this side of the fence hard with long-range sniper fire. I think this is where they're about to concentrate the attack. That's why I came over here to help." There were now large dips in the "ghillie hedge," which had appeared so well tended when the fighting first broke out. A lot of official letters of condolence were going to get sent out in the morning to the men's families.

"They're getting ready to rush us," Bolan said. For a moment, he wished he had not traded his Marlin for the H&K 9 mm subgun. But that was what had happened, so he would have to go with what he had. Reaching into his blacksuit, he pulled out the three extra 30-round magazines he'd taken from the Secret Service agent and laid them on the grass in front of him.

"You have any idea what those red armbands signify?" Glasser asked.

Bolan squinted through the binoculars again, then shook his head. "Not exactly," he said. "I suspect it's got to be a way of differentiating some of the robed terrorists from the others. Exactly who the guys wearing red are, I don't know."

"They've also all got those really long, scroungy Taliban-like beards," Glasser noted.

Bolan frowned. "That may be the key," he said. "They're Shias. Maybe al Qaeda, maybe Hezbollah or some other group. The red sashes around their arms are to keep from mistaking them for Sunnis. And there's only one reason that would even be necessary."

Glasser nodded. "They're on opposite sides. Maybe not in attacking the White House, but in general principles."

"My guess," the Executioner said, "is that Davis orchestrated this whole little soap opera of death. He wants the Muslims killing each other at the same time his own men are killing them."

Glasser turned to Bolan. "How can he be sure the Shias and Sunnis won't unite against his Rough Riders? They've got them outnumbered now, three-to-one."

"He can't be sure," Bolan said. "Which is why I suspect there'll soon be more Rough Riders showing up behind the guys in the red armbands. Probably more than we can count. Then Davis and his Nazi Rough Riders will have all of the Muslims, as well as any remaining White House guards, caught in between them."

"I think you're right," Glasser said as he turned his attention back toward the men in the red armbands gathering down the street. "At least about not being able to count the new Rough Riders."

"How's that?" Bolan asked.

"Because we're going to be too busy shooting these guys coming at us now."

The Executioner followed Glasser's line of vision and saw wave after wave of men with red armbands suddenly begin sprinting toward them.

Turning his subgun that way, he and Glasser began to fire.

But it was futile. Regardless of how many extra magazines they had for their weapons, and regardless of how fast they could shoot, even if every single bullet found its way into a terrorist's heart, they were about to be overrun. They had only one chance to save themselves, the White House and the President. They needed help, and that help would have to come from the most unlikely of places.

But during a short lull in the fighting, the Executioner heard the roar of dozens of vehicles approaching the White House from every direction. And he knew that their help— even though the men about to provide it didn't know they would be playing such a role—was indeed about to arrive.

DAVIS STEPPED OVER Ibrahim Nasab's body and walked to the closet against the opposite wall. Carefully, he pulled a stone-colored trench coat from its hanger and slid his arms into it. Then, making sure the garment was belted loose enough for him to reach his pistol, he topped his head with a conservative, short-brimmed fedora.

His Rough Riders were still fighting at the fences, and the Hamas men had stalled there, too. But the overwhelming number of Hezbollah warriors whom Ghassan had just ordered to move in would tear down the fences with their teeth if need be.

And, Davis thought as he straightened his hat in the mirror, they would all be trapped nicely along the fences for his second front of Rough Riders to mow down.

Things were going a little different than he'd planned.

But even though he was now going to be forced into using his backup plan, they were going well.

And they were about to go even better.

THEY CAME DOWN SIDE STREETS, alleys and Pennsylvania Avenue itself. Jeeps, HumVees and pickup trucks. Private automobiles, recquisitioned taxis and vehicles of every other shape and size. But they all had one thing in common.

They bore paint that looked still to be drying, and prominently displayed on every vehicle was a symbol still recognized, and loathed, by the vast majority of Americans.

The swastika.

Hundreds of men wearing red armbands were climbing the fence, and Bolan, Glasser and the Airborne units assigned to the trench on that side of the White House were firing as quickly as they could by the time the second wave of Rough Riders had surrounded the grounds. Bolan ran all three of his MP-5 magazines dry and listened to the bolt lock open, then turned to Glasser as he drew his Desert Eagle.

"We aren't doing a bit of good here!" the Executioner shouted above the pandemonium. "For every one we kill, two more appear."

Glasser nodded. In the dim light, Bolan could see that the Kansas City SWAT commander's face had turned gray with smoke, and suspected his had, too. "We've got to focus the men with the red armbands on the Rough Riders and vice versa. Then our primary goal is to get the President out of here whether he wants to go or not."

Glasser nodded again. He still had rounds in his M-16 and he moved slightly to the side, where he had a clear shot at a

Nazi-converted Jeep Wrangler with an M-60 machine gun mounted just behind the driver.

At the same time, Bolan moved the other way until he could see between the robed men climbing the fence to the Wrangler.

Both Bolan and Glasser fired at roughly the same time, and whichever bullet killed the driver was anybody's guess. But the dual rounds had their desired effect, and a Rough Rider in the backseat stood up to man the M-60.

A second later, the iron fence was being torn to shreds by the heavy artillery rounds, and men in robes and red armbands were dropping to the ground like so many swatted flies.

Now, up and down the fence, more high-powered weaponry entered the fray, aiming at anything wearing traditional Islamic dress.

Bolan and Glasser ducked into the trench until the first salvo ended, then leaped out on the side facing the White House. Their blacksuits evidently confused the newly arrived Rough Riders, because after a few initial rounds that whizzed by them, Bolan heard a voice yell, "Hold your fire!"

The Executioner and the Kansas City SWAT man took advantage of the fact that they wore neither BDUs nor Arabic robes and headgear to sprint back to the White House itself.

Returning to the hall that led to the Oval Office, Bolan found a half-dozen badly shaken uniformed Secret Service personnel. "We have orders not to let *anyone* in," said a slightly overweight guard who looked to be nearing retirement age.

"Those orders have just been countermanded," said Bolan as he and Glasser raced forward. In the corner of his eye, the Executioner saw one of the younger guards draw his sidearm.

An older Secret Service man grabbed his hand and stuffed the weapon back into its holster. "I know him," the older man said. "He was here before."

By the time the Executioner and Tom Glasser reached the Oval Office, at least two dozen men guarded the door. Again

Bolan was recognized and passed through with no commotion. Once inside the Oval Office, the Secret Service agent the President had called Al immediately appeared. "He with you?" he asked Bolan with his eyes on Glasser.

"He is," the Executioner said.

Al shrugged but his face looked far more serious. "The home office has sent in so many reinforcements whose faces I don't recognize that it makes me nervous," he said, then turned away from the Executioner and Glasser.

Bolan made his way to where the President was seated behind his desk. The Man's coat was unbuttoned and the ivory grips of his .45 could be seen sticking out of his belt. "Nice to see you again," the President said. He turned to Glasser. "I see you guys buy your clothes at the same place," he said, indicating the Kansas City SWAT commander's blacksuit. "You'll have to pick up a couple of those for me sometime."

Before Glasser could respond, he, Bolan and the President all turned toward the outer door where the voices had risen slightly. The Executioner saw a man wearing a small gray hat and the same kind of trench coat to which bureaucrats the world over seemed drawn. In his hand, he was holding up a credential case that looked like Secret Service issue.

"I told you," the man said with more than a little irritation in his voice, "they sent me down from the Boston office as backup. Don't you guys ever read your e-mail or memos?" Without further ado, he pushed his way into the Oval Office, took his hat off his head and held it in his left hand.

Bolan noticed how loosely the man's trench coat was belted as his right hand disappeared inside the garment. "Mr. President," the newly arrived agent said, "I've brought you a letter from our special agent in charge of the Boston office. Just let me…"

The Executioner's brain went into overdrive. Something was wrong *here—very* wrong. He didn't know what or how yet, but he knew beyond a shadow of a doubt that this man was not with the Secret Service and that he was here to kill the President. He also knew that within the confines of the overcrowded Oval Office, a round from either his 9 mm Beretta or his .44 Magnum Desert Eagle might easily pass through the impostor and kill an innocent agent.

The man in the trench coat had his hand halfway back out of the coat by the time Bolan trapped it against his chest, unsheathed his combat knife and drew it across the front of the man's throat.

Gasps of both surprise and outrage accompanied the blood that spewed from the man's severed arteries, soaking Bolan, Glasser and the President. Several guns were drawn, and the barrels all pointed toward the Executioner.

"Wait!" the President yelled. He stood up behind his desk at the same time the man in the trench coat fell to the carpet in front of it.

Walking around the desk, the Man reached inside the open trench coat and pulled out the lifeless hand he found inside it.

Still gripped in Benjamin Franklin Davis's fingers was the nickel-plated Colt Single Action Army revolver.

"Secret Service issuing these things these days?" the President asked sarcastically.

He got no response.

"Send this guy's credentials to the lab," the Man said, standing back up. "You'll find out that they're phony." He turned to the Executioner. "Thanks," he said.

"It's what I'm here for," the Executioner said simply.

# Epilogue

"Can we give this poor hitchhiker a lift back to Kansas City?" Bolan asked Jack Grimaldi as he and Tom Glasser tossed their bags in the Learjet's luggage compartment.

"From here in Washington, D.C.?" Grimaldi laughed. "Sure. It's right on the way."

The two men, both of whom had changed out of their blood-soaked blacksuits at the first opportunity, boarded the aircraft. Glasser took a seat directly behind Grimaldi. Bolan buckled himself into his usual position, next to the pilot.

"What exactly would you call that back there, Cooper?" Glasser asked as they taxied toward one of the private plane runways at Dulles Airport. "Davis double-crossed his Hamas buddy Nasab by bringing in Hezbollah. But Nasab had also planned to double-cross the Rough Riders by having his men kill all of them once they'd used them to get onto the grounds of the White House. But then Davis brings in a second, much larger and better equipped wave of Rough Riders to knock out Hezbollah. So it's not a double or even a triple cross."

Jack Grimaldi turned his head on his neck and spoke into the back seat. "Call it a fourple cross," he said.

Glasser groaned at the joke.

"I'd just call it justice," the Executioner said. "Especially since the President had time to call in our regular military troops—not just the guys inside the fence but the ones who blindsided the second group of Rough Riders when they arrived."

"I'll drink to that kind of justice," Glasser said.

"So would I, if I wasn't flying," Grimaldi agreed.

Bolan chuckled, but in his mind he reviewed what had happened since he'd dispatched Benjamin Franklin Davis with his knife. The men in the red armbands had, of course, turned out to be part of the Shia Muslim terrorist organization Hezbollah. The leader of all of the Hezbollah cells in America—a radical named Ghassan—had been found among the dead men at the White House fence.

Ibrahim Nasab, Ghassan's counterpart in Hamas, had been found dead in Davis's office shortly after Davis had been identified. The .45 Colt bullet that had killed the Sunni had matched up perfectly with the twists and grooves in the Single Action Army revolver with which Davis had also planned to kill the President.

Amad Nadir—who had proved to be a reliable informant every step of the way—was on his way back home to the Middle East flying first class, compliments of a grateful United States government. The man had also received a very healthy paycheck for his services.

Jim Ritholz and Shelly Cirillo had returned to Chicago, where they were trying to explain their unexcused absences for the past several days. But Bolan knew that wouldn't be much of a problem once Hal Brognola and the U.S. Department of Justice gave their chief a call. And if that didn't get them out of hot water, the President himself had promised to make a call to suggest the Chicago PD turn a blind eye to the two detectives' days of AWOL.

Turning in his seat, Bolan saw that Tom Glasser's eyes were half-shut and threatening to close the rest of the way. So he reached back and tapped the Kansas City SWAT commander on the knee with the back of his hand. "Tom, you awake?" he asked.

Glasser's eyes opened. "I am now."

"You sure you don't want to reconsider Hal's job offer as a permanent blacksuit?" Bolan asked. "He doesn't extend such invitations very often, and he certainly doesn't do it lightly."

Glasser straightened back up in his seat. "I'm honored that he'd ask me," he said. "But I've got men who depend on my leadership back in K.C. I'd be doing them a disservice if I didn't pass on all of the things I learned at the Farm. Not to mention while hanging out with you."

Bolan nodded his understanding and turned back around in his seat. It was just that kind of loyalty—as well as Glasser's proficiency as a fighting man—that had earned the Executioner's respect.

So Bolan closed his eyes. He could use some rest during the flight, as well.

The Executioner was almost asleep when he heard the radio mounted to the controls of the Learjet squawk. "Stony Man One to Flyboy One. Come in, Jack."

Grimaldi reached for the mike, held it to his lips and said, "I'm here, Barb. What's up?"

"Location, Flyboy One?" Price asked.

"About thirty minutes due west of D.C.," Grimaldi said.

"You still have Striker and our Kansas City friend with you?"

"That's affirmative," Grimaldi said.

"Well, see if you can touch them down in Indianapolis, Jack. They'll be briefed once they're on the ground."

Bolan turned in his seat again. "You up for one more mission on your way home, Tom?" he asked the man in the back of the Learjet.

Glasser's eyes opened wide, suddenly all of the fatigue Bolan had seen in them only a few moments before disappeared. "Oh, as long as it's on the way home, I guess I might as well," he said, grinning from ear to ear.

Bolan turned back around in his seat to face the front again. He couldn't help smiling himself.

The Executioner had heard it said that adrenaline was the most powerful of all drugs. And, as with other drugs, some men became addicted to it and needed more of it as time went by in order to achieve the desired high. Such men were often even called "adrenaline junkies."

But Mack Bolan was no adrenaline junkie, and neither was Tom Glasser. They did their best to right wrongs, protect the weak and help people because it was the right thing to do.

So the Executioner couldn't accept the theory that adrenaline was the strongest drug known to man. Because once you started helping people, you found that to be the strongest addiction of all.

# TAKE 'EM FREE

## 2 action-packed novels plus a mystery bonus

## NO RISK

### NO OBLIGATION TO BUY

**ROGUE ANGEL™**

Look for

# PROVENANCE

by **AleX Archer**

Finding the relic is a divine quest.
Even if it means committing murder.

When a mysterious man orchestrates an attack on
archaeologist Annja Creed and then offers her an
assignment, Annja is baffled.
She must find an object
that possesses a sacred
and powerful secret,
offering atonement to
anyone who uncovers
it…or wreaking havoc
on the world.

**Available March
wherever you
buy books.**

# ROOM 59

A research facility in China has built
the ultimate biological weapon. Alex's job:
infiltrate and destroy. His wife works at the
biotech company's stateside lab, and Alex
fears danger is poised to hit home. But when
Alex is captured, his personal and professional
worlds collide in a last, desperate gamble to
stop ruthless masterminds from unleashing
virulent, unstoppable death.

Look for

# out of time
by
# cliff RYDER